X (and *A*), but set in a world teetering on the edge of unraveling. Poignant, sincere, messy, kaleidoscopic. Brilliant."

— Tex Gresham, author of *Violent Candy* and *Sunflower*

Also by Sarah Colombo

Subterranean

why is marigold?

sarah colombo

Denver, Colorado

Published in the United States by:
Spaceboy Books LLC
1627 Vine Street
Denver, CO 80206
www.readspaceboy.com

Cover by Rachel Evans

ISBN: 978-1-951393-38-0
First printed November 2024

For Magnolia

CHAPTER ONE

marigold

The alligator's spine slides across the water like a snake, and then she turns her head toward me and she is not like a snake. She is like an alligator. I feel a thumping in my throat, my chest tight, and I am pleased. Before this moment of snake-spine, I looked at the water and saw algae and a floating, half-flattened coffee cup. Now there is the alligator, her tail swishing toward the coffee cup, her eyes on me. I stand up and walk backward from the bank, still watching her, as though my eyes can prevent her from moving toward me too quickly. Maybe that isn't the reason I am watching her. Maybe

I like the way it feels, my eyes on her, my breath shortening, my pulse fast. It's almost like feeling happy.

When the path bends parallel to the water, I feel safe to turn around. My feet kick up the dry dirt that falls quickly back into place, resistant to change. This is something I like, the swift return to normal. Dirt will be dirt. And I will be me, the same braided hair and kicking feet, even when my heart is beating fast and my body doesn't know if it is scared or happy. And I can be scared and happy and that is why I am always the same too, even when I am different.

Then I forget to feel scared or happy because I see Shelley moving toward me, slowly, carelessly. When I see Shelley, I feel everything all at once which is like feeling nothing. Which is like feeling myself.

It's the part of the morning where it stops feeling like night is ending and starts feeling like day is beginning. The sun stabs through the trees, the path mottled with the dark, stretched twins of the branches.

Shelley is still in her pajamas and her hair is greasy, pulled haphazardly into a bumpy bun. She sees me and stops, waiting while the dirt she kicked falls back to the ground, illuminated by a patch of sunlight. When I reach her, I notice the way the leaves pattern her face, making her look like something mysterious and half-present. Glancing at her toes, I see that they are coated in dirt. Her toenails still display an old pedicure, black paint grown out with a sharp line marking the end of the veneer.

She rubs her hands against her eyes and sighs. She is shaking her head a little, which I understand means she is annoyed at me for walking too slowly, but I also know she is choosing to play this part, the part of the annoyed person.

"I saw an alligator," I tell her

Despite the dry summer, the crumbling dirt and dying trees around us, the air is still normal: thick, wet, heavy. I feel it settle against me, like walking was keeping it at bay.

"What else is new?" she asks, unimpressed.

Acting unimpressed makes Shelley feel safe. Mr. Miller told me that.

We were in his classroom after school. I was thirteen or fourteen, still new. The desks were all slightly out of line from the ebb and flow of the girls. We were well-behaved students, so even the destruction meted on the classroom was at half-measures, everything a little out of line, a little scuffed, but no turned-over chairs or loose pens rolling around on the floor, maybe just the corner of a piece of paper fluttering from the air conditioning, a line of eraser dust on a desk.

"Why does Shelley say things that she doesn't mean?" I asked him.

He stood behind his desk, shirt untucked, khakis wrinkled, and polished his glasses on the tail of his shirt. He did this daily, and his glasses became progressively smudged, so that they were dusty grey circles by the time classes ended. He put them back on and blinked at me.

"It's her sense of humor," he said.

I was half-standing, half-sitting on one of the student desks, watching him out of the corner of my eye, but mostly turned toward the window, watching the girls walking across the lawn toward the dorms. It was our free time, a little pocket of semi-unregulated life after class and before dinner. Most of the girls used it to walk around half-dressed through the dorm halls, whisper, squeal and laugh, and run after each other for some fake fight. I usually spent it in Mr. Miller's room or with Shelley. Shelley and I kept our door locked and I read while she stared out the window, or I listened to her while she ranted about something, or she listened to me while I asked her some of my questions.

"It's not her jokes. It's the way she is," I said. I turned back toward him, let the girls become wriggling tadpoles at the edge of my sight.

He sighed. The sigh was fake, Shelley told me after she witnessed it. "He loves answering your dumb questions," she said, "but he also loves to act like you're some big burden he has to deal with."

"Some people," he said, "don't like to tell the truth. They don't want to show when they feel certain positive feelings. It's safer that way."

"Safe how?" I asked.

He blinked at me behind his smudged glasses.

"It's complicated," he said. "It can be a lot of things, but I think it's because if people know what you like, what makes you happy, they have more they can use against you."

"She thinks I'm going to use something against her?" I asked.

I turned back to the window. Most of the girls were inside the dorms now. A few stragglers still made their way across the lawn, curving along the fountain or leaning over to tie a shoe. They walked in clumps of two or three, except one who was alone, still far back, still mostly by the school building. It was Shelley. She was leaning against a tree with her arms crossed. I realized she was waiting for me.

Now, standing in front of her, heat pressing against us, I ask: "Why are you out?"

It is Sunday. On Sundays Shelley doesn't leave the house or bathe or change out of her pajamas. She lies on the couch and watches movies, sometimes eating, sometimes sleeping. When I come home in the evenings the whole place smells like her warm, damp body and Cheetos. I usually open the windows to air it out and she moans something about wasting her day or hating herself, but she doesn't seem to remember all that by the time the next Sunday comes around.

"Came to get you," she says. She waves a mosquito away from her face. "God, it's awful out here."

"To get me for what?"

I take a few steps back and to the side, seeking cover in the closest shade, but am still not able to completely protect myself. The trees are too sad and skinny to serve this secondary purpose. There is some relief from the heat on the top of my head, but somehow my collarbones now feel like they are burning.

"He's here," she says, pulling at the neck of her shirt.

A tightness forms somewhere in my stomach, and suddenly I am hungry and nauseated at the same time. It's a release of a feeling that's been lurking underneath, the dread that forgets to what it is attached. Now the dread comes to settle, finds its home, remembers him.

"He's supposed to come tomorrow," I say.

"Well, he came today."

I think she wants to throw her hands up at me when she says this, but instead she crosses them. She tries to be more understanding, to remember that I can't help the way I am. She's been trying for years.

Mr. Miller stressed that I needed to get used to people not doing what they're supposed to do.

"People forget," he reminded me.

This was a few years after the time he tried to explain Shelley to me. I was less new. We were in his classroom, supposedly waiting on LeBlanc, who was not going to show up. Free time was almost over. It was toward the end of fall semester, the lawn in the winter dark that fell earlier and earlier. Mr. Miller wore one of his sad, baggy cardigans with little moth holes along the arms. The holes made the girls feel a strange sort of guilt. On another teacher, such shabby attire would be ammunition for derision, but everyone liked Mr. Miller, so they just clucked over his pathetic clothes, said he needed somebody to take care of him. With this they often eyed me, suspicious of our afternoon meetings, jealous of what they perceived as favoritism, even though they knew he was required to meet with me, required to help me..

"They should remember," I said. I leaned my forehead against the cool window, the light in the room reflecting off it, making the yard and the dorm a fuzzed-over, far away vignette.

"Sometimes they remember, but something else comes up that they think is more important, and they do that instead."

"How do they decide what's more important?"

"Sometimes it's not actually more important, not technically, it's just the thing they want to do more."

I wondered what LeBlanc wanted to do more. Mr. Miller spoke to me in a kind, soothing voice, as if my feelings were hurt. For someone who was supposed to know so much about me, he often seemed to understand nothing. I wasn't upset about LeBlanc, not really, I didn't care if he thought working or some dinner with friends or anything else was more important than the holiday dinner party at school. I just liked things to go the way they were supposed to go. All day I'd planned my actions, my words, my clothes, my hair on the understanding that LeBlanc would be at dinner, and he was not.

Arriving a day early is a different way of not doing what you are supposed to do. Usually people are late.

"Where is he?" I ask Shelley, shifting to my left a little.

A patch of skin above my elbow starts to heat up. I like the feel of it, a distraction from the pain in my gut.

We are in a thicket of dying pecan trees. They still have little buds that sprout in spring, but no pecans. The branches fall everywhere during storms and hang low the rest of the time. Shelley reaches a hand up and pulls a twig off a branch, hurls it out into the trees. It doesn't go very far, just lands in some weeds a few feet away.

"He's at the Dollar Store," she says.

"What's he like?" I ask.

"Well..." she moves her hands to her hips, looks up at the tree branches, her face striped. "He's not like LeBlanc."

This can mean anything. No person is one way and LeBlanc certainly isn't.

"He's young?" I ask, because one way to describe LeBlanc is old.

She considers, twists her mouth to the side. "Yeah. He's young."

"He's nice?" I ask.

Another way to describe LeBlanc is mean. But that would be a simplification. Shelley likes to simplify things, though.

"Seems so," she says.

I wait, hoping the silence will call to her, the still, dry dirt, the dying trees and me.

She shrugs. "You'll have to see for yourself."

CHAPTER TWO

tom

As I drive through the compound, dread settles on the back of my tongue. I turn up the radio to drown out the worry. An emphatically dumb, boisterous country song fills up the space in my truck, and I roll slowly down the freshly-paved road—an opulent black with two bright, solid yellow lines running down the middle. On either side of the road there are palm trees, elephant ears, and azaleas. A whitewashed sign pronounces: "Live. Work. Play." in a bright-blue, flourishing script, a wave cresting beneath.

If it weren't for the plant, sitting heavy at the corner of my vision, a bell ringing against my brain, this place would seem like a retirement community or country club. The plant could be an unrelated thing, an unfortunate blight on an otherwise nice place to live. I try not to look at it, to keep up the illusion of niceness, a plastic-wrapped version of my new life I can conjure up to blot out reality. Still, the plant is there whether I turn my head or not, and at some bends in the road it is right in front of me, looking rusty and forgotten, a copper tinge to the holding tanks, the low-block buildings, and the looming stacks.

Once I pass the welcome center, the main road dips back to a previously paved level, grey with barely visible lines. The nice bushes and pleasant palms disappear suddenly, leaving only a scrubby border of weeds and trash.

This is more in line with what I pictured when I pictured working for LeBlanc: a Cherry Coke bottle, partially flattened and half-filled with culvert water.

It was always an assumption. "When you work for LeBlanc..." my father would say.

No one seemed curious about whether or not I wanted to work for LeBlanc.

I didn't like science or business or any of the other things I was encouraged to study. I liked fishing and reading. Sometimes I liked one more than the other. "It's no way to earn a living," my father would say. I didn't want to earn a living. I wanted to stay somewhere cheap and work as little as possible, but I understood there was something shameful in that.

It could be the shame that propelled me here: the bright sun bouncing against the hood of my truck, the air conditioner barely keeping up with the heat. Whatever it is—shame, fear—it mixes with the menacing presence of the plant and forms a hard, bumpy knot in the center of my stomach. I try to work against it, buff it into something more pleasant and smooth, by telling myself "you chose this." I repeat it over and over like it means something. Another thing, a childhood trick, is to envision. I envision a life here that I know I won't have: picture a pleasant fishing spot, a nice clean apartment, maybe a friend. None of it will stick in my brain, though. The images pop up, slosh around, then drain away, leaving the rusted plant and littered ditch.

Following instructions from Kenny at the gate, I turn down a gravel road marked by an algaed sign that is crooked and pointing in no particular direction. There is mostly just dirt along this road, with clumps of trees farther back, and packed dirt driveways leading up to weathered and sagging houses. The houses are raised several feet off the ground with slabs underneath where cars are parked, kids' toys are strewn, or chairs and beer bottles are scattered. Alongside each house there are wooden stairs leading to the doors.

Kenny told me I need to see Marigold, and that she lives in the yellow house on this road. I look for the yellow house, but they all look a little yellow, whether they are meant to be green or white or blue, a mix of the rot and the sunlight. Then I see it, yellow on purpose, a freshly painted house that looks more stable than the others, with monkey grass planted along the driveway and flowerpots lined up on the stairs. A deep freezer and a couple of camper chairs sit on the slab underneath.

I pull into the driveway and cut the engine. Heat pours into the cracks of the truck, smoking me out. I step out, slam the door, and stare up at the house. There is no evidence that anyone is here. I debate leaving. It wouldn't be hard to just get back in my truck, drive the way I came, speed past Kenny at the gate to avoid any awkward explanations, and return Monday like I was supposed to. If I come back tomorrow, I won't be standing outside a stranger's house, straining my ears to hear the sound of a TV. Instead, I'll be in some air-conditioned administrative office, filling out paperwork with a nice lady named Pam who has lipstick on her teeth and too much perfume. Maybe I won't come back.

The embarrassment of leaving, of this Marigold person catching me getting back in my truck, of Kenny at the gate flagging me down and asking what I'm doing, of anyone on the compound finding out that I was here, then left, then came back, seems just as embarrassing as being here, now, so I decide to stay.

I start up the stairs, listening for signs that someone is home. All I hear are the various bird chirps and bug hums that make up life and my own footsteps creaking on the wood. When I knock on the door, I hear nothing for so long that the world around me grows silent from my strained listening. Then I hear footsteps and my pulse gets fast and I gulp and grow impatient. The door pulls open slowly, the bottom sliding along a beige carpet.

A woman stands there squinting at me with dark eyes. Her black hair is half in a bun that is sliding off her head like a scoop of melting ice cream, the rest is matted to her neck and face. She wears an oversized t-shirt advertising a race from 30 years ago. It looks like she isn't wearing pants, but her shirt is so big it might be covering a pair of shorts. Her bare feet have chipped, black nail polish. She is short and sturdy. Her nose has a bump in it like it was broken once.

"Can I help you?" she asks.

I wish so much to not be here that the wish feels powerful, like if I keep trying, I might actually disappear. I'll be back in my mom's trailer, packing, preparing to arrive on Monday as intended. But I did not wait until Monday and am in fact standing here in front of a possibly pantsless person who is annoyed with me already.

"Hi," I say.

I grin at her, which makes me hate myself, but I can't stop. The grin has no effect. She watches me, silent.

"I'm Tom."

For a moment I see a flicker in her eyes, and I think she will get embarrassed, upset, run to put some shorts on or make some sort of joke about the fact that she is wearing them after all, but the flicker dies down and she just nods. I wait for her to say something, but she doesn't. She bends her toes and scrapes them across the carpet, then picks at a factory-issued sticker along the side of the door.

"Are you Marigold?" I ask. My voice comes out in a dry croak.

She shakes her head.

"No," she says. "She's not here."

She yawns.

I wait.

"OK," she says. She rubs her hand over her face. "Wait. Aren't you supposed to come tomorrow?"

I nod. The stupid grin again.

"Yeah. Sorry. I had an issue with where I was living. Had to get out earlier than I thought. LeBlanc said it would be fine."

The issue was my mother. She was manic from excitement or worry, I couldn't tell which. I had only been staying with her for a few weeks, just while waiting to move out here. Every day was tenser than the one before. She woke up at 5:00 a.m. and vacuumed the hallway, baked lots of things and burnt them, blasted episodes of Jeopardy she had recorded on VHS. I took longer walks around the trailer park, and then out to the garbage-filled woods behind when I got tired of answering questions from her neighbors on their porches: "How's your mom?", "How long you staying?", "How old are you again?", "You know anything about squirrels?" Out in the woods I would kick cans, look at leaves, and take down hanging vines with my pocketknife. The closer my move grew, the more anxious I became, until I called LeBlanc.

"LeBlanc said it would be fine," the woman in the door repeats after me. "Guess he forgot to tell us, but that's nothing new. Wait there for a second."

She closes the door. The bird and bug sounds suddenly reconverge around me and I feel like an intruder, a lone, silent mammal. She comes out of the door after a few minutes, wearing pink polka dot pajama pants with the same race shirt and flip flops, squeezes past me, and starts down the stairs. I follow.

"You need to go to the store," she says. She is speaking to me, but she doesn't turn her head, just talks to the air in front of her.

I nod even though I know she can't see me.

"We were going to go later today, stock up your place, but you can go ahead."

When we get to my truck, she goes around to the passenger side and stands there, arms crossed.

"Should we take my truck?" I ask.

"Unless you want to walk," she says, motioning around as if to demonstrate the lack of vehicle on the premises.

We get in and when I start the engine I try to quickly turn the music down so she doesn't hear how loud it is or that I am listening to something possibly uncool, but I am not able to do it fast enough, and it is in fact something uncool, a song about a sad little girl dying with no shoes at Christmas. I mash the power button quickly to turn off the radio and avoid looking over to see her reaction.

"Don't turn it off on my account," she says.

She sounds annoyed. I can't tell if she is annoyed that I turned it off, that I was listening to it in the first place, or that she has to deal with me at all.

We head back toward the main, paved road and head farther into the compound. The faded concrete seems to lead nowhere, no landmarks in sight, just the long, lean trees back from the road and the reflector lights down the center sometimes bumping against my wheels. Then suddenly a squat cement building comes into view. A yellow banner hanging from the roof says: "Dollar Store."

"Stop!" the woman says suddenly

I stop in the road, right outside the entrance to the parking lot. She opens the door and jumps out.

"Go ahead and park," she says. "I'm going to get Marigold."

She shuts the door and turns down a path that cuts into the trees on the side of the road opposite the store.

I pull into the parking lot, feeling jittery, like I drank too much coffee and didn't eat any breakfast. Then I remember that I did drink too much coffee and didn't eat any breakfast, but there's something else on top of it, a sense that I am dog-paddling my way through life and the undercurrent is getting stronger.

There are no other cars in the parking lot. It is more newly paved than the road, a bright black asphalt with straight white lines. The safety lights are still turned on from the night, their illumination bleeding into the natural light and disappearing. I sit there for a few seconds and lean my head close to the air conditioning vent, preparing myself to be blanketed by heat again. What I want to do is wait in my truck until she comes back, to be accompanied into the store like a nervous teenager going to a party, but then I imagine her returning and asking something like "Why are you still in your truck?" and I get out.

I walk toward the entrance, stepping on chip bags and shredded cigarette butts. The sign on the door says they're closed, and the clock on the sign has hands pointing to 9:00. I don't remember what time it is. Through the tinted glass, I think I see a figure moving. I lean against the door with my hands shielding my face, but all I can see is a shelf of canned tuna and chicken with mayonnaise jars stacked helpfully beside them.

Pacing around the parking lot, waiting, sweat pouring from my temples and down the back of my neck, settling between my shoulder blades, I realize I don't even know what I'm waiting for. For a Dollar Store to open. For a woman in pajama pants to return.

After walking the perimeter of the building, through the untrimmed grass crowded around the outer walls, over crushed beer cans and crumpled receipts, I go back to the door.

The sign still says "Closed."

I knock a few times, then try to look inside again. Still the mayonnaise, but I think I catch a little movement in a part of the store I can't quite see.

I step back from the door and it transforms into a dark and distorted mirror. There I am: slumped and pathetic with my hands in my pockets, layered over the cans of tuna and chicken, the mayonnaise and my elbow existing in the same plane. Then I see someone coming toward me. It looks like she is walking through the store, coming to let me in, but I can't figure out how she got in there. I realize it is another reflection, coming to meet mine. She is behind me.

I turn to see the woman in pajamas. She's saying something, I think to me, but I can't quite hear. She cups her hands around her mouth and her voice is louder now, but I still can't make out the words. I take a step toward her and start to ask her to repeat herself, but then I notice someone walking beside her. Something in the back of my brain rings at the sight of her. I know her. I think I know her, but the way that I know her, the place, the time, the circumstance, is a piece of detritus at the bottom of a dirty lake, just giving me glimpses when the wind blows, when the sun hits at the right angle. She is taller than the woman in pajamas, and thin, less imposing. Her blond hair is in a tidy braid thrown over one shoulder and she wears a long, white dress, with dots of gathered white thread all over and a wavy line of dirt around the bottom. They are right in front of me now and the woman in pajamas is saying something about the store and I realize there's another voice behind me, a man's voice, but I'm not following what is happening, just watching this person that I know but don't know how, trying to stick my head under the water. Her big green eyes blink at me.

"Marigold?" I ask.

CHAPTER THREE

marigold

"He won't open early!" Shelley calls to the man who is peering into the door of the Dollar Store.

We're about halfway through the parking lot toward the building. I see his shoulders stiffen at the sound of her voice. He turns toward us. He is tall, stocky, his haircut the type of un-styled shaggy that looks like he cuts it himself or has a mom or sister who does it for him. His hair sticks to his forehead and around his ears with sweat and his face is pink with the heat. He's dressed in what Shelley calls The Uniform. It is not actually a uniform but a style of clothing all of the men around here wear. The Uniform is jeans, a fishing shirt, and boots. Sometimes the boots are rain boots, sometimes work boots, sometimes cowboy boots. On a casual day, the boots might be exchanged for a pair of plastic clogs. The jeans may be worn-in or brand new, they may have intricate designs sewn on the pockets or they may be as plain as jeans can be. The man peering in the window of the Dollar Store opts for plain jeans, faded along his back pockets and knees, work boots, and a khaki fishing shirt.

Shelley adds: "Even if he's standing right by the door and he sees you waiting there, he still won't open."

She's yelling this in a loud, amused, way, hoping Randy the Prophet can hear her. Hoping to annoy him.

The man steps closer to us. At the same time a hand appears in the door and flips the sign over to read "Sorry, We're Open," and the door opens with the jangling of the bell overhead. The man looks at me, his eyes narrowing, and asks: "Marigold?"

Randy the Prophet steps out from the store, arms crossed.

"I open the store when it's time to open," he says. This comment is directed at Shelley, but he doesn't say it directly to her, just states it generally, looking at each of us in turn. "I guess that's a crazy idea."

Shelley shrugs. They pretend to be mad at each other sometimes.

Then she says: "Yes, this is Marigold," and motions toward me. "This is Tom," she says and motions toward him.

"Oh," Randy the Prophet says, and now he is speaking with seriousness because we were told that Tom would come and here he is.

"He's the one LeBlanc told us about," Shelley says, which is something we all know, but she is saying it for Tom's benefit, so that he will know we were prepared for his coming.

Randy the Prophet turns to Tom and sticks out a hand.

"Randy the Prophet," he says.

Tom looks confused. People often look confused when Randy the Prophet introduces himself because they can't tell what he is saying, because his name doesn't sound like a name but like the beginning of an explanation or a thought.

"That's my name," Randy the Prophet adds.

Randy the Prophet is getting old. He is not old. Not even close. He is middle aged, but I have known him years now and seeing him beside someone new makes me remember him, all of him, through each second and day and year and it causes the new him to layer over the old him and I can remember when he had less wrinkles around his eyes and a slimmer waistline. He has excellent posture and stands with his hands in his pockets, looking at Tom with a thoughtful frown. His black hair is pulled into a low ponytail. At some point, without me noticing, grey crept in, silver strands streaking the black around his face.

We all go into the store. Shelley circles around Tom and tells him what to buy, what not to buy. He chuckles and nods, but seems to be mostly ignoring her, filling his basket with Yoo-hoos, Bunny Bread, and Oscar Meyer bologna. Randy the Prophet waits behind the counter and I stand in front, picking up and putting back the plastic-wrapped pralines.

"I saw an alligator this morning," I tell Randy the Prophet.

I know it isn't interesting. Shelley pointed that out already, but still I want to say it. I want to say it to him to find out why I want to say it to him. It feels important.

He looks me in the eyes and says, "That's a good sight in the morning. Reminds you you're alive."

I nod. He sips on his Styrofoam cup of fresh coffee and pours me one from the pot, pushes the cup across the counter. I scratch at the Styrofoam with a finger, blow on the coffee.

"You don't need to get cereal," Shelley is telling Tom. "They have all kinds in the mess hall."

"Trying to run a business here..." Randy the Prophet says, but he says it with a sigh and sits down and opens a magazine.

"I like cereal at night sometimes," Tom says. He sticks a box of Froot Loops in his basket.

Shelley rolls her eyes at me and comes to lean on the counter. Randy the Prophet pours another cup of coffee, stirs in two sugars and three packets of Half-and-Half, and hands it to her. She brings it up to her nose, smells it, closes her eyes.

I take a small sip of mine. It is thick and acidic and still too hot. I roll the coffee around in my mouth to mix with my spit before swallowing. My tongue feels numb against my teeth, burnt a little.

"Marigold saw an alligator this morning," Shelley tells Randy the Prophet.

I stare at her.

"What?" she asks.

"I heard," Randy the Prophet says.

"That's a good way to wake up," Tom says. He is standing a little behind us with a basket that is overflowing, waiting for us to move so he can place it on the counter. No one responds to his comment. We aren't sure about him yet. Shelley and I take our coffee and move off to look at the magazines by the window while Randy the Prophet rings him up. He's added Maruchan Ramen and Chef Boyardee Ravioli to his basket.

"And just let me know if you have any troubles with your vacuum," Randy the Prophet says, handing him a receipt and pointing toward the doorway beside the counter, where a hand-painted sign says, "Vacuum Repair."

We squeeze into his truck, my knee pressed against the gear shift. The air conditioning is a weak, warm breath on my neck. Tom drives silently for a while, and Shelley leans her head on the window, eyes half-shut, ready to go back to sleep.

"Neither of you have a car?" Tom asks.

Shelley and I both speak at once, both saying a version of "No," mine briefer, Shelley's more wordy and annoyed. LeBlanc told me there was no point in me learning to drive, although I think there would be just as much a point as there is for anyone. Shelley can drive, but the prospect of picking out a car, paying the note, getting insurance, remembering gas, is more than she cares to deal with. The compound has a few shuttle vans and people are glad to let us bum when we need to.

Tom drops Shelley at our house, and we continue down a few houses to his place. All the houses are raised and identical except for the colors and the way each person chooses to arrange the items underneath. Sitting under your house is a big way of spending time here, that's how we visit and see who's walking by. Our houses have porches but most of the time they are hot and miserable places to be, the dried wood scratching your feet and threatening a splinter.

We arrive at his house. It is technically white but needs a new coat of paint. The cement slab underneath is bare save for a power strip, twisted and stranded. He pulls all the way under the house, and the air-conditioning suddenly gains more effectiveness. We sit there for a few seconds, enjoying the cold air against our sweat.

I notice that Tom keeps making a noise like he is about to speak. I can hear his mouth opening, a sigh, then he turns his head to look at something. Finally: "Why is that guy called that?"

It surprises me how informal he is being, both by referring to Randy the Prophet in such an offhand way and by talking to me, who he doesn't really know, like we're in on something together.

"Randy the Prophet," I say, to try to get him on the right track.

"Right," he says. He's quiet for a while, then tries again. "Why is he called 'The Prophet?'"

"He sees things."

I'm never sure what to say at this point. Randy the Prophet doesn't like any of the ways people describe what he does. "Sometimes he sees things about a person..." I trail off, feeling inadequate.

"Like the future?" he asks.

I nod, then shake my head. "Sort of. I can't really say, since I'm not in his head, but I think he sees little flashes. I guess they're related to the future."

"That doesn't sound like something appropriate to be happening on company property," he says.

I watch the side of his face. He has long eyelashes and I feel like I can hear them when he blinks. The way he says what he says, it doesn't sound serious. He says it like he is amused, maybe annoyed, but not like he actually cares what happens on company property. I look at his hands on the steering wheel: nervous, with long fingers and picked nail beds.

"LeBlanc approved it," I tell him. I don't tell him the rest, that LeBlanc doesn't approve *of* it. When I brought Randy the Prophet here and explained about him, LeBlanc said something like "Opiate for the masses," which was a rude thing to say, but in the end I got what I wanted, so I let it go. Letting rude things go is a good way to get what you want.

We get out of the truck and walk out from under the house, toward the stairs. He stops at the foot of the stairs and looks up, like he's not sure what to do, so I step in front of him and start climbing. The sun and heat seem crueler just at this moment, getting in a few last stabs before we are inside. When we get to the door, I punch in a code on a lockbox hanging from the knob, take out his key, and hand it to him. He puts his bags down. I shift my weight from foot to foot while he scrapes the key against the lock, puts it in the wrong way, then finally pushes the door open with a pleasant squeak of the spongey door liner.

The inside of this house is not new to me. Shelley and I spent the week cleaning and furnishing it in anticipation of Tom's arrival. LeBlanc likes to assign us these types of tasks, as if we are on some sort of welcoming committee. "Give the place a feminine touch," he told us. In our own house, I have no decorations, just a twin bed with a white blanket, a table with a telephone, and a shelf with books from Mr. Miller. Shelley has lots of stuff with no underlying theme or order, just magazines and DVD cases thrown everywhere, unfolded blankets, framed photos collecting dust.

We went into town early on a Saturday morning, looking for pieces of cardboard taped to stop signs that would direct us to the garage sales. Kenny drove us. We found all the necessary furniture, a couple of ugly paintings, and three wooden ducks. The ducks I insisted on. Kenny and Shelley said they were tacky, but I held them in my lap on the way back to the compound and examined their nicely painted wings, their yellow bills, felt the wood smooth against my hands.

I walk Tom around the house. First to the kitchen where he sets down his bags and puts some things in the refrigerator. I open the cabinets and drawers to show him the dishes and cutlery. He nods at everything with no reaction, as if it is all exactly as he expected, not better or worse. In the living room, I demonstrate how the futon folds into a bed. He stands with his hands in his pockets and says: "Hm."

In the bedroom, I walk to the slat shades and pull them open, so the sun comes in and suddenly the room feels like a nice place to be. The light falls in a square across the foot of the bed. The ducks follow each other in a neat row on the bedside table.

He stands in the doorway with his arms folded. "I like the ducks," he says.

I nod. "I picked them out."

We stand there for a few seconds. It feels nice. Shelley and I accidentally left the window unit in the living room turned down too low, so the entire house has a pleasant chill. The heat from the sun coming through the window presses against my back. I think of something else to say so I can keep standing here.

"What do you think about this place?" I ask.

"The house or the compound?"

"Both."

He shrugs. "They're fine."

"There's another room at the other end of the hall. It's empty. You can use it for your hobbies or guests."

He nods. His arms are still crossed. He is looking at my face, which I know is not socially normal. Mr. Miller was always warning me not to stare. Now I still get warned, usually by people I don't know who like to ask, "What are you staring at?" They don't really expect an answer. They know I am staring at them. They just don't like it.

"Why are you staring at me?" I ask.

He blinks, unfolds his arms, sticks them in his back pockets. "You just look familiar to me," he says. "Where are you from?"

"Up the road a little bit," I say. People talk this way. In generalities.

"Anywhere else?" he asks.

I shake my head.

"Ever lived up north?"

We are so far south that almost anywhere is north. But here people mean somewhere within a three-hour drive.

"No," I say. "Just up at the girls' school, then here."

"OK," he says. And this is nice, because I was prepared for more questions. People don't like to let things be.

CHAPTER FOUR

tom

In the mornings I stare at the ducks. They stay arranged the way they were when I moved in, circling my side table like a pond. Sometimes I knock one off, or brush one with an arm when I get out of bed, but I always make sure to rearrange them at night before I go to sleep.

Waking up, I still have to remind myself where I am. When I open my eyes I expect to see something else, but I'm not sure what. Maybe some amalgamation of everywhere I've ever lived—baseball participation trophies lined up on a red bookcase, a poster of a painting I know nothing about, a beige wall, the boxes my mother keeps in the guest room—but never exactly this: bright wooden ducks swimming by my head.

I wonder if she ever thinks about the ducks. The fact that she picked them out is one of the few things I know about her, so it has become a part of her identity: Marigold with the blonde braid, she picked out the ducks.

It is still dark outside. The weak overhead light in the bedroom casts everything in a soft yellow. The room has a vacation feel to it, not yet marred by my presence, no marks on the walls or balls of hair on the carpet. The smell isn't mine either. A cheap Dollar Store cleaner barely rises above a moist earthiness. I shower and get dressed, everywhere the morning dark pressing in, making me feel like I am sheltered, alone, anonymous.

At breakfast yesterday, Randy the Prophet told me: "Some people think Marigold's not trustworthy, but she's good. She's always been good and kind." We were in the corner of the mess hall, an air vent blowing hair in wisps around his face. We watched Shelley and Marigold make their way through the line, plastic trays sliding along the metal rail shelf. They were dressed for the work week: Shelley in black slacks and a white button down, her hair pulled into a tight, shiny bun, Marigold in a yellow dress that buttoned down the front, her hair in the usual long braid.

"Why wouldn't she be trustworthy?" I asked.

I watched her grab a carton of milk and place it properly in the square space on her tray. I was a little amused at Randy the Prophet's assertion that she had always been good, as if such things could be known.

"She's very close with LeBlanc."

He stopped looking at them, turned to his tray, and bit into a neat slice of omelette.

The words thudded against my brain, tried to swim in through the tributaries.

"Close how?"

"She's basically his daughter," he said, taking a sip of coffee. "Though she wouldn't claim it, and neither would he."

Now his words were swimming in my brain, but I couldn't catch them. I shook my head.

"LeBlanc doesn't have a daughter."

"Right. That's what I said."

I watched her and Shelley at a table by the window, the dull morning light draped over them. Marigold looks around my age, maybe a few years younger. I tried to remember when I first knew LeBlanc, but it was like trying to remember when I first met my parents. He was always there. Like every child, my knowledge of adults revolved around their relationship to me. LeBlanc ceased to exist when he crossed the boundaries of our home, my dad's job, a murmured fight between my parents. I knew he had a wife, but I didn't remember meeting her, and I definitely never heard about any child.

Outside, the cricket sound greets the end of night, or the beginning of day. I get in my truck with a cold Yoo-hoo sweating against my palm. I drive out to the staff beach, keeping the radio and air-conditioning off, my hand hanging out the window, a stale breeze forced by the velocity of the truck brushing my fingertips.

My father and LeBlanc used to talk about this place, before the plant was finished. The idea was that this patch of tropical living would increase worker happiness. I remember thinking how great it would be to have a beach at work. I was picturing a different kind of beach, the kind on postcards with white sand and crystal blue water. It's doubtful that many staff use their free time to wade out into the warm water or sit on the tree-less pile of sand, their workplace looming overhead, sucking out the water beneath them.

I park in the visitor parking lot and take the sandy walkway down to the beach, a beleaguered plot of shipped-in sand abutting the still and silty gulf water. There is no moon, no sun yet, and the stars aren't visible, still it is not dark here, so near the plant, with its safety lights and blinking indicators.

In the morning though, before first light, there is something of an escape here. If I turn my body away from the plant, and focus on the water, the sand, the empty feeling of a day that isn't here yet, I can pretend that I'm not here either. I'm not sure where I'm pretending to be. Nowhere, maybe.

My office is a trailer. It reminds me of in-school suspension: ramps, metal doors, peeling paint, cheap, thin carpet. Even the particle board desk with bubbled laminate is almost identical to the one our elderly ISS teacher napped behind.

Most people here share a trailer with a few co-workers, but since I'm in charge of something I get my own. According to the sign on the trailer door I'm Head of Sales. I forgot to ask LeBlanc what that means.

The inside smells like burnt coffee and mildew. When I first inherited the office, I tried scrubbing the sticky ring off the coffeemaker's heating plate, but it was part of the machine at that point. The mildew comes from somewhere under the carpet. When I open the door, I flip on the light and spray a Febreeze bottle that I keep by the entrance. The trailer is hot from baking all night with strange popping sounds coming from the walls. I turn on the window unit. The rattle and hiss dispel a silence I wasn't aware of before.

In one corner of the trailer stands my desk, random papers piled on top. In the center of the room is a rectangular plastic folding table with metal chairs around it. The coffee pot is plugged in on a low table by the only window, which has dusty blinds that rest on the air conditioner.

I sit down at my desk and fumble through some papers, then take out the grimy binder labeled "staff manual" and stare blankly at the pages, underlining words to try to make them stick in my mind.

Someone knocks on the door. It is such a soft knock that I think I might be imagining it, but I call for them to come in, just in case.

It is Marigold.

She says hello, then walks over to the window and opens the blinds, plumes of dust falling into the wake of the air conditioner and blowing around the room.

"That's my office," she says, pointing to the trailer next door.

She pulls one of the chairs from the folding table over and sits in front of my desk.

The contrast between her, bright and still, and the dingy, humming trailer is both exciting and upsetting. I feel a fluttering elation in my throat that has nowhere to land.

"I should have come to see you earlier," she says. "At first I thought you should come see me. LeBlanc made it unclear, and you are my boss."

"Am I?"

"Is that a joke?" she asks, not in an offended tone.

"No," I say. "I don't know whose boss I am."

"Mine."

"Well, get to work."

She blinks at me. "That was a joke."

"Yes."

"What's your background?" she asks. She crosses her ankles, places her hands neatly in her lap.

"What do you mean?"

"You have some sort of history with LeBlanc? He mentioned he's known you for a while. Did you work at one of his other plants?"

If something about her didn't make me feel embarrassed, ashamed of myself almost, I would laugh. There is nothing surprising about the fact that LeBlanc has told these people nothing about me, so I'm not sure what's funny, I guess that I'm surprised anyway.

"No, no," I say. I wipe a hand across the desk like I might be able to rub an answer out of it. "Nothing like that."

She waits. I'm expecting a question, the give and take of conversation, but I see that's not going to happen.

"I've known him since I was a kid," I say, finally. I shrug and flip through some papers. "I've known him forever. My dad and him... my dad was his second-in-command, I guess. Something like that. They worked closely together."

She nods. The silence is an undertow, and I'm trying to swim my way out, talking faster and faster.

"So, no, I never worked for him before. I just... know him. And he wanted me to work here. Always wanted me to work here, or somewhere, I don't know, probably anywhere, just for him."

She blinks.

"Randy the Prophet told me you've known LeBlanc a long time too," I say. "It was strange when he told me that, I thought we would have met at some point."

"You mean when we were children?"

I nod. I have a sudden flash of what it would have been like to meet her as a child. I probably would have been too shy to talk to her.

"I was up at the school," she reminds me. I like the way she says it, assuming I remember a past conversation, which I do.

"So, LeBlanc was... what? Friends with your parents?" I don't get the sense that she is withholding information, more that she can't tell what I want to know, or that I want to know anything.

"I don't have parents."

Most people would drop this bit of news ironically or with a wince, something to soften the blow, to forgive me in advance because I couldn't have known and now I must be feeling so awkward for asking. She just says it and watches me, looking almost curious.

"Oh. Sorry." I rub the palm of my hand down the center of my face.

"Why?"

I think it is a weird question.

"About your parents. That they..." I trail off.

The air conditioner makes a loud hiss and cuts off.

"LeBlanc started taking care of me when I was twelve," she says, and her voice is suddenly clear and loud in the silence, "but I lived at school. I stayed with him during vacations sometimes."

I make a noise of comprehension, pretending she's clearly explained everything.

"Sales," she says, as if this is a logical segue, "has just been me and Shelley up until now. There are some forms and things that LeBlanc usually signs off on, so I think we'll bring those to you, and sometimes with a more hesitant potential client, LeBlanc comes out and talks to them, so we'll have you do that. We have a map we work with, potential areas of expansion that sort of thing. I'll make a copy for you."

"OK," I say. "Thank you."

I laugh nervously when I say it, because I realize I am truly grateful, because I've been afraid, unmoored by this situation, thrown in by LeBlanc and expected to figure it out on my own.

CHAPTER FIVE
randy the prophet

Before I met Marigold and moved to the compound, I fixed vacuum cleaners out of my trailer. It made me mad how inconsiderate the people with their broken vacuum cleaners were, not taking the time to remove the bag full of fur and dirt and grass and hair. I never said anything about it, though, because desperate times and all that. I needed the money and wasn't even sure how I was getting any clients because all I did was steal a sign from someone's mayoral campaign and paint over it with: "Vacuum repair" and an arrow pointing to my driveway. Except I accidentally left off one u and had to add it in later when Gloria pointed it out. She put a little upside-down V, and the extra U above it and she said she learned that in school and it meant add the letter there.

The first vision came from the bag of a Hoover Constellation.

"Can you believe this thing still runs?" the guy asked when he dropped it off. It was spherical and compact; metal, with a blue base and silver lid. It looked like a planet with a nozzle that would suck up the universe. Like a friendly robot with a long nose.

"No," I said. I didn't say that actually it wasn't running, or else why would it be at a vacuum repair shop down a dirt road.

When I opened the Constellation's dome, there it was: a full bag surrounded by fuzz and sticky hair. I pulled out the bag angrily and the paper caught on one of the metal tabs holding it in place. As I yanked, the contents flew in the air: dirt and leaves and what looked like torn apart cotton balls. I let out a frustrated growl and slammed the bag down, but then I just stood there, the refuse from the bag around me on the floor, on the vacuum cleaner, on my shoes.

That's when I saw it, floating in the dust particles. I can't say what it was I saw. People always want to know. I guess I shouldn't say I saw anything, maybe I just felt it, but there she was all around me: this woman I didn't know and this feeling of her. This feeling of what she was feeling. It was something like when you're talking to a friend about something that's sort of sweet or sort of sad, but for some reason you feel it more. You feel extra sweet or extra sad and you start to get tears in your eyes a little and all you want is to make sure your friend doesn't see those tears or at least pretends he doesn't, so you don't have to talk about it. It was overwhelming, unexpected, and embarrassing.

The Hoover Constellation Man was very enthusiastic when he showed up a few days later to pick up his vacuum cleaner.

"Did you enjoy working on her?" he asked.

I just shrugged.

"She glides, you know."

I nodded. I wondered if this man really liked cleaning or what.

"Hey, so uhh..." I started.

The HC Man was right at the door, pulling the vacuum cleaner along by the nozzle, trying to show off the way it glided on the floor, I assumed.

"Your wife OK?" I asked.

The HC Man stopped. The stupid grin he'd worn since laying his eyes once again on his gliding vacuum cleaner drooped.

"What?" he asked.

"You have a wife?" I thought maybe I better back up.

"Did. Well. Do. Well. Don't know."

I waited.

"Don't know where she is, I mean."

I shuffled my feet and focused my attention on the roundness of the Hoover Constellation.

"Why are you asking about her?"

The HC Man didn't sound mad about it, just a little tired and confused.

"Just thought I..." I scratched the back of my neck. "I heard something that's all. Maybe. I guess I must have heard something about it in town."

"What town?" The HC man asked.

We lived in an unincorporated area made up of dead-end roads and discount stores.

"Down to the Dollar & More maybe."

"You were asking around about me?"

"No. No. I don't know. I'm confused, I think. All that vacuum dust, you know. Would you believe some people bring them to me with the bags still full? My nostrils get filled up and I don't think straight."

The HC man narrowed his eyes and picked up the vacuum cleaner, backing toward the door. "Thanks for fixing the Hoover, man," he said, pushing his way outside.

I stood in my living room for a moment, watching the dust float in the beams of late afternoon sun. Then I walked out to the porch, watching the HC man struggle to get the HC in the back seat of his car. I turned to go back in the house when I saw it again—

felt it—floating in the remnants of the HC's cat hair, lit up by the sun.

"I think she wants to see you," I called.

The man froze, one foot on the floorboard of the driver's side. "Who?"

"Your wife."

The man didn't say anything, just stood there, waiting.

"I don't know," I said. "Maybe not."

The man muttered something under his breath, hopped in the truck, and slammed the door.

I'd almost forgotten about all this when, weeks later, the HC man and his son and a woman that looked vaguely familiar knocked on my door.

"How'd you know all that?" the HC man asked, not pausing for niceties as he walked past me into the cluttered living room, his son and the woman in tow.

"What are you looking at, freak?" The boy snarled at Gloria who stood in the hallway, half in shadow, arms crossed. She shrugged, a sly smile on her lips.

"I found her at the Golden Nugget playing slots," the man said, as if in response to a question. "She said she was waiting for me to show up."

He sat on the edge of the couch, an empty Dyson box sliding slowly, sadly to the ground. "She said she was afraid to come home. Afraid I wouldn't..." he trailed off, as if he figured I knew the rest.

"This your wife?" I asked.

"You knew that, though," the man said. "How?"

The wife and son stood by the door, close to each other but not touching. I wondered what their reunion had been like: warm with lots of crying and sorrys, or cold, quiet, and awkward. I thought if Cynthia were standing there with Gloria, in a stranger's house who saw things he shouldn't, she'd have her arms around her, she'd play gently with the ends of Gloria's hair, curl them around her finger and let them go.

I shrugged. "Saw something," I mumbled, toeing the ratty carpet with my boot.

"Come on. I need to know. Hailey swears she doesn't know you. Don't you, baby?"

The woman, who must have been Hailey, nodded slowly, not looking at either of us, just staring at an old, stained painting of a cypress tree draped with Spanish moss, that hung crookedly over the couch.

"Saw her in your dust," I sighed. I didn't want to say it, knew how it sounded, but I wasn't good at making stuff up on the spot.

The boy snorted.

Gloria hissed: "Shut up."

"What do you mean in my dust? Like that aura shit or something?"

I winced. The thing about all of it, what was happening and what would happen, is that I was a non-believer. Not in the Christian sense of the word, or at least not just in that sense. I didn't believe in religion or astrology or tarot cards or tea leaves or numerology. If I were less of a positive person, some might call me a nihilist. I had too much love for my daughter, enjoyment of sitting outside and looking at things, and pleasure in helping others to fit the label. Life held meaning, I had no doubt, but it was not to be read in a sacred text or divined through a birthday. There was the dewy morning grass and the still water to be considered. There was the puffy face of my daughter when she just woke up, her childhood restored through 8 hours of sleep, her eyes unfocused, hair mussed. There had been Cynthia on Sunday mornings, staring out the window, drinking her third cup of coffee, still in her bathrobe.

"I saw it when the bag broke. Your dust bag," I admitted.

"You left that in there?" Hailey finally found her ability to speak. "Gross."

I nodded. "Yes, it is gross. I pulled it out and the thing sliced open and all the stuff flew out everywhere, and I sort of saw you."

CHAPTER SIX

marigold

A few weeks after I arrived, there was a back-to-school social.

"It's to welcome everyone back, or to welcome the newcomers," Mr. Miller explained.

Except me. I wasn't to be welcomed at this particular social.

"I don't think you're ready yet," Mr. Miller added. He winced when he said it, like it was painful for him.

I was only twelve then, new, and I didn't know much. So, I didn't ask him if he was OK, even though he kept frowning at me and fidgeting with his shirt and talking in circles. I just waited for him to stop talking, then I stared at him for a while, then I decided to say: "OK."

It didn't hurt my feelings, being uninvited to a school event. At the time, I didn't even understand that it should hurt my feelings.

Mr. Miller stammered some more, and then left me alone in my room, closing the door gingerly on the way out.

The actual dorm was another thing Mr. Miller decided I wasn't ready for yet, so my room was in an old janitor's closet—"Well, not a closet, exactly, more of a large storage space," Mr. Miller explained—that sat on the bottom floor of the dorm building. Also on my hall was the house mother who had a room that wasn't a "not a closet exactly," but just a regular room. She chose to pretend that I did not exist and walked past me in the hallway with a serene look on her face.

On the night of the social, the girls were giddy, not themselves. The brother school would be in attendance, and the idea of proximity to creatures unknown to them, made differently, put them in a state of drunken happiness. Their footsteps overhead rattled the books on my bookshelf and random shrieks and giggles interrupted my thoughts.

I'd spoken to LeBlanc once since arriving at the school, on a phone in the dorm mother's bedroom.

She stood in the doorway, her back turned to me, arms crossed while I sat on the edge of her quilted bed and enjoyed the sensation of running my hands along the coiled phone cable.

"What do you get up to out there?" he asked me. I couldn't tell that he didn't sound particularly interested.

"Mr. Miller takes me on walks. I sit in my room and think."

There was a long pause after this, then: "Think? What about?"

The words to explain what I thought about felt heavy against my brain. I didn't know how to say them. So, instead I said: "Goodbye," and hung up.

I was sitting and thinking at my vanity when the girls burst into my room. I wasn't sure what to do, so I just stayed at the vanity and looked in the mirror.

The first to come in was Mary Margaret. She was the tallest and most beautiful of the girls. I had never talked to her, or any of them, but I watched them and heard the way the others talked to her and about her, mostly like they were very afraid.

In the mirror, I saw Mary Margaret's face contorted in a painful-looking mixture of excitement and fear. I thought since everyone was afraid of her, maybe she was afraid of herself. She ran into the room while the others stayed by the door, watching with their arms crossed, looking slightly uncomfortable. I kept my hands in my lap and watched her. She came up beside me, but I didn't turn my head. After rummaging in the vanity drawer for a few seconds, she pulled out a pair of scissors, grabbed my braid, cut it off, and threw the clump of hair on the ground. Everyone ran back out of my room.

When Mr. Miller came to check on me that night, I was sitting on my bed with the braid in my lap. He got the vacuum cleaner from the closet down the hall and sucked up the little pieces of hair that peppered the carpet, then called the house mother, who took me to the bathroom, stuck my head under the sink, roughly combed my hair back, and evened up the ends as best she could. After she left, I sat in my bed, my still-wet hair dripping onto the collar of my dress. Mr. Miller sat in the vanity chair, watching me.

"Are you OK?" he asked

"LeBlanc won't be happy about this," I told him. "You should call for Anna Marie."

"Yes, we'll take care of that, but how do you feel?"

"He likes me to have the braid. It should go past my shoulders."

"Yes, I was told."

I made sure to breathe, and also tried something new: swinging my legs gently back and forth, my feet skimming the floor.

"How did you feel when she attacked you?"

The swinging stopped. I blinked a few times. "I felt unsure."

"Afraid?"

"No. I was just unsure of what would happen. I didn't understand what she was doing. I don't understand why she did it."

"Neither do I."

"How did I do?"

"What do you mean?"

"Did I act appropriately?"

"Oh no. Definitely not."

He shook his head, smiled a little. I picked up the faded, pink towel that the house mother had tousled through my hair and rubbed it against my neck.

"What should I do better?"

I noticed that my stomach muscles tightened. My heart rate increased.

"Remember when there's a fire in Laura's house in *Little House on the Prairie*?"

I nodded. Mr. Miller gave me plenty of assigned reading. "Literature is the key to the human condition," he told me. It was certainly easier for me to read than to try to be an actual part of the human condition by interacting with the girls at school, but I could find little connection between the static, plotted nature of the books and the actual behavior I observed in my classmates.

"Remember how she felt?"

I think he asked me these questions just because he enjoyed the robustness of my memory. "'Too scared to think.'"

"You should feel too scared to think, someone coming in your room, touching you like that. You can't be calm. You should have screamed and cried. When you looked in the mirror, saw your hair cut off, that would hurt your vanity."

"I look ugly?"

I can't say for sure whether I had vanity yet, but I felt a twinge of something as I ran my fingers through my shorn hair.

"No," he paused. The lamp in the corner buzzed. I breathed, and blinked, and swung my legs. "But I think if you were used to having long hair, and that's what the other girls here have mostly too, that you would feel self-conscious when your hair was gone."

I nodded. "I understand. Laura wasn't just scared for herself though, she had to take care of her sisters. Maybe she would be more scared than me. I only have myself to be scared for."

I placed my hand against my neck where it was still moist and rubbed the moisture into my skin.

"Can I ask how you feel now?" he asked.

I stood up, looked down and straightened the creases in my dress. "My heart rate is fast, my stomach hurts. When I breathe, it feels like I am breathing too fast."

"You feel scared now?"

"I think it is anxiety."

"About what?"

"I want to do the right thing."

"You're doing really well, Marigold."

I stared at him, then nodded. "LeBlanc will be unhappy. Anna Marie should come fix my hair."

Anna Marie came the next morning. She found me on the swing, alone. It was Sunday, which meant some girls were having visits with their families, while others were sleeping in, recovering from the social. The playground was dense with fog that morning. I kicked my feet and closed my eyes. On the swing, my body took on a lightness, and it was there, suspended just before the highest arc of the swing, that I felt most a self, most a brain and a heart and a body. The fog surrounded me, but I couldn't make sense of its presence, couldn't touch it or see where it started or ended. I kicked my feet farther and farther out and there was no parting or disturbance, only the fog and the legs, both there somehow and not bothering each other.

When Anna Marie appeared through the fog, I stopped kicking. I slowly came back to earth, and my feet dragged against the playground mulch. She looked different than how I remembered, walking casually, her face open and bright. She was looking around, at the fog, the playground, the school, the sky. When she looked at me, she stopped and smiled, putting her hands in the pockets of her jeans.

"Marigold," she said, excitedly. "It's nice to see you."

I stepped out of the swing and stood there, waiting for what would happen next.

"Do you want to say anything to me?" she asked, hopefully, nudgingly.

There was a swing-ness to me still, that made me want to do what I should, but still a newness that made me want things to be simple. Why did I need to say anything to her? Where was my hair?

Still, I said: "Nice to see you too."

I said it politely, coldly, even though it was something I felt. It *was* nice to see her. I remembered the fine lines around her eyes, her curls, the sudden eruption of her smile. She was the first person I ever met, and even though I couldn't access it then, couldn't combine that knowledge with the thumping in my heart and the lightness in my arms, the body-ness of swinging and the me-ness of standing there, looking at my first person, it did mean something to me. *She* meant something to me, something so safe and soothing that I carried it with me, the thought of her, throughout my life, tucked in my pocket like a shiny rock I could rub when I was nervous.

Anna Marie patted a white canvas bag that was slung over her shoulder.

"Should we get started?" she asked.

Back in my room, I sat at the vanity, facing the mirror. She stood behind me. I could see her reflection, and behind her the edge of my bookshelf and a sliver of the hallway through the cracked-open door. It felt like if I squinted hard enough the mirror would go on forever, and show me the grounds outside the dorm, the school building, the road, the river.

"It's nice in here," Anna Marie said, looking around at what little there was to see.

I nodded. It was nice. It had my books and my bed and my mirror. Sometimes in class, or out wandering the grounds, I would think of my room, the way it looked with just the lamp lit. When I moved in, the room was just a square with cement slab walls and tile floor. Mr. Miller brought me catalogs and I picked out the things I wanted. It was hard to say why I wanted the things—a white duvet cover with little pink flowers embroidered on it, a bed with a white iron headboard, curving and curling in the shape of leaves, a small, oak book shelf, a tatted rug in shades of red and pink, and the vanity, oak to match the bookshelf—but I did want them all, felt something when I saw each and when they were all arranged in my room I knew it was my home.

"What do you think about it so far?" Anna Marie asked. She was taking things out of her bag: scissors, a spray bottle, packets of blonde hair.

I didn't know what she meant by "it": the room, the school, life. So, I shrugged.

"I think you're doing well," she said. She opened up some of the packets of hair and laid them out on my bed. "When I saw you out on the swing, you looked almost happy."

Was I almost happy? I wondered.

She trimmed my hair to even it up from the house mother's attempt. Most of it was at my chin, but some pieces hung down longer. When she was finished, I looked like someone normal, a person who wouldn't wear a braid or white dresses, someone who would turn around and look at Mary Margaret and say: "Get out of my room!" Then she began to braid the new hair onto my head. I closed my eyes and felt her fingers in my hair—my real hair and my fake hair—and I felt something like being on the swing, and like when I first met Anna Marie, her face open to me, a face I trusted.

After a while, she sprayed and trimmed the ends and slung the hair over my shoulder.

In the mirror, I was swingless, braided, buttoned.

CHAPTER SEVEN

tom

The first time I thought about water, I was standing in it, thigh-deep. It was my eighth birthday and I was fishing with my dad, even though it was my birthday and my friends got to do what they wanted on their birthdays, and I did not want to fish. We went every weekend, weather permitting. Usually, I refused to participate, but I went. I wasn't the kind of kid to throw a fit or say something nasty or run away to try to get out of unpleasantness. I was the kind of kid who resigned himself to the inevitable. What I did was sit in the boat, lay in it even, my butt soggy from the water that sloshed in the bottom, my body lulled by the rocking.

Out in the water, my father said nothing. He did not ask me to join him, or mutter or cuss when a fish got away. He stood in the water and cast his line over and over again. Sometimes a fish would land in the boat, sometimes it would land on me. Then I would scramble up, toss it off, watch it flop around in the line of water at the bottom of the boat, watch its gills rise and fall, its one eye roll around.

What I hated most about fishing were the fish. I hated their desperate flopping and wild, one-dimensional faces.

On the morning of my eighth birthday, my mother shook me awake. It was dark like it was still night, but I guessed it was sometime early in the morning.

"Happy birthday," she said, kissing my forehead and rubbing my hair back over and over again.

The memory of her hand on my head was one I clung to. I kept it as a sort of mask I could use to overlay reality. It was one of the last times my mother acted this way: maternal, calm, wise.

I rolled over and grumbled.

"Tommy," she whispered.

I hated when she called me Tommy but didn't know how to tell her. I thought about it sometimes, but I knew how it would go, she would nod and smile, and say, "Oh, I'm sorry, sweetie," and I would see this little glint in her eyes, but I wouldn't know how to say the right thing, the thing that would mean: I still love you and you are my mom.

"Tommy?"

I grunted

"Can you actually try to catch a fish today? For your dad? It'd be like a birthday present."

I rolled back over and opened my eyes.

"But it's *my* birthday."

"Making other people happy is a present for yourself too."

I didn't say anything.

When I got up, I put on my stupid fishing shirt, lime green with vented armpits, and my stupid fishing pants, weird and swishy when I walked, and the ugly camo hip waders I got for Christmas but still fit me because I wasn't growing fast enough and would be short forever with small feet, I knew it.

When we got out in the water and my dad tied us off, instead of just sitting there and watching and drinking a Yoo-hoo, I got out and stood beside him and cast a line. I felt the way I couldn't feel the water in the waders, could only sense that it was there, pressing against me. Behind, the boat rocked arrhythmically. My dad taught me technique, how to reach my arm back just so, when to let go, how to jerk and shimmy the rod so that the bright blue fly swam along the top of the water. When something jerked my fly, my arm, me, my heart leapt like it too was being pulled out from where it belonged. I looked the fish in the eye, a shimmering red drum, felt the strange rigidity of its mouth as I pried it from the hook, and tossed it in the boat.

"Where does the water go?" I asked.

"The lake," my dad said, and kept fishing.

"Where does it come from?" I asked. I knelt down in it and sat back on my heels like an old man shooting the shit.

"I don't know, son, probably from some other river."

I leaned forward and stuck my whole head into the water. I thought about it coming all the way from some other river, how it was drops of water all together, but it was also one big sheet of something cold and moving.

CHAPTER EIGHT

marigold

The sun is gone. We make our way home by the scattered lampposts: some lopsided from the last storm, some dim, some off. The bulb on the lamppost marking the turn to our street hangs limply from a wire and hisses into the dark. Shelley trudges up the stairs, crinkling a Snickers wrapper in her hand. I stand under the house for a moment, on the slab of concrete with our chairs and freezer. The sky is purple over Mr. Kenny's house across the way. The air fills with chirps and hums and the absence of noise that comes from people sitting quietly in front of the TV, or sleeping, or night fishing.

A mosquito lands on my arm and I let it sit there for a few seconds. I don't get bit often, which they say is normal, some people don't, but it feels better to experience these things, the little aches and annoyances. When it starts to sting, I flatten it and wipe the black remains and spot of blood onto my palm, then onto my skirt.

I go upstairs. Shelley lies on the couch, the TV muted, colors flashing across the wall above her. I sit on the sliver of couch left by her feet.

She is in a bad mood, I can feel it cloudy and purple around her, in the way she doesn't move her feet for me or look at me. This is not an ideal situation. I know Shelley better than anyone, but she is not consistent. She is not a character in a book. Sometimes when she is angry she wants someone to ask her about it so she can talk. Sometimes she wants to be left alone until she feels better. Sometimes she wants to be left alone for a little while, then checked on later so she can talk.

"Are you OK?" I venture.

"Yeah," she says. She doesn't look at me. Slowly, she rolls to her side then pushes herself off the couch, walks to her room, and closes the door.

Shelley and I met when we were thirteen. It was the week before school started back after summer, and I spent the morning swinging on the playground, watching the other girls get dropped off, kissing and hugging their parents. Mr. Miller said I was ready to move into the dorms with the other girls. It was unclear what rubric he used to decide I was ready. The other girls still didn't talk to me unless trying to provoke me or if forced to in class. I was still strange in my body, slow and unsure.

"A new student is coming, and I think she'll be the perfect roommate for you," he said.

The playground was shaded by two live oaks that beckoned toward each other over the play gym. Even in the shade, the early August heat wriggled between the creases of my skin, in my ears and up my nose. The sunlight filtered through the branches and patched the ground. Watching the girls get dropped off, I wondered which one my new roommate might be. I wasn't able to worry about meeting her, just aware of the most likely scenario: she would not like me. No one liked me. Whenever I mentioned this fact to Mr. Miller he said, "I like you," but it wasn't true. He wanted to like me.

Later that afternoon, Mr. Miller called me to the dorm. We'd already set up my side of the room, put my duvet with the pink flowers over the twin bed and hung my dresses in the chifforobe. The other side of the room was now scattered with the contents of a couple half-emptied suitcases. A small girl with unkempt black hair sat on the floor between the two suitcases, holding a pair of jeans in front of her and frowning.

"Hello, Shelley," Mr. Miller said.

She lowered the pants and stared at us.

"This is your new roommate," he said. It wasn't clear whether he was saying it to me or to her. He elbowed me.

"Hi," I said. "I'm Marigold."

She made eye contact with me, nodded, then started folding the pants.

Mr. Miller made some excuse and left.

I moved over to the bed and sat down.

Having, as far as I could tell, only folded the one pair of jeans and put them in her dresser, Shelley climbed up on her bed and lay on her bare mattress, staring at the ceiling.

"You know they only put us together because we're both orphans," She said.

"I'm not an orphan," I corrected her. I was trying out sitting cross-legged on my bed, a casual pose I'd seen some of the other girls do when their doors were cracked open.

"Do you have parents?" she asked.

"No."

"Then you're an orphan," Shelley said. She didn't sound like a know-it-all. She sounded tired. She clasped her hands on her belly and blew air toward the ceiling.

But I wasn't an orphan. Heidi was an orphan. Mowgli was an orphan.

"I never had parents," I said. I moved so I was lying on my stomach with my chin in my hands and feet kicked up in the air. "An orphan is someone whose parents die."

Shelley rolled toward the wall and sighed.

"You're the worst kind of orphan there is," she said. She rolled off the bed, scooped up a bunch of t-shirts from her suitcase and shoved them in a drawer, slamming it shut with corners of fabric sticking out around the edges. "Like you said, you never had parents. No one ever loved you. Kids like that grow up to be murderers because no one hugged them when they were babies."

"I was never a baby. Mowgli was around a bunch of wolves when he was a baby and he turned out fine."

Shelley stared at me. "Mowgli isn't... Never mind. I don't even care. They told me you were going to be a freak."

"Who did?" I felt a twitch in my eye. I forgot to hold my casual pose and was now lying flat like a board on the bed, my cheek turned toward her.

"Mr. Miller."

"I don't think so."

"He didn't say 'freak,' he said you were different and unique which is the nice way adults call someone a freak."

In bed that night, I lay flat on my back and stared at a weakly illuminated semi-circle of ceiling from

Shelley's night light. I could tell from her breathing that she wasn't asleep. "They're dead?" I asked.

"Yeah," Shelley said almost immediately, like she'd been waiting for the question. "My mom... it just happened. Last year. My dad was when I was little. I don't remember."

"I'm sorry," I said. It was the right thing to say, but it wasn't correct. Why was it that I should apologize for something so unrelated to me? But I didn't just say it because I'd been taught to. I did feel sorry. I felt like there was something dark and sharp inside me that I could sand away with an apology.

I wait on the couch for a few minutes. A Western plays on the muted television—a man rides through town on a horse, tipping his hat to those congregated on the porches and behind saloon doors. A lovely woman in a high-necked dress smiles at him as she crosses the street. I turn the TV off and go to her room. The door is open a crack and the light is on.

"Can I come in?" I ask quietly. I try not to sound too sympathetic so as not to annoy her.

She makes a sort of humming noise that I think means it's OK. I come in the room and she is in bed pretending to read a book. I know she is pretending because she has been reading the same book since we were in high school. She prefers television. The book is called *As I Lay Dying* by William Faulkner and I loaned it to her. Usually she pretends to read it when she is mad. Sometimes she actually reads a little bit of it when she can't watch TV for some reason like a power outage and then she complains to me about how dumb and boring it is.

I stand in front of the door and wait. Eventually, she puts the book down on her lap and looks at me.

"What's up?" she asks.

Sometimes she is a lot of work.

"You seem upset," I say.

She shrugs.

I wait.

She throws the book on the floor and slinks down under the covers.

"What are we doing here?" she asks. Her eyes are closed.

My chest feels like it did when I saw the alligator. We swim around in this conversation all the time.

"I have to..." I start.

"You don't," she says.

Then I remind her that maybe I don't, but certainly she doesn't, and then she is quiet, because she thinks if I am here she needs to be, because we are all tangled up together in some way that I can't figure out. And I don't say anything either, because I think if you can't change it why are you worrying about it, but my brain, if it is a brain, is not like hers.

And the truth is I don't know if I have to be here or not and I don't have anyone to ask.

CHAPTER NINE

tom

I wake up in an orange glow, covered in sweat. I try to sink back into my dream. It swims away from me, slippery, leaving only a trail of color and light. I think Marigold was in it. This thought leads to another, one I keep coming back to: I know her from somewhere. The woman in the dream wasn't just the one who picked out the ducks, but someone else, an outline of someone, a blurry memory.

Standing up and raising the blinds, I see the row of houses across the street. Beyond them the plant and the gulf and the rising sun. It is like one of those cheap paintings they sell at stands in the middle of the mall: attractive and quaint at first, but the longer you look something turns in your stomach, a clash with the fluorescent lights and bleached floors, the scent of cheap food and cheap fabrics, the knowledge that it doesn't exist, the world of the painting, the quaint village or beautiful beach or house in the snow, not in the way it is shown, not simple and sparkling and easy on the eyes.

I stopped my morning wanderings once I started doing actual work. They were a small enjoyment for me, a connection to a life I thought I'd have, the one where I did little and put my attention toward enjoyment. After I looked at the files Marigold brought, called small town government officials, put my customized rubber stamp of approval on pieces of paper, I couldn't walk out into the brightening morning and hope to feel anything good.

Instead I stand at my bedroom window and try to mentally fast forward through the day. It helps if I can remind myself that in eight to ten hours I will be back here, alone, away from the phone and the papers and the plant.

"We've gotta be nice to him," my mom would always say. "He's helping us."

With this, she'd motion around her two-bedroom trailer, crammed full of the remainders of our life in a four-bedroom suburban home: too many throw pillows on the couch, clashing landscape paintings on the walls, and piles of boxes that had nowhere to go. The idea that living this way, with a standing-room-only shower and a comically small stove, was something she should thank someone else for made me laugh. Not really. I didn't actually laugh, but I did think it was amusing in a way that made me feel sad for my mother, and then angry with her, until I remembered LeBlanc was the one I was angry with, which started the whole conversation over again.

"The settlement is the settlement," I reminded her. "You can pretend that it's a good settlement if you want. It's not. But either way, how polite I am to LeBlanc won't undo it."

Sometimes it was hard to even get the word "settlement" out. I said it so often that it was exhausting to push the syllables across my tongue again, painfully boring like the third hour watching daytime TV in pajamas and unbrushed teeth. The settlement was the center of my mother's world, something she came back to again and again whether we were talking about what her neighbors were up to (having trouble paying rent—they didn't have a settlement, after all), or what she wanted to eat (we could afford some nice cuts of meat, thanks to the settlement).

Somehow after all the years that passed between the signing of the settlement and my adult life, I got folded back into it, became a bargaining point, an addendum.

After breakfast, I sit in my truck and watch everyone get into their vehicles and head to work. Some of them glance at me, some wave, most avoid looking in my direction. Randy the Prophet taps on my window as he walks past. Beside me, an unwelcome companion flat in my passenger side seat: a crisp manilla folder.

It's a small account. The Mayor-President just down the road. Marigold says he wants to see me specifically.

"He asked for the person in charge," she told me.

"That could be you," I said.

"It isn't, though."

It is hard to tell whether she is joking sometimes. It seems like she never is.

At the gate, Kenny nods at me and raises one hand lazily as he adjusts the dial on the radio he keeps on a cracked plastic table.

Once I turn off the property, once I can't see Kenny anymore, or the pop-up tent he sits under, or the rusted swinging gate, it is like I am nowhere. The plant, the bruising reality of it, is still there in the corner of my eye, but if I look the other way there are just trees and litter. Eventually even the plant is gone and then it's just the levee, the top of a few boats since the water is high. I forget to turn on the radio or feel bored.

The town greets me with a statement of fact: a faded green sign with the population count. There is no "welcome" or "you are entering." I drive into what another sign informs me is "Historic Downtown": a block with a boarded-up courthouse and strip mall. The directions Marigold gave me seemed unbelievable, but I follow them, parking in one of the faded, slanted spots in the empty strip mall parking lot, in front of a Dollar & More ("And more what?" I asked her). The front of the Dollar & More is comprised of ugly, square windows displaying summer-themed garbage that can be bought for a dollar. There are candles shaped like flip-flops, earrings shaped like flip-flops, and flip-flops. The sight of the flip-flops, stiff in non-committal floral prints, taps on a hidden memory and sends a soreness to the spot between my big toe and the one beside it. Above the windows, beside the lime green Dollar & More logo, someone has stenciled in a dirt brown, mater-of-fact font:"& Government Bldg."

I walk in and am surrounded with the scent of possibly hazardous cleaning products and plastic. There is no one inside except a young woman at the register, moon-faced and pale with lovely light-orange hair pulled into a tight ponytail that sits straight up on her head. She looks at me but doesn't say anything, both elbows on the checkout conveyor belt. She blows a large, pink bubble.

"I was looking for the government offices," I say. I feel nervous, like she might make fun of me for asking.

The bubble pops. She scoops it up where it is stuck to her face and crumples it back into her mouth.

"You want to talk to The Mayor-President?" she asks, like the question is barely worth turning into words.

"Is he in?"

She points over her shoulder at a door by the balloon stand, decorated with a hand-written sign reading: "Government Services."

I walk over and knock on the door.

"Not now, Martha," a gravelly voice calls.

"That ain't me knocking," Martha yells from the register, now circling furiously in a jumbo word search.

"Well then who the hell is it?" the voice asks.

Martha looks at me and flings her hands out.

"Um. I'm Tom," I say.

The voice behind the door says nothing.

"You can go in," Martha says, not looking up from the word search.

I crack the door open and give another light knock. "Hello?" I call.

As the door swings open, I take in the office: beige walls plastered with government notices and road signs, a desk piled with paperwork and plastic Dollar & More tchotchkes, a phone flashing in futility. Behind the paperwork sits a balding man with round, wire-rimmed glasses and a rumpled suit. He stands up and motions for me to sit, then pushes apart two piles of paper to form a tunnel through which we can see each other.

"Tom," the man says, as if he has known me a long time and finds nothing interesting about me being here.

"Are you the Mayor-President?" I ask.

He nods.

I tell him I'm from the compound.

He nods again. I try to read his facial expression. He looks blank, tired, resigned. I notice a half-eaten sandwich, squashed and unappetizing on top of one of the stacks of paper.

"Marigold said you wanted to meet me," I tell him.

"Yes, well, it was nothing against her. I found her a little odd, but it wasn't that..." he trails off, glances at the sandwich.

"Did I interrupt your lunch?" I ask. It seems early for lunch,

He waves a hand at the sandwich. "That's from yesterday." He takes off his glasses and rubs them against his shirt, then puts them back on. "I'm just a little concerned about this whole idea," he says. "But to be honest I don't know that I have another choice."

"How's your water?" I ask.

LeBlanc said that was all I had to ask. This was one of his major talking points after my father died, when he was trying to "prepare me for the real world." As if a teenager with a dead dad was remotely concerned about the inner workings of his business. When he started in on that, I usually just lay there, silent, staring at the pattern of lights my muted TV threw on the ceiling.

"It's not good," the Mayor says. "We've got some reports here."

He rustles around on his desk, pulls out a crumpled folder, and shakes it toward me with a knowing look as if the sight of it will convey the contents. "Some incidents. Sickness and such."

"Widespread?" I ask. I gulp. There is a tightness in my chest that I can't identify. I want him to say no, but I also want him to say yes.

"Pretty," he says. "Like for example the water here. Martha and I have both been feeling poorly. We started drinking the Dollar & More brand water instead and feel a little better. I don't know if that's real or just in our heads."

"Could be real," I say, my tone casual but concerned.

"There's been other..."

He opens a few desk drawers, closes them, stands up and walks around the desk then sits beside me and starts looking through the piles of paper on the edge of the desk. "Here's one," he says, placing a coffee-stained group of stapled papers in my lap. The top of the first page says "Official Complaint."

He goes back to sit behind his desk. "That's from a family that's been having seizures. All of them. Five people. Mom, Dad, Grandma, Brother, Sister. Never had them before."

I nod. I try not to remember LeBlanc telling me seizures are good for business.

"Sounds pretty serious," I say. It does, after all.

"Yeah. So, I heard about y'all. Obviously, I've known about y'all for a while, right down the road and all, but I started thinking about y'all and people were asking me," he points a finger at the papers to illustrate, "to reach out, so I am."

"I'm glad," I say. "I think we'll be able to help you."

I guess I am actually glad because whatever I am up to has to be better than grandmas getting seizures.

"Yeah," he starts. He says it like more will come, but then he shuts his mouth and watches me for a few seconds.

"You have some concerns?" I ask.

He would be stupid not to.

"We just don't have much," he says. "The town budget, the individual budgets of our people. It's not much."

"We've got something that will work for everyone," I say.

"I saw that was your slogan."

That makes me feel stupid, like I am even more fake than I actually am, but I didn't know that was our slogan or that we had a slogan. It wasn't even clear to

me as I was saying it that it was a line fed to me by
LeBlanc, which it obviously was.

CHAPTER TEN

gloria

It's sick," I told him. "What more do you need to know? It's disgusting. It's despicable."

"Any other synonyms you want to use?" he asked.

He lay on the couch with a pillow over his head. I wished he wasn't holding onto it, so I could pick it up and throw it at him.

Once, when I was about five, I cried to my mother: "Why does it feel this way?" I don't remember, but my dad likes to tell the story. I was pointing at my chest, where, presumably, I was feeling some type of pain. It was after a LEGO house I built didn't turn out right, and the pieces got stuck together when I tried to pull them apart. I ended up throwing LEGOs on the floor, stomping on the pieces, then screaming from the jabbing pain going through my bare feet.

"She took your little hands away from your chest and kissed them," Dad told me.

"Then she said: 'You feel things in a strong way. I'm like that too. Dad's a little different. He feels things too, but those feelings sort of spread out inside of him, it makes them easier for him to feel. For me and you, our feelings hit us right here,' she pointed to her own heart, then to yours, 'and they stay there until we figure out how to get them all out.' You told her: 'I don't want feelings.'"

I think some form of this every day. To feel what the world feels is nothing but a burden to me. I don't want to be empathetic and kind and compassionate. I want to be dull and numb, to take a nap, to hide my head under a pillow.

Right then, yelling at my dad while he tried to ignore me, all I wanted was to turn myself off, but instead I could feel the pressure building in my chest, the anger and resentment and sadness pulsing up into my brain, pressing behind my ears. I started to cry.

"Why do you have to act so fucking calm?" I screamed. I stood up and kicked the wall just to do something. My foot easily put a hole in the cheap plaster.

He sat up, putting the pillow down beside him, but he didn't say anything about the hole. It wasn't the first hole.

"You're leaving," he reminded me. One downside of having spread out feelings is they hide in the crevices of your body and seep out bit by bit. An upside is a person with spread out feelings can express those feelings gently. My dad mentioned me leaving once a day, as if it were a casual fact and not something that was floating around in his body like a small dose of poison, like the amount administered daily to a kid with a Munchausen-by-proxy parent.

"And that makes it OK to turn evil?" I asked. I was frustrated by my words because they sounded stupid and petulant in their simplicity, but they were what I meant, and I couldn't think of another way to say them.

"You're leaving, darling, and I don't need to stay here. I don't need all this space. I'm not making enough anyway. I never am. For once I could not worry about paying the rent, buying food. I could just work and go home and relax."

"I'll send you money," I said. I tried not to process what he told me because it forced me to see myself in a way I didn't like: whining about things he wouldn't buy me, ungrateful and snotty.

"Big bucks from the Mart."

"It's better than nothing."

"No, hon, you need it for yourself. You have to pay rent. It's not cheap in the city."

I rolled my eyes. He kept saying I was moving to the city. I was moving two hours away to a town that had traffic lights and a few box stores.

"Besides," he said. "It's not just that"

I really didn't want to hear what he was going to say next, because whatever it was, it was going to be weird.

"I have a feeling," he said. He looked me straight in the eyes when he said that. Weird.

"Great. Did you have a vision?" I didn't try to hide my annoyance.

"No, my cynical little turtle dove. It's just a feeling, like any person might have."

"So, you have a good feeling about working for people who are profiting off of our needs, basic human needs, and that makes it OK?"

"I didn't say it was a good feeling. Just a feeling."

He never mentions if that feeling was true, whatever it was, but I'm not that petulant teenager anymore, so I don't let myself ask.

When I pull up to the gate of the compound, Kenny grins and waves, comes over and waits for me to roll down my window.

"Well look at you," he says.

"Hey Mr. Kenny," I say. I say it like he's obnoxious and I'd rather not talk to him, because that's the way it should be. He's a nosy old country white man, but I actually like him, and I can't help it.

"You're all grown up," he says. He nods approvingly. Then shakes his head sadly. "Makes me feel old."

For some reason I hold back any rude responses which might include that I was already grown up when he met me, so I'm really just getting old which doesn't sound as cute. Instead I just shrug and ask after his family like the good country kid I am.

When he finally stops talking, Kenny walks to the gate and pushes it open for me, waving me off. The dread that built up on my drive down here grows exponentially once I get inside the gate. It's not just dread now but a pungent sort of anger balled up in the pit of my stomach. Something about the palm trees and the peaceful sign and the plant off in the distance. I want to burn this place to the ground, and have anonymously threatened to do so, but I can't because all that would do would give some rich asshole an insurance payout and take away some poor people's water.

I meet Dad at the store, and we take his truck deep into the compound, park off a gravel road and walk down a path into the bottomland. I'm walking behind him and watch his hand grab at palmetto leaves, brush against tree trunks.

We find a spot where the grass is flattened, and the dirt is dry and set out the beach towel I brought and some packages plundered from the store: Slim Jims, Star Crunch, Twinkies, Tobasco Cheez-Its, and one sad, brown banana that neither of us is going to eat. The swamp surrounds us, still and alive, the movement of the water barely detectable when a bug lands or the wind shifts. I like to see the crooked arms of the cypress bent into the water, they look tired and thirsty, and like they are finally getting satisfaction. Mosquitoes flit around us, but don't land since we're both covered in the sticky high-DEET spray that sits at the edge of the taste of the food on my tongue.

"So, there's new guy here?" I ask.

Dad takes a big bite into a Slim Jim and it makes a satisfying snapping sound. He nods and chews, swallows, then: "Yeah. He's a nice guy." He looks at me then, holds up a finger, takes another bite out of his Slim Jim. With his mouth still full, he says: "And don't start with me about 'if he's so nice, why's he here?' I don't know why."

I try not to laugh, because I am half-outraged, half-entertained. I dip a finger into the center of my Twinkie and lick it off. "I'm not in the mood to talk about that anyway," I say. "Just want to visit you."

"Will you spend the night?"

"Probably. I don't feel like driving back. I don't have another shift for two days."

A dragonfly lands on the towel between us, then dances around on top of our food packaging before flitting back amongst the trees.

"Well, that'll be nice," he says.

He sounds so happy that I feel guilty for not visiting more. He could visit me, though, I remind myself. And he could just not work here.

"You planning to hang out with Shelley?" He asks it like it's casual, like we talk about these things.

I blink and take a bite out of the Twinkie to buy some time, then shake my head. "Probably not."

"Well," he says. I think he regrets bringing it up, because he doesn't know what to do at this point. "Everything alright there?"

"Everything's fine," I say. I open the bag of Tobasco Cheez-Its so that there will be noise. It's an easy one to open, but I pull on the plastic for a while for extra crinkles.

I have no idea if everything is fine, or what it would mean for it to be fine or not fine. Sometimes I see Shelley and sometimes I don't. Sometimes I want to and sometimes I don't. I guess sometimes she wants to and sometimes she doesn't. The random alignment of us both wanting to see each other is rare, but nice. Sometimes I'll change my mind one way or the other. Looking out at the water, the way it sucks in the sun instead of reflecting it, I think I might change my mind this visit. "Maybe I'll see her later," I say into the Tobasco Cheez-It box.

Dad falls asleep in front of the TV before it is fully dark outside. I pull on my tennis shoes and try to leave without making the door squeak. It squeaks anyway, but when I glance back he is still asleep, or pretending to be. It occurs to me that he might have pretended to fall asleep in the first place to encourage me to go out. He usually stays up until past midnight, especially when he has a guest who has to politely listen to his night ramblings. My thought is that I will just walk around the compound and if I see Shelley then it is a sign and if I don't see her it's also a sign. I don't believe in signs, but I need some sort of narrative to build my evening around, otherwise I will stare out at the plant and break something in my dad's house.

Walking past Shelley's, my ears get red. Even though I know it is unlikely, I feel like she happens to be looking out the window just as I am walking by and is staring at me, judging. I cannot look at her house. I start to wonder how I walk, how my arms are supposed to move and whether I am slouching and if my face looks weird. These worries occupy me so that I don't notice that Marigold is walking toward me until she is right there, in my face, making her weird eye contact at me.

"Hi, Gloria, Randy the Prophet told me you were visiting," she says.

I greet her, then put my hands in my pockets and lean back on my heels a little. She stands straight, arms limp at her sides. Even though it is getting toward dark and she's been working all day, her braid is still perfectly smooth and in place, slung over her shoulder. I told my dad I think it's a wig, but he told me it's rude to even speculate about such things. I wondered since when did he expect me to be polite?

"Where are you heading?" she asks.

"Just walking," I say. I try to keep eye contact, because I feel like she is trained to know when people are lying or uncomfortable and breaking eye contact might be one way to tell.

"You should come up and watch a movie with us," she says. "We have popcorn."

I truly don't know which will be worse: walking in and surprising Shelley as she lies in some disgusting old t-shirt on the couch and figures out that I sought her out, or going home and thinking about the two of them watching a movie and eating popcorn and saying things to each other and knowing things about each other while I sleep on a futon in an otherwise empty room in my dad's house.

I decide to say sure and follow her back to their house. It's almost exactly as I imagined, except Shelley is standing in the kitchen eating Cool Whip in her disgusting old t-shirt. Her negligence toward her appearance is annoying. The sight of her hair tangled around a scrunchie makes me inwardly wince. She rudely doesn't act surprised to see me even though I haven't been to the compound in two months, and we only saw each other in passing at the mess hall last time.

"Hey," she says. She says it with her mouth full of Cool Whip.

I nod at her.

"I found Gloria walking around and asked her to join us," Marigold says.

Shelley doesn't react in any way, just takes a bag of popcorn from the box and sticks it in the microwave. "OK. I need silence for the next few minutes while I listen to the pops," she says. "You know I have to get it burnt a certain amount."

For some reason, Marigold and I both say, "I know," because we do know, but we say it like she's being completely reasonable, and we are happy to humbly submit to her request.

I decide to join in the casualness and spread myself out on the couch with a Coke while the two of them gather snacks in the kitchen. I watch their heads over the bar.

"What are we watching?" I call, like I've been part of this plan all along.

Shelley points to the coffee table where a ragged DVD case sits: *Peter Pan.*

"Marigold hasn't seen this one?" I ask. Generally the movies are a sort of educational experience for her.

"No," Marigold says, bringing a bowl of Doritos in and setting it beside the DVD case.

Once the popcorn is ready, we sit on the couch and Shelley presses play on the remote. I am sitting between Shelley and Marigold. Their couch is small and I feel very stiff and uncomfortable. We are quiet. When the opening credits start, I slide down onto the floor with my head propped against the couch. I feel much more relaxed down here. No one can see the side of my face or try to figure out what I am feeling.

It feels nice watching the movie. I eat too many Doritos and drink two more Cokes and feel happy with the way my body is overloaded with sugar and salt.

When we get to the part where Wendy sings "Your Mother and Mine," Marigold reaches for the remote and turns down the volume a little.

"Do you ever think about your mother?" she asks.

I can't tell which one of us she is asking. "Me?" Shelley asks. "Or her?" I don't look at her, but assume she's making some sort of motion in my direction.

"Either," Marigold says.

"I guess. Sometimes," Shelley says. She tries to say it with a yawn like it's no big deal. Maybe it isn't. My lungs hurt, and I hope she talks a lot so I don't have to.

"What was she like?" Marigold asks. I glance at her over my shoulder. She is staring at the TV.

I turn back to the TV. Wendy leaves the tree house and sees her brothers and the Lost Boys tied up. A pirate grabs her from behind.

Shelley blows out air before she speaks. It sounds like she was holding her breath. "Like a mom," she says.

"I don't know what that means," Marigold says.

Captain Hook lowers a package into the tree. At first, I wonder why they have never talked about this before, but then it makes sense: Marigold will ask about something when it interests her, Shelley will avoid talking about her feelings.

"You do too," Shelley says.

I turn my head toward her slightly, trying to avoid her notice. I see from the corner of my eye that she is straightening up a little. She pushes the base of her palms into her eyes.

"You've seen moms before with their children," Shelley adds.

"Yes, but the children never told me what it was like. I only saw it."

Marigold's feet are on the carpet beside me. She slowly drags her toes back and forth.

The pirates sing a song to the children about the benefits of becoming thieves and crooks.

"This is a hard thing you're asking me to do," Shelley says. She reaches for the remote and pauses the movie. The image freezes on the children grinning and Wendy with her nose stuck in the air. In the silence, I can hear the buzzing of the street lamps, a bug chirping, muffled voices down on the road.

"I know," Marigold says.

"It will help you?" Shelley asks.

"I think so."

My pulse is beating painfully in my throat. I press my hand there as if to stop the flow of blood. My mouth feels dry, but I am worried if I swallow it will be too loud and noticeable. I sit very still.

"I didn't think about it until a few years ago," Shelley starts. I hear her rustling around on the couch and turn to see she is clutching a pillow against her chest. "That she was a person, like me. She was only a little older than I am now when she died. I was just young and self-obsessed. I guess that's the way kids are. I hardly know what she was like as a person. She seemed to read a lot. I remember she had those self-help books and she would immediately start taking whatever advice they offered. This one week everything was about gratitude. At breakfast we had to say what we were grateful for, and she stuffed these notes in my lunchbox about how she was grateful for me. I wish she got old, so I could really see her, but I never did.

I try sometimes to... I don't know. I feel like if I think about her hard enough I can somehow find memories that I can't remember, and there will be some sort of hint to me about what she was really like, like what she would be like to a stranger on the street, or a friend, or her husband, or her own mom, but I can't get to that. I can't find it."

"Did she sing you songs?" Marigold asks.

This makes me laugh and I have to hold it in and turn it into a cough. Marigold loves these non sequiturs. She is often completely blind to the emotional moment.

"Sure. Yeah." Shelley says, she sounds a little amused too. There's something in this that gives me more confidence, so I turn my head completely toward her and she catches my eye and we both smile.

"Which one was your favorite?" Marigold asks.

"*Skinnamarinky Dinky Dink.*" Shelley says. She snorts. So do I.

"How did it go?"

"Seriously?

I start singing it first. My mom sang it to me too. I had this little yellow bear Dad won me in the claw game and she would dance the bear on top of my chest and then touch its nose to mine during the "I love you" part. Shelley joins in with me and we are sort of laughing because it's a goofy song, but we don't laugh too much, probably because our moms are dead.

Marigold goes to bed and I stay. I get back on the couch and Shelley and I sit there, each with our backs to an opposite arm, our legs running parallel to each other. We talk. Shelley tells me about the new boss, who she thinks is in over his head and is not a bad person. She rolls her eyes and shushes me when I start getting agitated and my voice rises. "Marigold's sleeping," she reminds me. I tell her about the efforts against LeBlanc, which she supports but thinks are pointless. "Why put so much energy into something that won't work?" We talk a little about the Mart and I pull out a few of the funnier stories that I unknowingly keep saved in the back of my mind for her—the man who wanted to know if I licked the produce because he "heard that sort of thing was happening," the kid who tried to steal a skateboard, the wheels sticking out from the top and bottom of his shirt. Sometimes she rubs her foot against my leg, and it feels nice and calming. We both start to drift off there, one of us throwing out a sentence, the other responding with a little noise or laugh, and in the moment before I am completely asleep I wonder why I was being so weird earlier, and I feel completely sure about what we are, and what we are is just this, and that is OK.

CHAPTER ELEVEN
marigold

The summer before I met Shelley, LeBlanc took me home with him. He lived in a big white stucco house in the city with tile floors and pots with leafy plants branching out of corners. There was a yard with a grove of citrus trees, but he preferred I stay inside. His silent central air conditioning unit kept the house chilled to a winter temperature, and I walked around in summer dresses with shawls and blankets wrapped around me. The house had windows that went from the ceiling to the floor and I liked to stand in them, glean some warmth from the sun, and watch the workers in the yard.

LeBlanc was gone most of the day to the plant which was under construction or doing other errands. When he had meetings at the house, I was asked to stay in my room until the visitors left. The room I had there was nice. That's what LeBlanc told me: "You'll like it here. Much more comfortable than what you have at school. Bigger bed. A rug. Your own TV, even." Those sounded like good reasons for it to be better, but I didn't tell him that Mr. Miller put a TV and DVD player in my converted janitor's closet room because he thought it was important for me to watch movies.

There was something about the room that I did not like. Now I might describe how I felt in it as lonely, but at the time I didn't recognize the feeling. When I looked around at the little basket of dolls, the fluffy pink pillows, the lacy curtains, the pure white rug, the marigolds in a vase, I felt like I was rewound back into my old self, my first self, knowing but not knowing, existing but not belonging. The room felt alien and unreal to me. What I wanted, when I thought about it, was to be back in my small dorm room, to hear the familiar sound of the faculty footsteps coming and going, their greetings in the hallway, to anticipate a possible visit from Mr. Miller where he would bring me a new book or tell me a story to which I was meant to react appropriately.

In the mornings, I would wake up in a panicked confusion, not recognizing the blanket on top of me, the smells around me, the ceiling. It was true that I didn't have any friends at school, or even anyone to talk to besides Mr. Miller, and sometimes the house mother who seemed to be battling her dislike for me by occasionally saying nice things about my hair or my clothes or the tidiness of my room, but at LeBlanc's I had no one.

Before LeBlanc came to pick me up from school, I asked Mr. Miller what he thought it would be like there.

"He probably just wants to get to know you," he told me. "You'll talk, like you and I do."

I tried to think about what it would be like to talk to LeBlanc. He visited me at school sometimes, but we were never alone together for more than a few minutes. A teacher was always around to keep the conversation going. I was asked about my lessons then left alone.

Mr. Miller was wrong. It wouldn't be the last time, and probably wasn't the first, but it was very disorienting.

LeBlanc only talked to me when it was necessary. On the drive to his house, he turned the radio up and rolled down the windows. When we stopped at a gas station, he asked, "Do you want anything?" and I shook my head. That was it.

Some days we might have a little small talk if we happened to pass each other in the halls, but I often didn't see him. We didn't eat meals together. I was told to eat in the dining room, but my place was the only one set. The maids would come in, lay down my food, then quickly leave. One time I managed to talk to one of them before she left. She said LeBlanc always ate alone in his study, and sometimes he didn't eat and the tray just got cold outside the door.

One day I waited outside the study until he came out. He jerked when he saw me, almost looking frightened. I asked him if I could have permission to go out in the yard for the day. There wasn't an official rule that I couldn't go out there, but on the day we arrived he said it wasn't an ideal place for me.

"Sure. OK," he said. He looked down at the tray by the door, then back at me, and gave me a weak smile. "Just stay where you can see this window," he pointed into his study, at the window there. "And wear a hat. I think you have some in your closet."

Without saying anything else, he picked up the tray and went back into the study, closing the door behind him.

I picked a wide-brimmed straw hat and went down the stairs and out the back door. My body was instantly hit with the relief of warmth, like getting into a relaxing bath or jumping into bed on a cold night. LeBlanc's study sat in the center of the house, so I dutifully walked down the main path of the garden, within his view. The path was interrupted a few yards in by a raised brick koi pond, round with clear sides, and lily pads floating on top. I looked up at the window of the study. The light outside and relative darkness of the room made it hard to tell if he was watching me, but I thought I saw his outline. I pulled a blanket out of my bag, laid it down on the ground by the pond, and sat beside it. Some of the fish were white, some were orange, some were a speckled mixture. Their scales contrasted with the purple water around them so that they almost seemed to glow there. I put my face close to the tank and a group of them moved quickly toward me, blinking and mouthing at me, their little whiskers wavering in the water.

"They think you're going to feed them," a voice said behind me.

I turned to see one of the gardeners, in a straw hat like mine, but worn and dirty, standing with his hands on his hips. I recognized this gardener from my days looking out the window. He wore overalls and had a gentle way about him, delicately trimming back the bushes, pulling weeds by hand, and patting the bark of trees as he passed by. I'd seen him kneel over the pond and feed the fish.

I looked back at the pond, at the little pleading mouths turned toward the glass, and felt a new type of energy inside me, not quite a quickening of my pulse, but an awareness of its regular beat. "Can I feed them?" I asked.

"Sure," he said. He reached into the pocket of his overalls, pulled out a lump of bread, knelt down, and handed it to me. Raising myself onto my knees, I knelt over the side of the pond and began crumbling the bread in. The koi swarmed to me like metal files to a magnet, their shimmering backs pressed up against each other in desperation. Their behavior made me feel a bit of unease, reminded me that they were living, breathing beings like me and that they were inside a tank and that they were hungry.

"Are they OK in there?" I asked the man.

"They like it," he said. "They're fish. They just like a snack like everyone else."

He knelt down beside me and started pointing out aspects of the different fish, how one had a big orange spot on its eye, how one had a damaged fin. He was telling me their names when a shadow cast over us. LeBlanc was standing behind us, arms crossed. I started to say hello, as did the gardener, but before we could get any syllables out, Leblanc said: "You should come back inside."

"I will," I said. "I just want to finish feeding the fish." I held up my hand, so he could see the remaining bread there.

He refused to look at my hand or at me. He looked in the direction of the koi. "No. You should come inside now," he said.

"I think I will finish feeding the fish first," I said.

Sometimes I try to get back to that version of me, to see whatever my eyes saw, but didn't recognize, but I can't. By now I am perfectly familiar with how LeBlanc looks when he is angry, and I can only imagine his lips were pulled tight against his teeth, set almost in a smile. His hands were probably clasped behind his back. His voice would have been cold and clipped.

"You will come inside. Now," he said.

The gardener stood up and walked away, giving me a small wave like everything was normal.

"I have to?" I asked.

"I have already told you several times what you are to do. Yes. You have to," he said, turning back toward the house and walking, then looking back to make sure I followed.

I stood up, the chunk of bread still in my hand, and walked behind him, palm up. With my other hand, I dragged the picnic blanket along the ground. I do remember noticing a stiffness in his shoulders, different from his usual more casual, confident gait. We went upstairs and when we got to the door of his study, he opened the door and asked me to come inside. I thought the timing was strange, but I guessed he was finally going to try to get to know me better like Mr. Miller said.

The office was dark and dusty. I don't think he let the maids come in there. It smelled like paper, dirt, and sweat. The walls were lined with bookshelves, the books on them askew, many knocked over, some lying open on the shelf or thrown on the floor. His desk was comparatively tidy with a single notebook and fountain pen and a framed photo.

"Didn't Mr. Miller teach you respect?" he asked.

I thought about the question. Mr. Miller explained to me that the teachers and staff at the school were older than me and they were in charge and so I should be polite to them and call them "ma'am" and "sir." He told me to respect myself and that meant to try to listen to what I was feeling and act and speak accordingly. He told me the other girls didn't respect me yet, but they would, and that I would need to try to respect them too, even though it would be hard because they'd been so mean to me.

"Yes," I told LeBlanc.

"But you don't show it to me," he said.

"I don't?" I can only imagine now how this question made LeBlanc feel, but at the time it was an innocent response.

"No. You don't. I asked you to do something. You didn't do it."

"That is respect to you."

I said it slowly, trying to help myself remember.

"That's respect to anyone!" he said. He slammed a hand down on his desk. That made me realize that he was angry. I tried to pay closer attention so I could figure out how to make him stop being angry.

"I'm sorry," I said. It was all I could think to do.

It was silent for a few seconds. Some of the dust in the room floated in the sunlight that came from the windows. Maids in the hallway were speaking quietly to each other. LeBlanc looked down at the notebook on his desk and tapped on it with his finger.

"It's OK," he said. "You need to work on your listening skills. Mr. Miller will work with you when you get back."

I got back the next day. LeBlanc said he had too many work projects going on and didn't have time to spend with me. When we pulled up to the school, Mr. Miller was waiting on the front steps in jeans and a t-shirt. I had never seen him look so casual before. His car was parked right in front and I saw suitcases in the backseat.

After LeBlanc left, Mr. Miller and I sat on the steps, looking out at the empty parking lot and grounds.

"Are we the only people here?" I asked.

CHAPTER TWELVE

tom

So, why are you here, anyway?" Shelley asks me. We are sitting in the mess hall after dinner. She's lazily eating half-melted vanilla ice cream. I'm leaning back in my chair, regretting the ice cream I already finished. She and Marigold sit across the table from me. Marigold is just sitting still with her hands in her lap. She has an ice cream in from of her too, mostly melted as well, but she isn't eating it.

"At dinner?" I ask. I know what she means, but I want to delay the conversation.

Shelley understands this type of behavior and doesn't allow for it. She doesn't even acknowledge it.

"You seem to have some level of disdain for what we do, and maybe even for LeBlanc. It's confusing to us."

Marigold nodded.

"LeBlanc made this big deal to us about you coming here, but I can't believe he would even trust you."

I start to think of what to say, settle on something, begin to talk, then she cuts me off.

"I mean, what's your background, anyway? Are you qualified for this job?"

I wait a few seconds before trying to respond. She cuts me off again.

"Marigold's more qualified than you. We all know that."

"I don't mind, though," Marigold says. "I wouldn't like to be in charge."

Shelley waves her comment away with the back of her hand. "It's the principle of the thing."

I consider telling them the truth. It would be easy because Marigold wouldn't look at me or respond emotionally, and Shelley wouldn't care, wouldn't internalize any of it or judge it. I could let the words bounce up against them and float down the garbage chute and that might be something, might feel like something.

Instead, I say, "I needed a job. LeBlanc's known me a long time. He helped me out."

Shelley rolls her eyes. Marigold nods.

After my dad died, after the initial sadness and shock and dealing with my mother's sadness and shock, I had a creeping feeling that LeBlanc wasn't going to let me go. He kept coming by the house. At first, he came with lawyers and HR and sat back quietly while my mother signed papers and listened with a glazed look to the various benefits she would be able to take advantage of. Sometimes Leblanc would come out from wherever he was, maybe in the kitchen pouring a cup of coffee, or in my dad's study, looking at his books, and put a hand on my mother's shoulder, or pat my back, both of us stiff and still beneath his touch.

Once the papers were signed and the house was sold and we moved into our trailer, he started visiting on his own. My mom dissolved fully into the self that had already begun to waiver around her years before Dad died, sullen and detached, hiding under blankets, watching families argue on daytime TV. When he came to visit, I answered the door. He would look in on her briefly, chat while she stared at him and nodded agreeably, the TV muted, her hair damp from sleep and sweat, stuck to her face. Then we would go on a walk or a drive. During the walks, we meandered through the trailer park, LeBlanc obnoxiously obsequious toward all the neighbors, greeting them, learning their names, asking after their dogs or their grandmas. On the drives he took me out to the river where my dad and I used to fish, me staring at the water while he talked endlessly. I was only ten and I didn't know whether it was OK to feel the way I did toward LeBlanc, a hot and bubbling hatred that seemed to surround and compress my lungs, so I stayed silent while he filled the air around me with his voice, meaningless noises corresponding to his schemes. I deployed the same politeness my father taught me, my yes sirs and no sirs, my recall and repetition of the last few sentences spoken before a question.

In my late teens, things changed. I stopped feeling like a helpless child. I started to really see my mother: eating cold macaroni and cheese at four in the morning while watching infomercials for various machines that did everything to food all at once, and to understand the blaring, dusty loneliness that floated around our trailer and settled on the baseboards. LeBlanc bought me a truck for my sixteenth birthday and on the days he came for a visit, I drove off before he got there. I liked to loop around the camps by the river, to see the old men out back with their poles, or the families running around the yards, the hand-painted signs with the corny pun names: Reel-ax, Aquaholic, Hooker Haven. Sometimes I parked where we used to fish, the same spot LeBlanc liked to take me, but it was different without him. The dark water and rustling trees calmed me. I didn't really believe in any kind of after life or ghosts or spirits or good vibes or whatever, but I did like sitting there and remembering my father.

I drove and drove until it got dark. Sometimes I stopped for an ice cream at the truck stop, watching the soft-serve squeeze out while I pushed the crank, tinny country music playing in the background, a rack of bedazzled cowboy hats beside souvenirs for a place no one visited on purpose. When I got back home, my mom was usually asleep on the couch, the creepy repetition of a laugh track washing over her.

I woke up one night in a deep and painful panic, my breath caught in my throat, my chest heavy. I felt like I couldn't move. There was someone in my doorway. I could see his outline against the light leaking down the hall from the living room.

"You're being very disrespectful," the shape said. It was LeBlanc's voice. He sounded amused.

I didn't say anything. I couldn't. My body was still rigid with fear. I tried wiggling my fingers, which went well and started the flow of blood to my arms.

"I promised your dad I would look after you. That's not something I'm gonna turn my back on. You think it's OK to disrespect the dead?"

I could tell from the way he was talking that he didn't expect an answer, and I still wasn't sure I could speak, so I just lay there and listened.

"Me and you, we've got a bond. Nothing's happening to it."

I wondered if this was a speech he memorized from a movie. If I hadn't just woken up, if there wasn't still fear dripping out of me, I might have laughed at the idea that LeBlanc and I were bonded in any way other than through the pathetic monetary payouts my family received. If I was bonded to him, it was in a way he couldn't understand, through the repetition of his name in my house, from the two syllables signifying something bad had happened or was going to happen.

"You'll be here," he said. "When I come by tomorrow."

I drive Marigold back to her house after dinner. Shelley is staying in the mess hall to play cards with some of the engineers. I keep the radio off—because I am not sure what kind of music she likes—and tap my finger on the steering wheel. It's a short drive. When I pull into her driveway, she sits there for a few seconds and doesn't unbuckle her seatbelt.

"I think what Shelley was trying to say is you don't seem to belong here," she says. She doesn't turn toward me, just looks forward out the window, somewhere in the vicinity of the empty underside of the house, the security light shining on nothing.

"Most people I meet here don't seem to belong," I say. It sounds different from how I mean it, like some sort of political statement or emotional teenage speech. "I just mean... I guess if I was picturing who would work here, it wouldn't be you, it wouldn't be Shelley, it definitely wouldn't be Randy the Prophet."

She nods. "What about everyone else?"

She means the workers. What I call them in my head. The people that don't administrate or manage, but do the actual work. The people I don't talk to that much, just see going back and forth doing their business. "I guess I take them for granted. They seem in the right place to me, but I don't know most of them."

"You really think I don't' belong here?" she looks at me this time, stares at me, actually. I try to meet her eyes for as long as possible, but it starts to make me uncomfortable. Her eyes are a light grey and she has short, brown eyelashes. She keeps blinking without losing eye contact. I look down at the gear shift.

"Yeah," I say.

I look up and she is still staring. The end of her braid hangs loosely over her shoulder and for some reason I want to reach out and touch it. I think it would feel smooth. For a moment touching the end of the braid is all I can think about and the desire to do so blocks up my breathing with excitement, like I've found something that could solve all my problems.

"Yeah," I swallow. I keep eye contact for as long as I can, then look back at the gear shift, and her hands in her lap beside it. "But you more than anyone, I think."

"Is it because you think I'm strange?" she asks.

I feel a sort of surging compassion for her then, and another urge to touch her braid, but in a different way.

"No in a bad way," I say. "Being strange compared to this place is a compliment."

Other things I don't say. That the sight of her inside a mildewing trailer is like noticing the pearlescent underside of a lumpy, gray oyster shell. Or that I dream about her, and in my dreams there is a light that comes from nowhere, glowing softly around her, and in that light I gain an understanding that I lose when I wake up. That touching the end of her braid might cause my heart to stop.

"Like how you said it about Shelley and Randy the Prophet."

She puts her palm flat against the stick shift.

"Yes. I meant that as a compliment too."

She puts her hand up to her braid and throws it behind her back. I feel a sudden desperation to see it again and turn briefly to press my forehead against the driver's side window. She doesn't react in look or word. Instead, when I turn back to her, she is meeting my eyes again and she says: "I really am meant to be here, though."

I shrug. Thankful for such a pointless statement so that I can have a pointless reaction. "If that's how you feel." Again I hold the eye contact for a while, then poke at the change in the tray under the radio.

"It's not about how I feel," she says. "It's about why I'm here."

"To you it's a calling," I say. It's annoying how I say it, like I know what she is thinking, when in fact I have no idea. In reality there is a fear I can't name growing inside of me that makes me not want to know what she means, not want to hear what she will say next. Maybe she understands that this is how I feel, because she unbuckles her seatbelt and says goodbye, quickly stepping out of the car. I give her a wave through the window and wait, watching her go up the stairs. At first, I can see her outline clearly in the radiating glow of the security light, but she disappears with each step up the stairs.

CHAPTER THIRTEEN

marigold

I'm supposed to be able to sleep. I am able to sleep. But it never lasts very long. No one can tell me exactly what it is that happens to them when they sleep. "How should I know? I'm asleep!" Shelley told me the one time I thought it was a good idea to ask. Whatever happens to other people, I don't think it happens to me. I don't wake up breathing heavy, rubbing my eyes, like Shelley. I don't wake up, turn over, pull a blanket over my head and go back to sleep. I've never taken a nap. Even though Shelley doesn't want to tell me exactly what it's like, I think to her it is something warm and comforting to fall into. It seems like, late at night when we are watching TV, that she is waiting calmly for the sleep to overtake her, happy to meet it where it meets her, unhappy to leave its company. For me it is something else.

When I go to sleep, I do not feel like it is anywhere nearby. We are not meeting halfway. It is more like I am walking down a long road all day and someone's told me that at some point the road will end, and that I'll see a little green sign when I'm close to the end, and so I walk and I walk and then finally, when it gets late and I'm in my bed, I see the little green sign far off, and I walk and I walk some more, and then I get to the sign, but the sign is just to tell me that I'm almost there, but I'm not yet, so I keep walking and then I don't know when I get to the actual end. A few hours later I wake up. I usually sleep for about four hours. Waking up is very simple. My eyes open. I get out of bed. I turn on the light.

What else is there to do but wander around in the dark if you wake up before anyone else? I do other things too, but there are plenty of hours in the day and only so many ways to fill them.

When I first get up, I sit in my bed and read a book. Mr. Miller still sends me books, even though my education is technically complete. He and LeBlanc say I should be a "life-long learner." I also have a catalog that I can order books from for myself, but I never tell Mr. Miller about these books, because he laughed at me once when I talked about them. When I didn't understand why he laughed, he apologized, and then said that those books just weren't very serious and weren't going to help me very much. I asked Shelley about it and she said he was just a snob. That was how I learned there are good things to like and bad things to like, and that whatever things you like are the good things, and whatever things you don't like are the bad things. The things you like can make you feel like a certain type of person, can make you feel pride, and even though you feel that pride, you should still try to take that pride away from someone else by pointing out that there thing is not as good as yours.

The thing I like is these books where women fall in love with cowboys.

Mr. Miller says they are smutty, but that is because he hasn't read them. They usually don't have any sex in them, and if they do it is at the very end and very vague so that if you didn't know about sex already you wouldn't be exactly sure what was happening. I know about sex because Mr. Miller gave me a long book about it when I was twelve and starting my period. Then Shelley showed me some movies like *Legend of the Fall*, because she thought I needed to understand more. Shelley doesn't have sex that way, with men, but she says she doesn't ever want to watch a movie with me where women have sex because I will ask her creepy questions. Shelley says the problems with the catalog books is that they are bad for women, because the women in them are helpless and obedient and waiting around for these cowboys to tell them what to do. I understand logically that she is right, but I also understand that everyone is always telling me what to do, including about these books, so maybe that is why I like them. The books make a simple sense of the world. The man doesn't like the woman, or the woman doesn't like the man or they both don't like each other, and then they do. I know that they will, and I don't have to worry about it. I can just read and enjoy the descriptions of riding around on horses and eating nice meals and going on walks in pastures. I like knowing how things will end up.

The books Mr. Miller sends me are classic and respected literature about the way people think and the way people feel and often they don't end with people falling in love. If the people are in love it doesn't work out, but often instead no one is in love, but people die or kill themselves or nothing happens except a lot of thinking and wandering around. That is what life is actually like, so that is why it is good art. Art should represent life Mr. Miller says, but I don't know why I should read about the things I do every day, the things I already know.

This morning neither option appeals to me. I have a book from Mr. Miller about a woman who doesn't like her life and talks to people about her feelings and thinks about what to do. I have a catalog book about a woman who is in love with a man who hates her, who is shockingly mean to her every time they interact, it is almost hard to believe that they actually will end up together at the end.

I leave the books on my bedside table and get dressed. For my walks I like to wear pants and long sleeves, because I sometimes walk deep into the woods and get scratched by plants and there are lots of mosquitoes out, especially closer to the water. LeBlanc doesn't like for me to wear pants, which Shelley says is as messed up as my books. She says I like those books because LeBlanc is like a character from them, but I don't know if I like LeBlanc, so that doesn't make sense. I'll change back into my normal clothes before work anyway. I like the pants. They are black and tight against my waist. I feel like a different person when I wear them, like Shelley or some of the girls we meet at bars who say rude things just to laugh.

In a tray by the door are my keys with a little flashlight keychain. I grab them and spray myself with the bug spray that sits beside the tray. The spray goes straight into my lungs and eyes and I step outside wheezing.

There is a freshness to life at 4:00 a.m. on the landing. The smell outside is not night and not day, but a clean in-between, mixed with the citronella in the bug spray and the sweat that formed and dried against my skin while I was sleeping. The sky is light purple and looking at it I feel a prickling up the side of my face like something good will happen. This is my favorite time, and no one knows it, because no one else is here to see it. They don't know what it's like to be awake at 4:00 a.m. and think for a time that life is starting over.

I was never one. Or zero. I was new once, but they told me I was twelve. Later I learned that babies don't remember being babies. They learn things, words and faces and relationships, slowly and with repetition until the world starts to form around them and their minds begin to dig a well to store it all, so that they don't just look at their mother and think "that is my mother" but they might also think "I remember that time my mother sang *Skinnamarinky Dinky Dink*."

I don't work that way. The first day I existed, when I was not zero but also twelve and new, I understood and I remembered. I didn't understand everything. I didn't know where I was or who I was, but I could understand language so that I could begin to understand those things.

"Hi," a woman said. The woman stood right in front of me so that when I opened my eyes for the first time her face was all I could see, save a light behind her ear that haloed her curls.

"I'm Anna Marie," the woman said. She stepped back and now I could see a room, bright white with lots of lights and tables on wheels and a bleach smell.

And I knew already these things: white and tables and bleach.

"Who am I?" I asked.

Anna Marie smiled at this. It was a big smile. She looked surprised, giddy. Her hands fluttered to her cheeks, then she reached out and put both hands on either side of my hair, smoothed it softly. I knew it was my hair.

"You're Marigold," Anna Marie said.

I thought that maybe I knew I was Marigold. The fact didn't jolt my brain in any new way, just floated around with everything else.

The street lights along the road are siloed ecosystems: funnels of light pouring down on their kingdom of bugs and dirt. I stay away from them, in the in-between place where the lights fade into nothing.

Once Shelley drank too much and stayed up until it was time for me to go out. She came with me down the road for a while, but then turned back. "It's too creepy out here," she said with a wave, then ran back to our house.

Creepy is a word she uses a lot and it's one I haven't quite figure out yet. I know what she means, of course, but I don't know exactly how she feels. I don't know how someone would feel scared on the road they walk down every day, just because it is darker. There's nothing new there. Mr. Miller says you have to have an imagination to feel scared of unrealistic threats, and since I don't have one, I don't get scared.

He tried once to help me understand imagination.

"When you wake up in the morning, what do you think about?" he asked.

"I think about getting out of bed and turning on the light."

"And then?"

"And then reading a book or getting dressed."

"And then?"

"And then going to class."

"And then?"

"And then in class I think about the next class."

"So, when I wake up, I might think: 'It's cold out today,' and that will make me picture the day. I picture the other teachers in sweaters and the students in the school crest scarves. Then, let's say it is Wednesday and I know I have the Freshman English Literature class on Wednesdays, so I think about the students in that class and then I think about one of them who has been difficult lately, and I imagine some smart response she might make to something I say, and then some smart thing I might say back."

"You think about things you don't know, and you pretend."

He laughed. "I guess so."

If I had an imagination, while I walk down the dark street and past the street lights, I would think that out there where the light doesn't hit, where I can't see, something dangerous is waiting. It doesn't need to be anything specifically dangerous—a murderer or a ghost or a clown or an alligator or a warthog—just a generally scary thing that wants to do something bad to me. What I see in Shelley is that what she is really afraid of is being afraid in the first place. She would never say "I think something is out there waiting to get me," because she knows it is probably not true, but she feels it anyway, and she doesn't like the feeling. It's the feeling she's afraid of.

Out on the main road the light is stronger, coming from tall industrial light poles that don't flicker out and are regularly maintained. Here there is not light and not-light, everything is washed in the light, unless I go onto the shoulder, behind the light, and even then, some of it spreads onto me. I walk this part quickly, because I feel like a glowing thing in the dark, exposed in an empty space.

I choose a path. It's one I haven't been down in a while. One I don't like as much as the others, which is good because I don't have it memorized. After a few seconds of walking, I am far enough away from the street lights to need my keychain flashlight. It's a small flashlight, but it is pretty powerful. Randy the Prophet got it for me after I tripped over a root one morning using a weak flashlight. I like the way swinging the light back and forth changes the things around me from nothing to something. I like the way the light makes the trees look like faint impressions of themselves. They are versions of trees that are only there when a flashlight is directed at them.

At some point, I grow tired of walking and choose a tree and sit beside it. This is what I do out here. Anyone who knows I come out here asks that first: "What do you do out there?" I walk and then I sit by a tree. "So... you just what? Think?" they ask, or something like that.

I don't know. Am I thinking? Not really. Am I not thinking? No. There are thoughts in my brain, but I am not thinking them. I am sitting by a tree. My flashlight is turned off. It is mostly dark around me, although it is not completely dark, because the plant is nearby, and its lights sort of smudge the sky and make the stars dull and the moon only just another figure, not the bright and pressing presence it was when I was at school.

There comes a time when I decide that I have sat long enough, so I get up and walk back. The walking back is different because the sun is coming up. The world turns grey. The fresh in-betweenness of 4:00 a.m. is slowly rubbed away to reveal the day.

I was brand new and also twelve when I met Mr. Miller. LeBlanc held my hand as we ascended the steps of the Evangeline School for Girls. I wore a white linen sheath dress, white socks rolled down with waved edges, shiny patent leather Mary Janes, and a big white bow at the end of my French braid. LeBlanc wore a seersucker suit, which I later realized was a sort of outfit for a character, a visual representation of the type of person he fancied himself. Mr. Miller met us at the entrance, swinging forward one of the heavy double doors, dressed in khakis, scuffed loafers, and an untucked polo shirt. His wire-framed glasses fogged up as the humidity spilled into the foyer. He took them off and wiped them on the front of his shirt.

"This is her," LeBlanc said once we were seated in Mr. Miller's classroom. His voice was too loud and cheerful for the empty room. It ricocheted off the scuffed floors and short desks and settled sadly over our three heads. It was a strange thing to say, but I think LeBlanc felt he had to say something because Mr. Miller was just sitting there watching us.

"It's nice to meet you," Mr. Miller said. He was sitting behind his desk. LeBlanc and I sat in the children's desks. He balanced on a tiny chair.

I stared at Mr. Miller, my mouth a straight line. He took his glasses off again and twirled them in the air by his head. I understood what he was saying, that he was speaking to me, greeting me, that I was one person and he was another and we had to reconcile this, but it didn't seem necessary to do anything about any of it.

"Can she talk?" he asked LeBlanc.

"Yes, but she doesn't always. You can ask her a question, though. She'll answer you."

"How are you today, Marigold?"

I stared at him. My hands were set peacefully on the desk in front of me, perfectly symmetrical and still.

I tried to explain it to him later, what it felt like to be me then, what happened in my brain, but it was difficult to put into words. I was new, but I wasn't a baby. The words people said and the things they did weren't entirely new to me. I understood that a pen had a cap that could be twisted off. I could tie my shoes. When Mr. Miller asked, "How are you today?" I understood this as a social question one person asked another in order to express interest in her general well-being. This knowledge circulated in my brain as I watched and listened. Absent was any feeling that the things I knew had something to do with me. If asked a question about myself, there was no social contract to respond, no feeling of the tension it might cause the other person to be stared at in silence, no sense of obligation. If I didn't have an answer to a question, I didn't say anything.

"Not that sort of question. Something more... factual," LeBlanc said.

"OK. Marigold, how's the weather today?"

"The temperature is 97 degrees," I said. "It is overcast."

Mr. Miller told me later that he thought I had some special internal thermometer or something I was using to find this information. Actually, I heard the temperature reported on the radio during our drive over.

"I see," Mr. Miller said.

"It's going to take some time," LeBlanc said, patting my head, "but she'll get there."

"Is she your... have there been others?"

"She's my first. I've met others, of course, some pretty good ones, too, but there's no team like mine. She'll be the best there is. You'll be a part of that."

"You're part of something," LeBlanc liked to say, and I couldn't tell if that something was me, or the concept of me, an achievement for some obscure journal, a paragraph buried in the back of a newspaper.

LeBlanc pushed his way out of the short, metal chair, the rubber-capped feet leaving black streaks on the floor. "I need to get going. You have any questions, give me a call." He put his thumb to his ear and pinkie to his mouth in an imitation of a phone.

Mr. Miller nodded. I turned my head to look at LeBlanc, then turned back to the front of the room, my hands still on the desk.

On our own in the classroom, Mr.Miller and I sat in silence. He rubbed his glasses on his shirt, blew on them, rubbed them some more. I stayed still. He squinted at me.

"You need to remember to breathe," he sighed.

I took the note quickly, making my chest rise and fall beneath the flowers embroidered on my dress.

"And blink."

I did.

"Not quite so regularly."

I cocked my head and stared at him.

"It might take a while, just watch me and the others, watch our eyes, you'll get the idea eventually."

I blinked some more.

"Now you need to nod or something, to acknowledge what I said."

I did.

He took me to my room on the faculty floor.

"I didn't think it would be a good idea," he said apologetically, as I looked around the empty closet, "for you to live with the other girls yet. They might have a bad reaction. I wouldn't normally just say that to a child, but I think you need to understand that. They might not like you."

I nodded. He felt it important to be acknowledged.

"Very good!" he said. "No matter what happens at first, they'll warm up to you. We just need to ease them into it all."

I blinked and nodded.

"You're not breathing," he said.

CHAPTER FOURTEEN

tom

His image creeps up on me. I see LeBlanc, sitting in our living room after dinner, drinking something amber poured by my mom. "We do good, you know," he said. I was sitting on the floor, trying to watch TV, even though the volume was down so low I could barely hear it. My dad sat on the couch beside him. My mom disappeared somewhere. I tried to ignore him. I knew I'd have to hear everything he said a second time, when my mom quoted him, and she and my dad fought. I wasn't looking at them, so I couldn't see my dad's reaction, but he didn't say anything.

"Tom," LeBlanc called to me. "Come over here."

I turned to look at him, then turned back to the TV briefly. "Tom, come on," my dad said. He sounded annoyed, but I couldn't tell if it was with me or LeBlanc.

I climbed onto the couch between them and looked at the knees of my jeans where they were worn and grass stained.

"You understand what we do?" LeBlanc asked me.

I nodded.

"Yes, sir," my dad reminded me.

"Yes, sir," I repeated.

I think I was about seven. I didn't understand what they did, except that it had something to do with water and that my mom thought it was "pure evil," but only when she was really mad, and LeBlanc visited for too long.

"Good," LeBlanc said. I glanced at him from the corner of my eye.

"Sit up straight," my dad said. I did but tried to keep my eyes on the TV. It was small, and all the lights were on, so it was hard to make out what was happening on the screen.

"That's good," LeBlanc said again. "Your dad's very important to me, and one day you could be too, if you make good grades and don't get into trouble."

People were always warning me about not getting into trouble, and I never understood what they could mean.

"Yes, sir," I said. He was one of those people who held eye contact for a long time. His eyes were a painful, pale blue, with blonde eyelashes. I met them for a moment, then looked back at the TV.

"We do good in the world," he continued. "We help thirsty people. You ever been thirsty?"

I nodded without looking at him.

"Imagine being thirsty all the time, and then when you get something to drink, it makes you sick."

I waited a few seconds, then decided I should say: "That would be bad."

"That *would* be bad. Wouldn't it?"

"Yes, sir."

"And that's why the world needs people like me and your dad, so those thirsty people can drink without having to worry."

That night the sound of a fight woke me up. I went to my door, cracked it open, sat on the floor and listened.

"He can't have him," my mom was saying.

"Jesus, he's not a kidnapper," my dad said.

He was a nice person most of the time, but when he was upset he liked to talk to her like this, like whatever she was worried about was just about the dumbest thing he'd ever heard.

"I gave them you already. They have you already."

I heard her feet pacing.

"They? What are you talking about? No one has me. It's just a job."

"They. Him and her. They've got you. That's that. I've accepted it, but they can't take him too."

The footsteps stopped then. The talking stopped too. After a while I saw the light leaking from the crack under their door go out. I sat in the dark and hated LeBlanc.

CHAPTER FIFTEEN

marigold

I like to be in my trailer. LeBlanc wanted me to share it with Shelley, but I asked him to reconsider several times and he relented. I don't ask him for much, as he admitted, so it was hard for him to turn down this small favor. She won't say either way, but I think it is a favor for Shelley too. We are together so much.

My trailer is not cheerful. Ms. Odette who manages the secretarial pool has a cheerful trailer, or at least that's what other people say when they go in. "It's so cheerful in here." A place can't actually be cheerful, but it can make people feel cheerful. Ms. Odette's trailer makes me feel the same as any other trailer, but I think what makes other people feel cheerful is it is full of very bright colors and encouraging words in frames and some sort of scent she sprays around it in the mornings that settles and moistens the carpet and makes me sneeze.

My trailer is mostly empty. "You need some decorations in here," is what people usually say when they come in, even if they have been coming in for years and probably know that I am not going to suddenly put up some decorations. What is in my trailer: a desk, a filing cabinet with three drawers, three chairs, a prayer plant in a clay pot, and a watering can. The desk is very cheap and old and ugly, but still in good condition because I clean it every morning and try not to scratch up the laminate. It is a brown color that does not make people feel cheerful, which is probably why Ms. Odette covered hers with floral-printed fabric. One of the chairs is a tilting, black rolling chair with scratchy fabric. That is my chair. The other two chairs are white, plastic folding chairs that are for guests to sit in. The filing cabinet is off-white with silver handles and lock and it is a little shorter than me. The prayer plant sits by the only window, where I keep the shades rolled up for a square of light to come in. In the morning, it opens its leaves.

What I like to do in the morning before I start work is stand by the plant and look out the window. All I can see through the window is the trailer on that side of me which is Shelley's. I like to see if her light is on to know if she is in there, but I don't like to see her, so if I think I see a movement near the window, I walk away. Usually she doesn't come in at that time, so I just stand by the plant and look at the trailer or up at the sky: gray and flat. After this, I go to sit at my desk. I keep a notepad and pen in the top drawer. I pull it out, then go in the next drawer for the keys to the filing cabinet. I get out the files I need for the day, then I pick up the phone and start calling people.

The summer when I was sixteen, Shelley and I were given the opportunity to work for LeBlanc.

It was the summer after the new plant opened.

Opportunity was the word LeBlanc used. Shelley disagreed.

"What's our other 'opportunity'?" she asked. "Staying with my drunk aunt?"

That's what Shelley usually did in the summers. I asked LeBlanc if she could just come stay with me at his house, but he didn't like that idea. Even when I inevitably got sent back to school early and Mr. Miller came back to stay with me, it wasn't allowed by the school for Shelley to stay there too. "Special provisions have been made on your behalf," was the only explanation I received from the headmistress.

Despite not thinking of it as an opportunity, Shelley did decide that she would prefer to come with me to work at the plant over staying with her drunk aunt, who mostly just slept in her dark house, but sometimes woke up to yell at Shelley. Shelley wouldn't admit that this hurt her feelings or made her feel any sort of emotions, but she did say her aunt didn't ever have enough groceries and she had to eat peanut butter sandwiches for most meals until the peanut butter ran out, then she had to steal money from her aunt's purse when she was asleep and hitchhike to the store and hope her aunt stayed asleep that whole time or she would yell at her when she came back.

Mr. Miller drove us to the plant. "I'd like to see it," he said, but he always took me wherever I needed to go in the summer, because LeBlanc didn't like to come pick me up.

It wasn't a very long drive, but Shelley still made Mr. Miller stop for snacks, and by the time we pulled up to the gate the backseat was filled with Snickers wrappers, Coke cans, and Cheez-It crumbs.

Before we got to the compound, we were nowhere. The scrubby trees and wilting bushes along the road, the trash-filled culverts, started to feel like they were repeating. Then there was something. It wasn't anything particular at first, just a general tapering off of the way things were so that it felt like we were reaching the end of the world. I understood that we were getting to the ocean, but I couldn't see it, could just sense it.

When the plant came into view it felt sudden and frightening. It looked like a trick, like I was seeing one thing superimposed on another, this series of concrete and metal, new and authoritarian, and this simple, shabby landscape.

"Shit," Shelley said.

"I didn't think it would be so big," Mr. Miller said.

We were not there, though, and had to keep driving looking at the thing, as the land grew sparser, more sky and less trees. The road ended in the gate to the compound. A man sat at the gate listening to the radio and reading a newspaper. He was lanky, with muscular arms and a mismatched protruding gut that stuck out optimistically over his belt. He came over to the car slowly, carelessly. Gave us all a friendly wave. Mr. Miller explained who we were and the man walked over to swing open the gate.

"Not a lot of security here, huh?" Mr. Miller asked him before pulling through.

"No one's gonna mess with this place," the man said. "We need it." He placed a hand over his heart. "This place's gonna save a lot of us. I'm from here, you know," he waved his hand toward the road, so we could get a general idea. "I was so proud when I heard LeBlanc was coming here. So proud and so relieved. Relieved would be the word. Bless that man."

Mr. Miller didn't seem to know what to say to this, so he just mumbled something polite and we drove on into the compound, the man swinging the gate closed behind us.

LeBlanc put us to work in the secretarial pool. We worked out of a large, carpeted room on the middle floor of the main building, with wide windows overlooking the gulf. We were set up on long tables with telephones and folders and we were mostly given numbers to call to "just let you know we're in the neighborhood." The days were long and slow except for lunch and coffee breaks. A waterspout sighting was the only excuse besides sanctioned breaks and emergency bathroom visits for leaving our seats. Someone would call it out, usually just a "Look!" or "There's one!" and we would all push toward the window and stare at the slow gray funnel, the water below churning, the sky above looking like it was trying to pour into the earth. We felt a satisfied type of fear, facing something dangerous that posed no danger to us.

One day LeBlanc came to visit the floor. Everyone was nervous, talking jittery on the phone, blushing and staring straight ahead when he walked past, as if they couldn't see him.

He sent his assistant to fetch us when our shift ended. He brought us to LeBlanc's camper, where he lived while the plant was being built, and where he decided to stay for the time being. He had a picnic table set up under the camper's awning and he grilled us hamburgers and chatted happily while we sat and sipped the lemonade his assistant brought us.

Things were different between us by then. We did talk regularly, although not in the way Mr. Miller predicted. LeBlanc skipped over the parts where we got to know each other and just talked to me how he talked to everyone else, like he already knew me and knew what was best.

"You're actually very good at speaking on the phone," LeBlanc said.

"Me?" Shelley and I both asked at the same time.

"Marigold," LeBlanc said.

Shelley tried to just smirk at this, but her eyes bulged a little and her neck looked red. She got a kind of pleasure in being slighted, but she also liked praise in whatever form, from whatever person.

"You're terrible on the phone," he added. "But you're very bright, I can see that."

She kept her lips together and didn't allow herself to look pleased.

"What do you guys think about this place?" he asked, as if the previous comments required no further discussion.

This was our third or fourth week there. We were living in a cheap and quickly built apartment building at the very back edge of the compound, sharing a two-bedroom apartment with two other secretaries. We slept in a bunk bed. At night, one of the secretaries had long phone calls with her boyfriend in which she yelled at him or cried, but usually ended by telling him over and over again how much she loved him.

"It's not very nice," I said. "But I do like being at work, and the grounds are pretty if you get away from all the buildings."

"It's depressing," Shelley said.

LeBlanc stood in front of the grill, the hamburgers sizzling beside him, spatula mid-air. "I knew I could depend on the two of you for an honest answer," he said. He tried to sound like he was amused, but he looked a little angry. "You really are quite the pair," he continued, turning to his burgers, not looking at us. "Normally people pair up to balance each other out, but you two, you're like two kids sitting on the same side of a see-saw."

"We don't know what that means," Shelley said.

"I mean," LeBlanc said, turning toward us and waving his spatula, "that Marigold was being rude, and normally another person might feel awkward around the rudeness, and say something polite to mitigate it, but since you are just as blunt as her, you just helped her double down."

"Why did you ask us what we thought if you didn't really want to know?" I asked. I don't know why I asked. This was a question I'd posed many times by that point in my life, to all the people who didn't like my answers. They never had a good response. The response they couldn't say, but that I figured out, was that they didn't want an honest answer, they wanted a specific answer that would confirm whatever they already thought.

"Because I'm trying to help you two brats," LeBlanc said. The word brats came out in a not-amused way. I think he felt a little embarrassed by it, so he gave a weak chuckle and poked at his hamburgers.

"How are you helping us?" Shelley asked. We both knew it was the wrong thing to ask at that moment.

"Hand me your plates," he said, reaching his hand out to the side, pretending like it was so important to keep his eyes on the burgers that he couldn't glance at us.

We brought our plates over and he stuck hamburgers on our open buns. We loaded them up with the condiments and toppings laid out beside the grill, then went back to the table.

LeBlanc sat across from us and looked back and forth, making eye contact as we ate. He had a burger in front of him, but he didn't touch it. He was starting to go gray, his sideburns silvering before meeting the rest of his copper hair. He had big, smooth hands with neatly manicured nails and a pinky ring with an insignia from some club he was in during college. His arms were freckled, sticking out of a fitted white polo shirt. For his age, he was in pretty good shape, thin and muscular. I noticed a few gray chest hairs poking out of the top of his shirt.

When his blue eyes met mine, I held his gaze, chewing on my hamburger. People didn't meet my eyes that often. I tried to see what was behind his. That was something Mr. Miller taught me to try to help me understand empathy. Try to figure out what is behind the face a person is making. What do they really mean? But I think of it more like the brain is behind the eyes, so I am literally trying to see through their eyes straight into their brain. I wished so much to be able to do this. Then I could know exactly what he wanted from me when he narrowed his eyes. The only thing I could figure out his brain was doing was thinking very fast, and hoping I would look away. There is always that when people look into my eyes, a pained wish to look somewhere else. Then his look shifted into something else, a sadness, and I felt like he wanted me to feel this sadness too, like he was trying to bridge his brain to mine, but I couldn't quite catch it. Then he did look away, back at Shelley, then back at his hamburger, his hands folded in front of it.

"I know the two of you, you're still young," he said. "You probably have big plans."

Shelley snorted. She didn't like plans. I didn't have an opinion about them.

LeBlanc ignored Shelley's snort. "But I want you to know, there's a place for you here."

We looked at each other.

"Don't worry, you won't be in those terrible apartments. I'm building homes. Nice ones. There will be a chef on site. Just something to keep in mind. This place will be here for you."

At school, the other girls' lives revolved around plans. The current moment seemed to offer them nothing. Some plans were as simple as who they might flirt with at the upcoming dance, others as complicated as where they wanted to live, what they would do for a living, whether they would have children, and how they would spend their inevitable riches. Each girl was preoccupied with her plan. She would find any excuse to insert it into a conversation, find it relevant in any situation. Mostly plans were discussed at night in a circle on the floor of someone's dorm room. Shelley and I weren't exactly invited to these gatherings, but we weren't explicitly excluded. Sometimes we wandered in, sat on a bed or in a back corner and listened.

"I can't wait until I'm a famous actress," Mary Margaret proclaimed one day, hugging a pillow to her chest and lying down on the floor.

The girls around her nodded as if this was a perfectly reasonable thing to say.

"Have you ever acted?" Shelley asked.

Mary Margaret didn't say anything. The other girls rolled their eyes at Shelley or turned and gave her pointed looks.

"Why are you even here?" Mary Margaret asked finally, keeping her eyes on the ceiling.

Shelley colored a little but kept her face straight.

"*Have* you ever acted?" I asked. I thought from the way Shelley asked the question that she knew she hadn't, but I was curious about the trajectory of this dream.

"Everyone here knows I can act," Mary Margaret said, rolling onto her side and propping herself up on an elbow to look at us. "I do scenes from movies all the time."

"You probably won't be a famous actress, though," I pointed out. "I think that's pretty hard to do."

"You can be anything you set your mind to," the Headmistress told us on career day.

Shelley raised her hand. The headmistress winced. "Yes, Shelley?" she asked.

"You can't really, though," Shelley said.

Everyone in the class giggled, except me.

"You certainly can," the headmistress replied, not even bothering to sound argumentative. "We live in a free country filled with opportunity. All you have to do is work hard."

"What if everyone in this room wants to be president?" Shelley asked.

The giggles continued.

"I think that would be great," the Headmistress replied, her lips forming a smile, her eyes hard.

I raised my hand.

"Yes, Marigold?" the Headmistress motioned toward me with a lazy hand.

"It wouldn't work," I said. "We couldn't be what we wanted to be if we all wanted to be president. There are too many of us and not enough years. Even if each of us only served one term, one of us starting at the minimum age of eligibility and going on from there, we'd run out of time, and that's assuming no one outside of this room also wants to be president."

The Headmistress sent me and Shelley out in the hall.

The reason I am good at calling people, according to LeBlanc, is that I lack a certain nervous energy that can ruin a sales call. In other aspects of life, I've been encouraged to adapt the most common behaviors, to seem to feel more than I do, but in business my natural behavior is considered beneficial. Shelley finds the leads, I make the calls. Shelley is good at finding leads because she understands people. Sometimes others are confused by this revelation, because she can be so cold, but beneath all of her straight faces and quick responses, she is finely attuned to the nature of others.

LeBlanc sends her out on the road every few weeks. She drives around in some rural and waterless part of the state, scheduling meetings with holders of small power: the mayor-president, the town clerk, city council members. There is a list of questions she asks them. LeBlanc came up with the list. Their answers don't matter that much, according to her, it's more their attitude, the tenor of their voice. When Shelley finds a promising lead, she places a star by the name and brings it back to me.

I take the list and make the calls. The main thing about making the calls is to flatter the person I am calling by pointing out how smart they are for taking this opportunity. These are words LeBlanc coached me on. They aren't the ones I would use. The tone is mine though, and most of the responses thereafter, because I can be honest about most facts, which are that the municipality will profit, that the leadership will look good, and that the water is top-quality.

It surprised me to find that the leadership will look good, but it is true. The residents have the initial impression of something positive happening—their water system is getting fixed—and then later, if things go wrong, their anger can't figure out where to land, or they don't have the time, the energy to express the anger. Untangling a new problem isn't as easy to process as the initial relief of having a problem fixed. They will be disgruntled, probably, they won't be able to pay for the water sometimes, maybe, but this results in a general unhappiness and unease, not usually in any fingerpointing, except among a minority that will be quickly ignored because their anger makes everyone else feel uncomfortable.

Today I have five phone calls to make before lunch. Two of them result in a clear yes, two are maybes, and one is technically a maybe, but probably a no. Between the calls, I walk the length of the trailer a few times, then stand by my plant and look at Shelley's window.

CHAPTER SIXTEEN

tom

On Fridays, people go offsite. They carpool. Randy the Prophet and Kenny pick people up. I've heard everyone in maintenance has company trucks that they're technically allowed to drive offsite, so they offer rides when they're in the mood.

It took a month for anyone to invite me, but here I am idling at the end of the road. According to Shelley, whoever wants to go will come out and jump in my truck. I'm supposed to wait fifteen minutes. A group of teenagers come running up the main road and turn toward my truck. "You got room?" one of them asks me through the rolled down window. I nod. No one else is in the truck besides me. They jump in the bed. I think some of them are kids of workers, others are in the internship program. "Two more coming," someone calls from the back. I look in the rearview and see Shelley and Marigold, walking and talking intently, not hurrying.

Marigold looks a way I've never seen before. Her hair is down, the loose waves hit just below her shoulders. Instead of one of the light dresses, she is in black pants and a black t-shirt. Shelley, beside her, also has her hair down, straight and grazing her shoulders. She wears a red dress with thin straps, tied at the waist.

When they get closer to the truck, Shelley sticks her thumb up. I reverse a few feet and they get in the passenger side, Shelley squeezed in between me and Marigold.

"Am I supposed to take these teenagers to a bar?" I ask them.

"They'll hop out and run around town," Shelley says. "They'll be sitting in the back of your truck again by the time we're leaving."

The sun is setting. The night shift guard, whose name I can never remember, is working the gate. He waves to us disinterestedly as we pass. The teens whoop at him and he rolls his eyes.

Although the area around the compound is spotted with little populated segments that are technically towns, "going to town" for the people on the plant means a specific town about 45 minutes away. It is the town that has more than one bar and a few restaurants and a real grocery store. After so much time on the isolated compound, the sight of the stop lights, cars, and bright storefronts makes me lightheaded. There is a temporary release from my body, a floating happiness that I used to feel as a teenager. An expectation that something good will happen. A hazy trust in the future.

Shelley directs me to pull into a parking lot in front of a strip mall with a dilapidated hobby store, a Chinese buffet, and, lit by a string of Christmas lights, a storefront that just says "BAR" in black block letters.

When I park, the teens hop out of the truck and run off.

"Where are they going?" I ask.

"Some street corner or parking garage where they can find other teens," Shelley says.

In front of the bar, people stand on the sidewalk and in the parking lot holding their drinks, gesturing and talking loudly over the rock music streaming from a speaker propped up on a bar stool. Some look at us, some call out greetings to Shelley and Marigold. I recognize a few faces from the plant, others I guess are just people from town. This town is one of our bigger local clients. I look at the smiling, drunk faces of the people around me and imagine them drinking our water.

Inside, softer country music streams from a jukebox. It is almost too dark to see. I stand still for a few seconds, so my eyes can adjust, then I take it all in: the black bar, the grimy mirror behind it, the rows of liquor and the tap with a few cheap beers. Above the bar, a TV flashes a cartoon. The others have left me standing here, so I look around and try to find them. The walls are lined with black Naugahyde booths. The middle of the room is scattered with tables, some low-tops, some high, with an opening around the jukebox where one couple is dancing: two men swaying slowly with their heads on each other's shoulders. I find Shelley and Marigold with Randy the Prophet and a man and two women from maintenance in a booth. I walk over and sit on the edge of the booth seat beside Marigold with one leg sticking out into the aisle. In the corner a few tables up from us, I spot Martha from the Dollar & More with some similarly bored-looking women, all darting their eyes around as if hoping for someone better to talk to.

Randy the Prophet motions a waitress over and orders a round. The jukebox starts playing something sad and sliding, a song that starts to tinge the surroundings. I start to see everything around me as if it is a setting for a dramatic movie, every person in the booth with me a character.

Marigold doesn't sway to the music or look around the room. When the waitress brings her drink, a plain glass of whiskey, she slowly sips it and stares straight ahead, looking in between the two women from maintenance.

"Your hair looks different," I say.

She turns toward me and cranes her neck a little bit, shaking her head and pointing to her ear. She can't hear me.

I lean toward her, press my thumb against her ear to drown out the jukebox, and say it again. She doesn't turn to look at me but tucks some hair behind her ear. The song ends and suddenly the space the music filled is replaced with the chatter of loud people used to talking over music, clinking glasses, and the background music from the cartoon on TV.

"Shelley likes for me to wear it like this when we go out," she says. "She says it makes me look normal."

"I didn't realize you looked abnormal, "I say.

She looks me in the eyes and blinks.

A new song comes on, this one jangly and upbeat. Randy the Prophet takes Shelley to the clearing in the middle of the bar to dance. A few other couples go out to the floor, the group two-stepping in circles.

"Do you like to dance?" I ask. I try just yelling over the music.

She shakes her head. "They look happy, though," she says, nodding toward Shelley who is laughing and dancing out of rhythm with the music, spinning around Randy the Prophet.

I let the music take over the space, so that I can be silent and not feel uncomfortable. Hiding inside the sound, I feel like I am someone else, like I am watching someone live my life. The bar doesn't feel like a place I know or like it exists in a time I've lived. There is a sense of unimportance, a pleasant acceptance of the current moment. The walls are covered with askew posters of women in bikinis holding up beer and race car drivers holding up beer and football players holding up beer. A digital display over a cigarette vending machine in the corner flashes: "Smoke 'em if you got 'em." I decide to buy some.

"Would you like a cigarette?" I yell at Marigold.

She looks surprised by the question, widens her eyes, then shakes her head.

I walk over to the machine, put in my money, and select a pack decorated with a blue waterfall. When I look over my shoulder, she is still sitting at the table, watching me.

I find a door at the back of the bar that goes out to an alley full of other smokers, or people on dates who want a quiet place to talk. I take out a cigarette and light it, inhale and cough. When I was a teenager, I smoked a lot, just to have something to do. My dad did it and his friends did, and they seemed to like it. I haven't smoked in years and am not sure why I wanted to, except for the same need to have something to do. There is only so much blinking and nodding and straight forward conversation I can have with her. I walk down the alley a bit and sit in a plastic lawn chair with a missing front leg, carefully pushing my weight toward the back of the chair. The conversations of the people around me are a meaningless noise that I swat away from my mind. I stare down at the ground and smoke my cigarette.

"I hear those are bad for you," a voice says. I look up to see Shelley, shining with sweat, loose hairs frizzy around her face, smiling and breathing heavily. She is holding two beers. She hands me one and sits down on the ground.

"Can I have one?" she asks.

I shake the pack toward her, she pulls one out gingerly, puts it in her mouth, and leans forward for me to light it. I stub mine out and light another. We sit in silence, breathing smoke into the stale, hot air.

"Marigold doesn't seem to like it here," I say. I say it just to say it. To put her name in my mouth and try to make something happen with that. She doesn't seem to dislike it really, she seems the same as always.

The door to the bar opens. It is Martha and a couple of her friends. I nod at her, but she pretends not to notice, and walks to the opposite end of the alley.

"It's sort of beyond her regular training," Shelley says, smoke curling from her fingers. "But I feel like coming here is training in a way. Maybe eventually she'll be leading a line dance or singing on top of the bar. At least maybe she'll smile at people."

"Training?" I ask.

"Humanity 101 or whatever."

She taps her ashes out delicately on the asphalt.

"I don't get your joke."

"Well I don't think there's a real name for her sort of performance plan, so I just gave it that name. It's not that clever. I wouldn't call it a joke, exactly."

I look down the alley at Martha and her friends. I feel sorry for them, their dullness, laughing unhappily in the sticky air, but I also envy the ability to lean against a wall, be unconcerned, be miserable and not know it. Is it misery if you don't know it? Shelley blows smoke toward my knee.

"Performance plan?" I ask. I feel stupid. This sort of thing happens to me a lot: not knowing terms used on the compound, being ignorant of basic facts about the employees.

"So she can be a real girl, or whatever LeBlanc wants."

"As opposed to?"

"Well... you know..."

She is smiling at me, and then she is not.

"Oh," she says. "You don't know."

I lean down and stub out my cigarette.

I drink too much and Shelley has to drive my truck back. I lay in the bed of the truck with the teenagers giggling and shouting around me, watching the sky. If I was Martha or one of her friends in the alley, I might know my astrological sign, might see its shape there and find some comfort. Instead, the pinpricks of light puncture the darkness and tell me nothing.

When the truck stops at my house, Shelley and Marigold lean over the bed and look at me. Their faces are smudges in the dark.

"You OK in there?" Shelley asks.

I say yes or make a sound similar to it.

"You need help getting inside?"

I shake my head, rolling the back of my skull against the ridged bed.

Their smudges disappear.

I close my eyes, but I don't know if I am asleep or not, if I am dreaming or thinking. I see Marigold with her hair down in an empty room. Maybe it isn't an empty room so much as an empty space, a fading nothingness around her. She is looking me in the eyes. She is blinking.

CHAPTER SEVENTEEN

leBlanc

He was raised a certain way: his parents loved him, his mom ironed his t-shirts, his dad never told him not to cry, that sort of thing. I could tell all of that when he walked up. I was in my office, on a phone call, staring out through the glass at the back of my receptionist's head. She was always very put together, but she had this little cowlick at the end of her part that I found endearing. I wondered if she even knew it was there. He came up to her desk and started chatting with her and the cowlick bobbed up and down. There was just something about him, about his perfect smile—not perfect in that he had perfect teeth, although he did, but perfect because it wasn't too much or too little, not forced, not shy, just right— and his wrinkle-free trousers and his fitted suit jacket. This was a person who did everything right.

My receptionist turned toward me a little and pointed, I guess explaining that I was on the phone, and I waved to them both, trying to indicate I'd be off in just a second. He stuck his hands in his pocket and nodded. That respectful nod. That son of a bitch. When the call was over, my receptionist ushered him right in. I had the feeling she'd been hovering over the phone, waiting for the light by my line to go off, eager to get this man where he needed to go as soon as possible.

The first thing I noticed when he came into my office, besides his pleasant scent, was that he had on the type of watch that said: "I have money and taste, but I'm not a show off."

We didn't seem so different. My suit probably cost a few hundred more dollars than his. My watch was slightly nicer, but also not flashy. My shoes were freshly polished. But it was not easy for me. Could people tell? When I looked in the mirror I found it impossible that they couldn't. There was this perpetual sweat at my temples. My shirt was always coming untucked, my tie askew. At the end of the day, I was covered in a film of grime and sweat that I could only attribute to overexertion. This man looked like he never sweat, never tried, never worried.

I was interviewing him for a job, but it didn't feel that way. It didn't feel like I was the one being interviewed, either. It felt more like I was some strange animal in a zoo and he was an expert, come to observe me.

He sat comfortably in the chair in front of my desk, legs spread casually open. My wife called that the power stance. She claimed she hated it.

"I like how delicately you sit," she told me once. I looked down to see my ankle crossed over my knee and quickly undid it.

The interview went well. He knew the right things to say, the right time to make a joke, the right way to assure me I was making the right decision. He kept checking his watch like he had somewhere else to be, and I found myself trying to wrap things up for his benefit. Still, it was customary for me to add a social component to these interviews, so I asked if he'd like to get lunch. He checked his watch again and then agreed enthusiastically. Easy.

I took him to an oyster place attached to a gas station off the service road. I thought I'd get some satisfaction out of it. The way someone like him might wince the minute we pulled into the parking lot: seeing the Y missing amongst the wooden letters spelling OYSTERS, leaving just the shadow of itself. Looking at the dirty reflective glass on the doors that obscured the interior. The sign in the gas station window for $4.00 fried chicken baskets. But he was perfect there too, at ease.

When I opened the door and the briny smell of oysters mixed with the choke of the deep fryer and he took in the stained plastic tablecloths and the casually dressed clientele, he rubbed his hands together and said, "I'm starving."

We sat at a narrow two-person table in a corner by the bathrooms. Our table had been hastily wiped down, wet crumbs still clinging to the tablecloth. Above us, peeling from the wall, was an old poster for a long defunct beer endorsed by a long-retired athlete.

I tried to clean off the table with the pathetically thin paper napkins that shredded as I pulled them out of the holder and disintegrated once they touched the wet patches on the tablecloth. He looked intently at the laminated menu, warped and grimed.

"Everything looks great," he said, and I really felt he meant it. "What do you recommend?"

We ordered three dozen raw. The waitress laughed at everything he said. Not a polite, silly giggle, but a deep belly laugh, like she was at a comedy show. I was laughing too. I couldn't even tell you why. I don't remember what he was saying.

When she brought out the trays, ice starting to melt under the half-shells, cracker packets and little sauce containers and lemon wedges gathered in the middle, he tucked a couple of those cheap napkins right in his shirt collar, flung off his jacket, and went to town. He sucked them right out of the shell with nothing but a dash of hot sauce. I felt ashamed, picking them out with the tiny fork, placing them carefully on a cracker, adding my horseradish and cocktail sauce on top. It was the eating equivalent of crossing my ankle over my knee.

After he gulped down about four oysters in silence, he seemed to suddenly remember I was there. He wiped his hands and looked at me seriously.

"What do you think?" he asked.

I had an oyster on a cracker half-raised to my mouth. I set it down on top of an empty shell, the ice underneath all water now.

"About?"

"Me," he said. "Do you think you'll hire me?"

That self-satisfied bastard.

He smiled at me then, and kept eating his oysters, waiting for me to answer.

I ate my oyster, the cracker crumbling on my pants.

"Yeah," I said. "I guess so."

We shook hands out in the hot parking lot, my palm sweaty, his cool and smooth.

When I got home, I found my wife in her room, staring out the window from her lounge chair. From the window, I knew she could see me drive up, so I was slightly annoyed that she hadn't bothered to come down and greet me and didn't even seem to be waiting for me to come see her. She lolled her head slowly toward me. A book lay open on her lap.

She was the most beautiful person I'd ever seen. In such moments, when I happened upon her in her natural state, that beauty struck me in my stomach, made me feel nervous and excited and afraid. It was still early afternoon and the bright light from the window surrounded her, made her something faded and apart. All she did was wait. She waited to see what I would say. There was no question, no inquiring look, just a maddening passivity.

'Think I got my new guy," I told her.

She nodded. "That's great," she said.

She didn't say it in a dismissive way, but she didn't sound like she cared all that much, either.

"He's a real charmer," I told her.

I still remember telling her that.

It was the first thing I remembered, years later, when I found them there, in that same chair.

CHAPTER EIGHTEEN

marigold

Our junior year at the Evangeline school, there was a prom. No one was allowed to bring dates and there were no limo rides or fancy dinners, since the dance was held in the auditorium and only attended by the boys from St. Joseph's. The cafeteria served a pot of gumbo and plates of potato salad. The boys shuffled in awkwardly in their tuxedos and the girls tucked napkins down their beaded dresses and stuck the corsages they bought themselves in the middle of the table because they made it hard to eat.

After dinner we crossed the lawn to the auditorium, lovingly decorated by the events club to reflect the year's theme: "Light up Your Life." Banners displaying the theme, the words draped in Christmas lights or surrounded by spotlights or lamps, covered the walls, and a small table sat awkwardly in the middle of the floor holding a rotating, round, multi-colored light. The auditorium swallowed up the music coming from the small sound system, notes and unheard words floating along the floor. I watched the faces of my classmates and the boys as they were intermittently striped by the spinning light and tried to figure out what they were thinking. They looked scared and bored but also happy, nervous.

I found a seat at a table by the punch bowl and watched as couples formed: someone walking toward someone else, a nod of the head, then a strange moment of walking separately toward the dance area, around the table with the light, not touching until the moment came to dance, then figuring out where to place hands, how close to stand.

Shelley drank vodka from a flask and watched the unfolding events with a frown.

"These guys are all boring," she said.

She liked Laura Ellen who was a grade below us and not at the dance. Laura Ellen would be at the dance if Shelley took her as a date, but she never asked, even though Laura Ellen kept saying how much she wished she could go to the dance and that it wasn't fair that the lower classmen didn't get to go. Shelley ignored these comments, which even I understood as hints. Laura Ellen finally stopped her comments when Shelley sighed one day and said, "Them's the breaks, kid."

I couldn't tell anything about the boys: if they were boring or not, or smart or not, or good at telling jokes. They all seemed in a state of petrification that prevented them from showing any type of characteristics.

"Watch out," Shelley said, taking another drink and then sticking the flask back into her sequined purse. She nodded toward an approaching body, one like the others, with floppy hair and slumped shoulders.

When he got to their table he leaned on it for a second, as if out of breath, not looking at either of us. Then he looked up at me and asked: "Wanna dance?"

I turned to Shelley.

"Don't look at me," she said. "Do you want to or not?"

Mr. Miller took me aside earlier in the week to discuss the dance.

"We don't normally tell kids to do what other people are doing, but in your case, at least for a while, it's a good idea. If other people your age are doing it and they seem like they're having fun, and it's nothing dangerous or illegal, you should do it too, just to try."

I told the boy I would dance with him.

He didn't express anything when I said it, just turned around and walked toward the dance floor. I stumbled out from behind the table to catch up with him. As we got closer to the speakers, the music actually sounded like music, the thump of it echoing in my body. He put a hand on the small of my back until we found a gap in the other bodies and he turned toward me, grabbed one of my hands, and put his other one around my waist.

The song was something pretty and light—a woman singing about loving someone, an eerie in and out of synthesizers under her words. The boy didn't look at me or talk, but I found my body moving closer to his, until my head was on his shoulder, his breath heavy above my hair, his chin brushing against the top of my head. There were faces around me, watching as we swayed, curious about me, always curious, but I closed my eyes and felt the music swell.

When the song was over, he stepped away from me, said, "Thank you," and retreated to a corner with some other floppy-haired boys. I stayed on the dance floor for a moment, the new song fast and loud, the students around me jumping and laughing and vibrating with it, their bodies sometimes knocking into mine, then I went back to Shelley who was asleep, her head on the table.

The boy came back three more times, and each time I walked behind him, waited for him to turn, and moved my body against his. After the fourth dance, he kept hold of my hand and mumbled, not looking at me: "Want to go outside?"

"OK," I said.

Some of the girls stared as we walked past. The boys mostly grinned. Mary Margaret grinned too, but it wasn't the same sort of grin as the boys, it was one that gave me pause, like Mary Margaret knew something I didn't. His hand was sweaty and hot against mine, our fingers interlaced awkwardly. I wanted to adjust my hand but was worried that wasn't the right thing to do, even though my wrist felt bent and my arm jutted at a strange angle.

He took me to the playground and we sat on the swings. He twisted toward me and I mirrored him.

Eventually he had his hands on my knees, over the silk of my dress, then he moved them up to my waist and they stayed there. He looked me in the eyes, but we didn't say anything. I wasn't so ignorant that I didn't know about kissing, I'd seen it at other socials, heard Shelley talk about it, read about it in the books the other girls passed around that Mr. Miller told me weren't worth reading—"then again maybe they would be, there's definitely a necessary human element there"—but I hadn't given much thought to the reality of it happening to me. When the boy closed his eyes and pushed his face toward mine, I stayed frozen. At first, I thought he was asleep and was going to fall on top of me. When his lips touched mine, they were cold and dry and I tried my best to do what I thought kissing was. I puckered my lips and pushed them against his. He seemed to like what was happening, making a pleasant humming sound and breathing sharply through his nose. Eventually he stuck his tongue between my lips and I wasn't sure what to do next, so I just opened them and let him move it around inside my mouth, which increased the humming sounds.

"What the hell?"

I heard Mary Margaret's voice somewhere nearby and tried looking for her by just straining my eyes, not moving my head.

"What the hell?" she asked again, and this time the boy was startled and pulled himself away from me and jumped up from the swing.

It wasn't just Mary Margaret, but some of her friends and some of the boys they'd been dancing with, all standing a step down from the mulch bed that surrounded the swing, looking back and forth between us and Mary Margaret to see what would happen.

"What?" the boy asked. I didn't know if he was scared or mad because I didn't know him.

"Are you having a nice time?" Mary Margaret asked.

The boy shrugged, but she wasn't asking him. She was asking me. I stared at her and pushed my legs out slowly, swinging a little.

"Come on, Benji," one of the boys called. "You better come on."

"Why?" he called back, but he started walking toward them, not looking at me. When he got to his friends they put their arms around him and began muttering and walking him back toward the auditorium. The girls giggled and followed behind them, but Mary Margaret stayed where she was, her hands in fists by her sides.

I watched her.

Mr. Miller told me there were no rules for interacting with people like Mary Margaret: "Try to avoid being alone with her."

"Why did you do that?" she asked. She sounded genuinely upset, not fake-curious in the way she sometimes did when she was trying to trap someone into saying something embarrassing.

"Do what?" I asked.

I kept swinging.

"Kiss someone," Mary Margaret said.

"He wanted to kiss me."

Mary Margaret stayed planted, her fists tightly pressed against her body.

"That's because he doesn't know about you," she said. She narrowed her eyes at me as if that might help her catch a reaction. "Now he does."

"OK," I said.

"Go away!" I heard a slurred voice call in the dark.

It was Shelley, who materialized beside me, picked up some mulch, and threw it at Mary Margaret, hissing. The mulch didn't get anywhere near her.

"You want to act like I'm the mean one all the time," Mary Margaret said, to whom, I wasn't sure—to Shelley, to both of us, to the world at large—"but I'm the only one who is honest around here and I'm tired of it!" With that she turned and faded into the dark.

"You OK?" Shelley asked.

It was not a normal Shelley question.

I thought about it. I didn't know. I shrugged.

"How was it?" she asked.

"Sort of dry, and then sort of wet."

"Was he nice?"

"I couldn't tell."

"Oh well."

"The dancing was nice, though."

"Oh yeah. That's a good part."

We went back to our room and watched the boys load up on the bus in the parking lot. I thought I saw the one I kissed and pressed my head against the window, wanting to see some sign of how he felt: humiliated, excited, indifferent.

"Why didn't you tell him?" Shelley asked. "You tell everyone, whether they want to know or not, usually at an awkward and inappropriate moment."

The boy or maybe not the boy got on the bus and I pulled my forehead away. "At first I didn't think to say. I think I felt normal, maybe. Then I did think to, but I wanted to know what it would be like."

CHAPTER NINETEEN

tom

We didn't go to church on Sunday mornings. It was the only day my dad was guaranteed off. I would wake up to the smell of bacon, eggs, and biscuits, and the sound of my parents' records. My dad sang loudly and off-key, while dancing around, trying to distract my mom while she cooked.

One morning, the song *Wurlitzer Prize* came on. I'd heard the song so many times, I couldn't remember not knowing it, but for some reason it was the first time I'd paid attention to the words.

"What's a Wurlitzer?" I asked.

"Company makes jukeboxes," my dad said.

We were done with breakfast, dirty plates spread over the table with orange-juice-glazed cups. My mom sipped her coffee and leaned back in her chair, staring out the window. My dad sat with his hands resting contentedly on his belly.

"Why do they give out a prize?"

I liked asking these types of questions. They were the kind where an adult had to explain something complicated, something that had to do with being an adult. It was like peeking into the future. When I asked these kinds of questions, my parents got these indulgent smiles on their faces, like my ignorance gave them pleasure.

"They don't, it's just his way of exaggerating to illustrate a point. He's saying they should give him a prize because he's put so much money into the jukebox."

"What's a jukebox?" I asked.

This was a less fun question to ask and for my parents to answer. It was a simple question with a simple, non-interpretive answer.

"It's a thing plays music. You've seen them before. They have one down at the diner. The rainbow thing with all the buttons."

I nodded. I wasn't sure what he was talking about, but I decided I didn't want any more explanations.

My dad could tell somehow.

"You don't remember?" he asked.

I shook my head.

"We'll go there for lunch?" he asked, looking at my mom.

She nodded and shrugged.

The diner smelled like a greasier, smokier version of our house that morning. As we followed the waitress to our table, my parents stopped suddenly. I was behind them and couldn't see what was going on. "Hello," a familiar voice said.

I stuck my head between my parents and saw LeBlanc sitting in a booth with a blonde woman across from him. The woman turned toward us and offered a quick wave, only smiling with half of her mouth, then went back to her food.

"Hi," my dad said.

My mom didn't say anything. We walked to our table.

After we ordered, my dad took me over to the jukebox. We walked past LeBlanc again. He didn't look up, but the blonde woman turned her head slightly.

"This is it," my dad said, motioning to the bulky box with a rainbow tube arching over the top and big stained buttons along the front. "What do you want to listen to?"

"The Wurlitzer song," I said.

I thought this was the kind of smart thing I should say, that showed I paid attention, that I was following a narrative that had been planned for the day, but my father didn't look pleased or impressed. His mouth got tight and he stuck his hands in his pockets. "That's a good idea," he said, but I could tell he didn't mean it.

He showed me how to scroll through the album covers and find the song and punch in the right letter and number. As the song started, we went back to our table. The blonde woman with LeBlanc got up and walked toward us. Just as she passed, my dad said, quietly: "Sorry."

I thought he must have bumped into her.

CHAPTER TWENTY

marigold

So he knows now.

He knows.

Everyone knows, Shelley says in my head.

He was going to find out eventually, she says.

Why do you even care? She asks.

Why didn't you tell him yourself? You tell everyone.

I have long hair that is not in a braid. I wear jeans and a t-shirt. I am good at talking on the phone. I am not technically human.

CHAPTER TWENTY-ONE

tom

"I don't see why it matters," Randy the Prophet says. He is so disinterested in what I'm saying that he doesn't even bother to look up from his crossword puzzle. The sound of his stubby pencil scratching against the rough paper lies pleasantly under the jangly wordless version of a popular song leaking from the store's sound system.

"It doesn't *matter*," I say. "Well, it does matter. But I'm not saying it matters in a bad way."

I don't know what I'm trying to say, so I just stop talking. I'm leaning over the counter in the store, drinking a Yoo-hoo. It does matter of course, but it's hard to explain why. I was deceived, is one reason.

"We thought you knew," Shelley told me last night.

So, then, I wasn't deceived, really, or not by anyone but myself. It's not like I'm so ignorant that I don't know about this type of thing. I even knew LeBlanc was interested in it. Had heard him talk about it before.

I guess it matters the same way that it matters where a person's from or whether they grew up with both their parents or went to private school or had a dog. Facts about us matter, don't they? Facts about me certainly matter, but no one seems to be interested.

"Let me ask you this," Randy the Prophet says, putting down his crossword, like he's finally begrudgingly decided to give me the time of day. "What does it change for you?"

I shrug. I can't say that. I'm not sure how to say it to him or to myself. "It just changes the way I think about her, I guess. Same as it would for anybody."

He nods. I like talking to him because I think when he found out it probably didn't change anything, but he is able to understand, instantly, how I am different from him, and it doesn't bother him or make him think any less of me.

"Well, I can understand that," he says. "But you'll accept it soon enough. You're thinking it subtracts something, but really it adds something if you ask me."

"She is impressive," I concede.

"She is."

He goes back to his crossword. My Yoo-hoo is done, but I stand there with the empty bottle in my hand, turning it around and reading the label. I want to keep talking about her, even though I know there's nothing else to say.

Maybe he senses this, or maybe it's just a coincidence, but he puts his pencil down, looks at me, and says: "I saw you, you know."

"Where?" I ask, confused. It's a weird thing to say. There are plenty of times he's seen me, of course. We see each other almost every day. The way he says it makes it sound like he saw me doing something I wasn't supposed to.

"You know," he circles his hands around his head and moves his fingers like he's pulling something from the air around it. "I saw you."

I shake my head. "What?"

"You know about me, how I see things."

"The name..." I say, not wanting to add anything else.

"Right. Right," he nods seriously at this, his hands still above his head. He lowers them. "Well, I had a vision about you. I wasn't sure if I should tell you or not."

"Why not?"

I am peeling off the edge of the Yoo-hoo label.

"Well, I get the impression you're not into that sort of thing."

I keep looking at the label. I like Randy the Prophet. He is very sincere and kind and I enjoy talking to him. He is also good at reading people. I don't want to look him in the eyes where he can see how silly I think all of this business is. "I think it's fine..." I say quietly.

"It's OK if you don't believe in it or whatever," he says. He laughs a little. "Pretty sure my own daughter thinks I'm just doing it for show. Doesn't hurt my feelings. I'd be skeptical too. But if you want me to tell you, I'll just tell you, and you can take it or leave it."

"Do you think I should know?" I meet his eyes.

He twists his mouth up and squints at me. "There's no way for me to know that. I don't know what it means myself. I can tell you and if it means anything it will mean more to you than me."

"Just tell me," I say. I go back to peeling off the label. I don't believe in it, whatever it is he does, but I want to know. I want to know so badly, I feel like Christmas Eve or getting ready for a school dance or entering a contest. My hands buzz with excitement, so I just grip the bottle and look into it.

"So, you know you brought me that vacuum?"

I nod, let down. I think maybe he's decided not to tell me after all and I feel painfully disappointed, because I know I won't ask him if he changes the subject. There was an old vacuum cleaner in the hall closet of my house. I used it one time, lazily, vaguely running it around the house, over the furniture. The second time I tried to vacuum, it started spitting out dust all over the floor. I brought it in to Randy the Prophet to fix. The pile of dust and hair is still on the floor in the hallway, I step over it multiple times a day.

"The bag was overflowing," he says.

I can feel his eyes on me. My heart goes all the way up into my throat, then down into the pit of my stomach. He is not going to tell me. I set the bottle down on the counter and make fake eye contact, look at a sun spot on his forehead.

"Was that the problem?" I ask. I try to sound interested in the vacuum cleaner, not disappointed.

"That's the problem with you," he says. "It's rude to bring it to me like that, then I have to get all that dust and hair everywhere."

"Sorry," I say. "I honestly think that was the first time I've used a vacuum cleaner. I didn't know about the bag."

He snorts.

"Really. Sorry. OK?" I ask. I know I sound rude and petulant, but I need to get away from him. For some reason my frustration at not hearing the vision is so strong I am afraid I will cry. "I'll see you later, man, OK?" The "man" sounds strange coming from me to him. I've never called him that before. I turn to leave.

"You're not getting out of it so easy," he says.

I turn back around.

"Why don't you sit?" he asks. He points to the two lawn chairs he keeps behind his counter for slow-time visitors. I walk around and sit beside him. He pours each of us a cup of coffee and we look at each other over the steaming Styrofoam. The wrinkles around his eyes crinkle up as he blows on the coffee. His hair is down, smooth and a little slicked back, hitting just at his shoulders. He's one of those people who doesn't seem to care about his appearance, but always looks put together, tidy, even if his clothes are old and unfashionable. Today he wears one of three shirts I've seen: a long-sleeve button down in a canvas color that looks like it is made out of denim or another similarly thick material. The shirt is tucked into a pair of black jeans with a black belt. His shoes are thick, black work boots, polished. The outfit is way too heavy for the weather, but he doesn't look remotely sweaty, in fact he gives off a pleasant odor of spicy aftershave, chewing gum, and cigarettes.

I look down at my own scuffed boots and jeans with mud around the ankles and make a mental note to get myself together, starting by picking up the pile of dust in the hallway. There is no way Randy the

Prophet would leave a pile of dust in his hallway, or wait weeks before vacuuming his home. He certainly wouldn't use a vacuum cleaner without understanding how it worked.

"The thing is," he says, pausing to sip his coffee. "Sometimes with the vacuum cleaners, especially if the bag's left in them, I see things."

I can't tell if he's back to the vision or if this is just about vacuum cleaners. I nod and hold the coffee still between my hands, the unnecessary warmth in the barely cooled store somehow comforting.

"Yours sat with me for a while. That happens sometimes."

"You kept the bag with you?" I ask. I've given up on hearing about the vision but try to politely maintain the conversation.

"No, I mean the vision."

Again, he pauses to drink. I'm afraid if I drink any coffee my heart will beat straight into my brain, so I keep the cup where it is and scrape a fingernail against the Styrofoam.

"I don't know. 'Vision' isn't the right word for it really, but that's the closest I can think of. Usually it's more of a feeling. But what I mean is sometimes, I get to the bag or some dust or fur or whatever and I see something there, floating in the air around me. Sometimes, though, nothing seems to happen, and I go about my day like normal and then eventually I feel it, something settling into me, slowly, like all the dust

181

and hair and dirt and carpet fibers were floating around me in a cloud all day and they just decided to come down so I could take them in."

"It's from breathing them in or what?"

I don't know what to ask, but I don't want to be rude. I appreciate his openness to whatever is happening to him, an openness I don't possess, cynical and negative as I am. I don't want any of that cynicism to come across.

"No," he says.

Now we sit in silence for several seconds as he drinks more coffee. I reach up, set mine on the counter, sit on my hands, and start rocking back and forth.

"I wouldn't say it's anything like that," he says, finally. "But I can't say what it is really."

A group of kids comes in, yelling, teasing each other, tennis shoes squeaking on the floor. It's late Saturday morning and the store is in an oversaturated haze from the morning sun and the fluorescent lighting. The kids look golden, shining in the light, smiling and careless. Randy the Prophet stands up to chat with them. He knows most of them by name and asks about their parents, their school. They pick out snacks and drinks and he rings them up while they partially answer his questions, partially ignore him and keep talking to each other. I stay in the lawn chair, watching the procession of tops of heads and foil wrappers.

Randy the Prophet stays standing at the counter until the last kid leaves, then he sits back down and drinks more coffee.

"Anyway," he says. "What happened with your vacuum cleaner. After a day or two, I started feeling different. An accumulated difference, like I'd been getting different slowly, every second, but then I got to a point where I could feel it, could look back and see Point A from Point B. Then I remembered it was you, or felt it, or whatever you want to say. Remembered that disgusting vacuum bag. And I felt you alongside me, inside me, ahead of me, behind me, all of that." He holds his hands up now, like he's being accused of something. "Or that's what I thought. I understand if you don't believe me."

I make a vague hand gesture for him to continue.

"What I felt was like I was getting heavier and heavier. Like even my fingers weighed a ton and they were pulling off my hands, but my hands were pulling off my arms and my arms were pulling off my shoulders. And I also felt something else, like my insides were all mixed up, fighting with themselves, tangled. And I saw something, but I couldn't be sure what it was, it seemed like a muck or a fog that covered my eyes, tainted everything."

I wait. He drinks more coffee and looks at me. I stare at the spot on his forehead.

"And that's what? That's how the vision feels or that is the vision?" I ask. I reach up for my coffee and take a few sips, no longer feeling nervous, just completely let down.

"It's both," he says. "That's how the vision felt, and that's what the vision was."

"Does it mean something?" I ask, sure that it doesn't.

"I would have no way to know," he says.

I hold up the hand that isn't holding the coffee and wiggle the fingers in the air.

"They don't feel heavy," I say. I immediately feel bad for saying it. I don't think I sound mean, but I know that I feel mean.

Randy the Prophet just nods and sets his coffee on the counter, watching me. "I know it's all silly," he says. "It might all be fake. No way for me to know."

"Anything you say ever come true?"

"It seems that way sometimes, but I believe in coincidences."

"Do you like being called Prophet?"

"I've been called worse."

He pauses and pushes his hair behind his ears.

"I've been called better, too."

CHAPTER TWENTY-TWO

The realization sinks in every once in a while. Usually when I'm at work. Usually when I'm doing a particularly monotonous task. Today I am folding men's t-shirts. Folding t-shirts is one of my favorite tasks. It doesn't take any thought. I am a good folder, a natural, my boss says. There are always shirts to be folded, especially in the men's section, because they just walk over and rifle through them like they are a bunch of mysterious documents on a desk in a creepy old mansion, and then they walk off without picking one out or even trying one on.

I folded all the laundry after Mom died. Dad used to fold it with her, and he hated it after, couldn't even look at it. It was nice for me, because being around him could be overwhelming. He was an open book that I wanted to close sometimes. When it was laundry time, I'd go into my room and turn up my music and sit on the bed alone and fold slowly. I would unfold and refold the t-shirts until they sat in perfect square piles. It's strangely similar at the Mart. Headphones are banned so I'm listening to whatever terrible music comes piping through the intercom system, and instead of my dad trying to avoid a reminder of his loss, it's my co-workers trying to avoid doing any work, but either way t-shirt folding is my alone time.

The shelf display I'm working on contains the Beach Ready colors: painful oranges, lime greens, unnatural blues. I fold and stack with the smallest sizes on top and the biggest on the bottom.

Thinking about the beach makes me think about the plant with its lazy facade of tropical paradise and sad staff beach. When I think about the plant, it's like my brain is a clear sky and the thoughts are clouds, and they come in and bump against each other until sometimes two clouds look like one, and I know the sky is still under there, and that the clouds are separate, but I can't get to any of it. Then I just feel angry.

"Anger with nowhere to put it is very dangerous," LeBlanc told me.

This was in one of our meetings. He liked to call me into meetings. As the leader of the protest group, I was his official enemy, and he liked the gracious appearance of us breaking bread together.

"Yes, it is, and it will be dangerous for you," I said.

We were in his camper office on the plant. He just showed up when he felt like it, set up his little camper, and had meetings. The camper looked at least twenty years old, with outdated paisley-printed fabric covering the little nub of a couch and dark wood cabinets in the sliver of kitchen. We sat at the kitchen table. He poured us both whiskey in plastic cups printed with cartoon characters from different shows.

"Got these at the flea market," he said, raising his cup toward me.

I raised mine too, and we clacked them together in a sad cheers.

"Honey," he said. He smiled a little when he said it. I winced. "You can't do shit to me and you know it."

He drank the whiskey all at once and I followed. Then we sat there and looked at each other.

"I've gotta try," I said.

"Yeah," he said. He looked down at the cup, swirled around what drops of liquid were there, as if that would conjure up more. "I get that."

I know he met with me so he could say that to me. I understand that he wants to get in my head. His whole act like he gets me and we're so much alike and he just feels sorry for me is transparent. But it works, doesn't it? Because when I'm sitting here folding a t-shirt that is the same color as a traffic cone, I can see myself tomorrow, and the day after, and years after, all these little versions of myself, overlapping at the edges, still folding these stupid shirts. The only thing that will change will be the colors. Maybe the fabric. The Mart will get fake eco conscious and use some supposedly recycled plastic. Maroons and grays will be in for the fall. But I'll be in here folding shirts and wanting something. Wanting to do something about the plant and LeBlanc and the thirsty, but I won't have done it, because I can't.

What I can do is this: letter campaigns, meetings at my apartment, phone calls to my representative, phone calls to the mayor-presidents, town hall meetings at the library. And it all looks good. Or it sounds good when I tell people about it. People at work seem impressed. "Wow, you're really passionate," Guy told me the other day. Guy has greasy blonde hair that he is constantly rubbing away from his face before and after picking at zits on his chin and rubbing his nose. He likes to work in produce, because he thinks it's important to separate out the unripe from the ripe avocados and no one else cares about doing it that way.

I am passionate, that's true. And it's nice for Guy to be impressed. But what would Guy think if he came to my meeting at the library? Me trying to look professional, wearing a little less eyeliner and a cheap, unraveling black dress I got at the Mart from the discard rack we're allowed to take from. It has little buttons running down the middle that don't button or serve any purpose other than to dangle there sadly. Two of the buttons already fell off before it got to the store, which was why it was on the discard rack. The discard rack has a misleading name because we still have to pay for the items, they are just 90% off. I paid two dollars for it. I stand in the lobby with my clipboard hoping to see someone walking in from the parking lot who looks like they care about this sort of thing, but it's all moms busy with their kids and old men who want to use the computer. Sometimes I can convince someone walking by to just come in and hear me out. They'll sit in one of the library's uncomfortable seats, shivering from the over industrious air-conditioning, and nod and smile nervously at me. The minute I pause in my talk they usually make some excuse about meeting someone and get out of there.

The meetings at my house aren't much better. It's just a few of my friends who aren't really that committed to the cause but want to come over and eat the discount bakery items I get because they are misshapen or past the expiration date. I try to keep the conversation on topic, but they start to make me feel embarrassed, like I'm being a drag or something, so I start to let them interrupt more and more until we end up watching a movie or listening to some long story about someone's break up.

All this passion isn't for anything, is what I remember as I lay a medium traffic cone shirt over a large traffic cone shirt. It won't get me anything but late nights at the library and respect from Guy. Worse, it almost seems to get me closer to LeBlanc.

When Dad first started working for him, I'd never even met LeBlanc. I didn't know his name. The compound and what it stood for was just a nebulous evil that my rage dripped into like rain on a pond. Now LeBlanc is someone who knows my birthday—he sends me cards—and my interests and my moods. LeBlanc is the worst of it. Because I can't be who I need to be around him. When I face him, I try as hard as I can to be just as angry and indignant as I always feel, but it slips away from me. I toss off a few insults, roll my eyes at him, keep my arms crossed, but I end up slowly deflating until I'm drinking his whiskey, toasting, smiling grudgingly at his stupid jokes. It's like he's just any other person. I know that he is human now and I can't forget it.

Besides all that I am just one girl with a clipboard and a few friends who might write a letter if I beg them. I am nothing. I can change nothing.

When Dad told me about a new municipality that was about to sign up, I called the mayor-president right away. He was a nice guy, sounded a little tired, a little worried, but he genuinely seemed to care about the crappy little town he was put in charge of.

I'm bad at this part.

"You don't have any tact," LeBlanc told me.

I tried to have tact. I asked the mayor about the water situation in town and listened patiently, making the appropriate polite noises as he spoke. When we got to the money was when I lost my tact.

"And you understand how it's going to work, financially?" I asked.

He asked me what I meant.

I explained, even though I knew he knew what I meant, he just didn't want to say it in case I didn't actually know anything.

"He did say there'd be some increases due to the maintenance we need," the mayor conceded.

The rates would go up and up and up until some people couldn't afford them anymore. Until their water got cut off and they were buying bottles at the store and boiling it for their baths, or going to a neighbor's, or putting iodine pills in the river water and hoping for the best. And then, when they decided they couldn't do it anymore, when they came to the mayor-president, now in a slightly less depressing office, now with a full-time secretary who only called in a third of the time, when they threatened to oust him if he didn't take care of the water problem, he would try. But LeBlanc would say his hands were tied. He was doing a good thing for these people. He came in, replaced the municipality's failing water system, and what did they think? That was cheap? It took money to maintain and there was always something new, something broken he didn't know about, a new staffing need, and all of that had to be paid for somehow didn't it?

I don't think I was yelling. Maybe I was breathing a little hard.

The mayor-president thanked me for my time and hung up.

"Everyone just thinks you're crazy," LeBlanc told me. "That's what they always think about people who tell the truth too plainly. The truth sounds crazy."

I fold a turquoise shirt and think about the sound of the mayor-president's voice. He almost sounded like he felt sorry for me. I can't blame him. I feel sorry for me too. I think about myself like I'm not me, but some acquaintance: alone at the library, yelling into a phone, harassing my friends, crying in bed at night, folding t-shirts for a living.

CHAPTER TWENTY-THREE

marigold

He comes to see me in my trailer on Monday morning. I'm standing next to my prayer plant, staring at Shelley's window. The morning light darts into the trailer and illuminates the dust. The leaves on the prayer plant open up, thankful and hungry.

"How are you?" he asks.

He is standing half in the door. I keep looking out the window, listening to the sound of his voice and his breathing, trying to gauge how I should act. His voice sounds polite and slightly ironic, like we are both in on a joke that we don't want to talk about.

"I'm fine," I say.

I turn toward him. The plant is between us, even with my torso. I think I must look nice standing there with the sunlight and the plant. I feel nice at the moment. He looks the same as always: worn in jeans, untucked shirt, dirty boots, uncombed hair. He does not look nice like I do and that makes me feel a positive feeling toward him, like he is a child that needs a little care.

He smiles at me. He has this funny big smile that doesn't match the mood.

"You can come in," I tell him, and he finally puts his other foot inside the door and closes it.

Now he stands in front of the door, rubbing his palms against his thighs.

I wait a few seconds to see if he will say something. He doesn't.

"How can I help you?" I ask.

"I was wondering if there were any accounts I need to sign," he says.

He barely bothers to deliver this in a believable tone.

"I bring them to you when they're ready," I say.

He nods and starts to turn back to the door. I know that he wants to talk to me but can't figure out how to do it.

"Let me check, though," I say. "I might have a couple ready. I sometimes forget over the weekend."

I walk over to my desk, sit down, and start looking through the small pile of papers on my desk. He sits down in the chair in front of the desk, leaning forward with his hands clasped between his knees.

"Nothing quite ready yet," I say, stacking the papers back up and looking at him.

"OK," he says. "OK."

We are silent. The air conditioner cuts off.

"I heard about you," he says finally. He stares down at his hands when he says it, then looks up with that same strange smile. The smile is something you put on your face when you see an old friend or your grandmother.

"I know," I say. I try to hold his eyes, but he darts them back down toward the floor. "Shelley told me. But I could tell anyway at the bar."

He makes a sound in his throat that might be a laugh or a suppressed cough.

"How could you tell?" he asks.

"You just started acting a little differently toward me, watching me more closely, being a little less friendly. That's how people normally act. Unless they've known me for long enough to get over it like Shelley or are just good people like Randy the Prophet."

This time the sound definitely sounds like a laugh, but when he looks up he is not smiling. "I'm not a good person?"

"Not as good as Randy the Prophet," I say.

He nods.

I don't feel the need to make him feel better.

"It did surprise me."

"Well that's good. It means I'm being the right way."

The laugh cough again.

He shifts around in his seat until he is leaning back with his hands in his lap. Our eyes meet, but he looks away again, at my forehead.

"Being the right way is a funny way to put it."

I shrug. "You're right."

"I wonder why no one told me."

"They probably assumed I told you."

"Why didn't you?"

It's my turn to avoid eye contact. I look down at my papers and poke them until they are a little straighter. I suddenly feel very tired and wish that he was gone and that I could lay down under my desk and take a nap. It seems impossible to say all the words I need to say to explain myself. And another thing, something I find hard to admit: I don't know how to explain myself. This human attribute of talking around a thing, of accidentally saying something the wrong way or something you don't mean is one that has frustrated me my whole life.

"Why weren't we designed to read each other's minds?" I asked Mr. Miller. "It would be so much more efficient. There wouldn't be any problems. No wars or divorces. Probably no marriages in the first place."

Still, with Tom, I try to figure out what I am thinking, how to say it, and something else new: what I will say and what I will not. I discover that I don't want to tell him an entire truth. I will give him some parts of truth.

"At first I thought you did know."

That is true.

"You know LeBlanc pretty well. I assumed when he gave you the job he explained about me. Then when we met I really thought you knew, because you kept staring at me in a strange way, which happens sometimes, but you said it was because I looked familiar to you. After a while, I realized that you probably didn't know, because you just didn't treat me that way."

The air conditioner cuts back on and I am thankful for the buzz behind my words that feel like they are otherwise floating around doing nothing. Tom is watching me blankly, still looking at my forehead.

"The main thing that you did that was different from other people is you seemed surprised by my behavior. If I was blunt or rude or waited too long to answer a question, it seemed to bother you. Most other people don't seem to be bothered by me or anything I say, like the way I act doesn't quite count as much, so it's not worth getting worked up over. Once I realized you didn't know, I should have told you. I'm sorry."

He flits his eyes back down to mine and sighs, then the smile comes back, big and nervous. He is jiggling his leg. "I don't think you should apologize to me. It's your choice, I think. To tell someone or not."

"I guess Shelley doesn't think so," I say.

"Are you mad at her?"

"No," this is true. I don't think I can be mad at Shelley. "She thought you knew. It was a mistake. I think she feels bad, even though she is acting like it's a big joke to her."

"That's just how she is."

"Yes."

"So, then you knew I didn't know, and you just didn't want to tell me."

"Pretty much. It was the first time I had a relationship with someone who didn't know. It was interesting."

This was sort of true.

"Interesting?"

"I always wondered how someone would act. I was able to find out. It was nice."

"Nice?"

"I felt like I was doing a good job, because you didn't even seem suspicious. That was nice."

He nods, rubs his hands on his pants a few times, then stands up, walks behind the chair, and leans forward on it.

"I want to ask you something, but you can tell me if it's rude or makes you uncomfortable."

I watch him and wait.

"Why did he do it?"

"Who?"

"LeBlanc."

"Why did he..."

"Why did he make you?"

For some reason, I can't stop looking at the prayer plant. Its pale green leaves, marked with a darker green, welcoming the sunlight.

When I learned about photosynthesis, I asked Mr. Miller: "Why don't humans work that way?"

"What way?"

Why can't they live off sun and water? Why can't they absorb what they need into their skin?

He didn't know.

If I worked that way, I would also not have to talk. I couldn't talk. I could sit in the sun all morning, then fold up and relax all night, and that would be all there was to being.

"I don't know," I tell Tom. It is true, and no one has ever asked me that before.

"What did he tell you?"

"He didn't tell me anything."

"Ever?"

I shake my head. I am still looking at the plant. Something momentarily obscures the sunlight. A cloud or a plane. The room becomes a pleasant gray, then lights up again as the object moves away. I never thought to ask LeBlanc why. I think I knew he wouldn't tell me something like that. I think about all the ways in which Mr. Miller encouraged me to analyze my life and the people and things around me and try to think of a time we ever discussed why someone might exist.

"Never," I say. I look back at him. His expression is hard to read. The big smile is gone, but it isn't replaced by anything, just a blankness.

"Did you ever ask?"

"No."

This answer seems to make him upset. He takes in a sharp breath through his nose, sits down, rubs his hand across his face, then looks back down at the ground, tapping his toes against the carpet.

"Why not?" he asks.

I don't know the answer to this question, but I am curious about something: "Did you ever ask anyone why you exist?"

He thinks about this for a few seconds. The toe tapping stops.

Another sharp inhale, some shifting in his seat. "You mean why my parents wanted to have me? Or if they even did? No, I've never asked them that, but it's not the same, is it? Because they were just doing what people do. They probably don't know the answer themselves. They got married, they had sex, here I am. They didn't have to..." he stands up again and walks over by the prayer plant. In the sunlight he looks like a faded memory. "They didn't have to think about it that hard, is what I'm trying to say. I don't know what LeBlanc had to do... I don't know about all that, but I'm sure it took more work."

"Well," I say. My voice sounds strained. I clear my throat. "I don't really see how knowing the answer would help me. I'm here. It's LeBlanc, so he probably just wanted to do it to do it, you know? He likes to be part of this type of thing, to be special."

"So, you're never going to ask him?" He touches one of the plant's leaves gently.

"No."

He turns to look out the window. "Why not?"

It is interesting to me that he thinks I will do something just because he suggests it. I am trying to figure out if it is a good suggestion. I am trying to figure out if I care why LeBlanc did it. The thing LeBlanc did was make me, which is a strange way to think about it.

"I don't know if I care," I say. "I'll think about it, though."

"You don't know if you care."

He repeats it to the window.

"Why do you care?" I ask.

"Why do I care."

Again, he is talking to the window.

"I don't think I can answer that," he says.

"Because you don't know the answer, or you don't want to tell me?"

"Both. I think."

I ask Shelley what she thinks.

We are out at the dock over the ocean. Our shoes are sitting beside us and our toes are in the water. Down the dock, some people from town are fishing. LeBlanc gives out a certain amount of passes a year. On the day they're given out, there's a line miles long leading out of the compound. Some kids are playing tag down on the scrubby land where the dock ends. Their cackling and screams mix with the calls of the seagulls. A pelican lands on a wooden post in front of us, inflating and deflating its beak.

It is a long summer day, one where it feels like the sun will never go down. We are full of dinner and tired from work, but it is still light outside.

"I asked once," Shelley tells me.

"Asked what?"

"Why you exist."

She kicks the water, and it splashes along the knees of her pants, and on my bare knees beneath my rolled-up dress.

"I asked Mr. Miller. When he told me about you, that we would be roommates and all that."

"What did he say?"

"He said it wasn't any of my business."

I make a little sound at the top of my throat to indicate that I believe it. Mr. Miller didn't end up liking Shelley, even though it was his idea to put us together. He liked me to ask lots of questions, but he thought Shelley asked too many, or the wrong kind.

"Why did you ask him?"

"I was just curious."

"Are you still curious?"

"Of course."

"Why didn't you ever ask me?"

"It seemed like a rude question."

"Did you think I knew?"

"Yeah."

One of the children down in the grass catches another one and they shriek and fall down. Something green floats by my foot. "Got one!" a man shouts, leaning back and reeling in his fishing pole.

I never asked, "Why am I?" on that day Anna Marie greeted me. When I opened my eyes and went from not being to being.

I'm in my room, cross-legged on the bed, skin still salty from our visit to the dock. I close my eyes and try to get back into my new brain. My new brain, now my old brain, was something different from what I have wobbling in my head today. The main thing I feel about my old new brain is that it wanted to exist. The minute it became an entity that knew it existed, it wanted to keep on doing that, to keep on seeing, thinking, hearing, smelling, and learning.

Why would a brain want to not be? Being is what it is there for. Asking why you exist is allowing for non-existence, making non-existence an option. So, my brain just kept going and going, getting my mouth to ask questions and my ears to listen, but never that question.

Of course there is a reason. I know that. I have to know that. But did I ever think about it? Did I ever look at LeBlanc and wonder why this man brought me here? This man who seemed to have little or no interest in me.

For the first few years of my life, LeBlanc would barely look at me or talk to me. When I reached my teens things thawed between us, but I never understood exactly what changed. I decided it was because I was better.

The first time I realized I was better, I was in English class. When I raised my hand to answer a question, Laura Leigh reached up and pinched the skin on my neck. Normally, this would happen over and over again, and I would think about it and remind myself to be angry, then I would turn around and try to frown and ask Laura Leigh to stop. But this time, I actually was angry. When she pinched me, I turned around, glared at her, and said "Don't touch me again." The class fell silent. The girls who had been entertained at Laura Leigh's antics had strange, frozen smiles, with scared eyes. The girls that hated Laura Leigh had a different type of vindictive smile. Shelley, who sat across the room from me, gave me a thumbs up. Mr. Miller cleared his throat and continued the lesson.

The next time I saw LeBlanc after the Laura Leigh incident, he didn't turn on the radio the minute I got in the car like he usually did. Maybe it was because when I got to the car I sighed and said, "I really wish Shelley could come with us," or because I rolled my eyes at him when he asked if I was excited about the visit. I actually did roll my eyes on purpose, not because I was better, but because I liked it when the others did it and wanted to see how it felt. Rolling my eyes felt just as good as it looked when the others did it: like you could express everything you were feeling and get away with it.

On that drive, LeBlanc talked to me, like Mr. Miller said he would years ago. He asked me questions. I told him about classes, about the people on my hall, about Shelley and Laura Ellen. I told him which teachers the others liked and which they didn't. I liked all the teachers about the same, although I could recognize that some knew more than others. Strangely, the ones that knew less were often the favorite, probably because they allowed the class to get off track, encouraged it even, I can only assume to cover up their lack of knowledge. As the car ride continued, an ease grew between us. I could see his shoulders relax. He started driving with one hand on the wheel, gesturing with the other. He told me about the plant that was almost done and about the dinners the chef would prepare for me during my visit.

The dinners were the thing that changed the most. LeBlanc started eating with me. He didn't show up every night, but at least once or twice a week we would have dinner together. The staff were very nervous whenever he arrived, clattering dishes and waiting anxiously behind him for any request, but he was always casual, usually in jeans and a t-shirt, leaning back in his chair and exclaiming over how good the food was.

So then I was better, I thought, and LeBlanc liked me. Maybe he didn't like me, exactly, but he was interested in me to some extent. Maybe that was when I should have wondered, or asked: "Why am I here?"

Back at the docks I had asked Shelley: "Should I ask him?"

She stared down at the water, making zig zag patterns with her bare toes. "I don't think he'll tell you."

She was right. If he wanted to tell me he would have by now. What LeBlanc wanted you to know, you knew.

I open my eyes and slink down on the bed, then roll over to pick up the phone. I call Anna Marie.

CHAPTER TWENTY-FOUR

tom

I start to think that Randy the Prophet's prediction was right. Not a prediction, he would say. A vision, but he might say not that either. Whatever it was that he felt or saw and told me about. Something about being tainted by muck.

I lie on the couch with Yoo-hoo sweating in my palm and watch courtroom television. It might be 7:00 p.m. or maybe 10:00 p.m. or maybe it's already 2:00 a.m. It's Saturday—unless it's 2:00 a.m., in which case it's Sunday—and I've been on the couch for hours, getting up every once in a while to get a snack or a drink. I'm wearing the same t-shirt I slept in, sour with my night sweat, and a pair of loose plaid pajamas.

The judge on TV lectures the defendant: "You will address the court with respect."

The audience boos. I think they are booing the defendant, but they could just as well be booing the judge for her command of respect.

The muck. I can see it, I think.

I just want someone to acknowledge that he is a bad man. LeBlanc. They all know it, I'm pretty sure. How could you work for him, live with him, do whatever it is Marigold did with him, and not see it? I think what I want more is to go back to my five-year-old self and make him admit it. I'd get down on my knees in front of myself, look at my little sticky, pink-cheeked, innocent face and say, "That man is bad." Because that's somehow what bothers me most, the adoration I had for him before I knew better.

And what do I know better, anyway? That's the thing about LeBlanc. I don't know anything. It's less knowledge and more of a hunch. I got the hunch when I was a teenager. Sure, all teenagers have hunches that authority figures are bad, but that hunch balled up in my stomach and grew and grew and beat against my insides every time something happened with LeBlanc that wasn't quite right, but wasn't quite wrong enough.

I finish off the Yoo-hoo and put it on the floor beside some other empty bottles and food wrappers.

The muck is holding me down. I can't get off the couch or talk to anyone. My phone rings on and off all morning. I sit here and watch TV. The muck makes it hard for me to see, hard for me to hear. I can't follow the courtroom drama. I can't even tell what the commercials are trying to sell me. Someone knocks on the door and the muck makes it impossible to answer. I lie there and listen to the knocking.

"It's me," a voice calls, finally.

It's Marigold.

"It's Marigold."

The muck doesn't leave, but some of it slides off enough that I sit up and call: "Coming."

When I answer the door, I wish I had at least changed my shirt.

She is clutching a folder.

CHAPTER TWENTY-FIVE

marigold

When the package from Anna Marie arrives, I hide it from Shelley. I don't know why. In the days that pass while I am waiting for the package, I do not plan to hide it. I do not think about showing it to Shelley or not showing it to Shelley, but I do choose not to tell her about the phone call I made or about the package that is arriving. She doesn't mention our conversation on the dock. That is how things go with us sometimes. I do not want to acknowledge to myself that I am hiding anything from her, but every day since my phone call with Anna Marie, when the post office opens, I am waiting outside the door to get our mail, just in case she tries to go before me, even though both of us rarely check the mail and always end up carrying back a load of unwanted catalogs and coupons.

Since I have checked the mail every day all week, the box is nearly empty, the silver walls shining at me, save the stiff yellow envelope leaning to one side. I slide it out and look around. Only a few other people are getting mail at that time, and no one is interested in what I am doing anyway. I put the envelope under my shirt, which is when I realize I am keeping a secret. It is Saturday, steamy and unpleasant outside, even in the morning. The envelope scratches against my skin and I feel a square wet spot form under it as I begin to sweat. When I get back home, I walk swiftly through the house, hoping the sound of me leaving or returning hasn't woken Shelley. In my room, I close the door, pull the moist envelope out from under my shirt, and throw it on the bed, then stand there looking at it. I wait a few seconds and listen to the house to make sure Shelley isn't stirring. The doors here don't have locks. The dorms at school didn't have locks and neither did my room at LeBlanc's. I've never been able to lock a door.

The envelope is nothing special. It is that boring orange-yellow color of all workplace envelopes: a rectangle slightly bigger than a piece of paper. It looks full, but not bursting with contents. The corners are bent, and my name and address are written in Anna Marie's small, tidy handwriting in the center.

The envelope is two things. Right now, it is a not-special, ugly, bent, sweaty thing sitting on my bed. Once I open it, it will be something else. Once I open it, it will still be ugly, bent, and sweaty, but it will be the envelope that carried information to me, information that I will learn once and know forever. Knowing only works one way. Knowing undoes not knowing, but you can't not know to undo knowing.

I lie on the bed on my stomach and open the envelope. It has that gold, metal grommet that goes into a matching gold, metal hole, but it wasn't used to seal the envelope. Rather, it is taped shut with several layers of packing tape, the grommet lying flat beneath. Inside the envelope, there is another office supply: a manila folder. It is bright and clean with nothing written on the tab, not a folder that was plucked from its alphabetical place in a filing cabinet. Inside the folder there is a group of papers held together at the top with a blue binder clip.

On top is a photocopy of a page from some sort of textbook. It has an anatomical drawing of a person with each part labeled. There are more pages like this, with drawings, graphs, charts, and dense text explaining best practices, past failures, and important research to reference. Some of this I actually already knew about, because Mr. Miller and the science teacher thought it important for me to understand myself and did a little summer session with me when I was fourteen after LeBlanc got busy and sent me back to school like he always did.

I flip through the papers. There are resumes and background checks for people who worked in the lab. Their special skills related to the project were highlighted on the resumes. Since these were photocopies, the highlighted parts were harder to read than the rest: gray with the letters beneath fading. Anna Marie's highlighted section was a part of her previous work history: hairdresser.

There are letters from Mr. Miller to LeBlanc. I always assumed such things were written. Their contents aren't particularly interesting or revelatory, they say the types of things Mr. Miller would write in a letter to LeBlanc. How I am progressing so well. A list of books he was having me read. How this endeavor really made him question life, its meaning, its makeup. If LeBlanc ever wrote him back, those letters aren't here.

There are my school photos, always in front of the same strange, marbled background. I normally wore a white dress on those days: some years eyelet, some years lace. The dresses appeared outside my door the morning the photographer arrived. I look OK in the later pictures, not altogether convincingly normal, but I have a sort of half-smile that some might find friendly. In the early ones I looked inanimate. My eyes are wide open, my mouth a straight line. I remember staring into the camera, where the photographer pointed, and waiting for the interaction to be over. "Smile, please," the photographer pleaded, but when I did the smile was big and fake and didn't match the rest of my face. "OK. Maybe don't," he said.

The first of these photos, from my first year at the school, is stapled to a letter from Mr. Miller. "I realize this isn't an ideal photo," I see as I skim the letter. I trace my finger along the brow of my younger self, feeling a fluttering pity.

The last thing in the folder is a folded letter. I unfold it and a photograph falls out. It is not a copy of a photograph, but an actual glossy, color photograph. I don't recognize it. I look at my face there, shiny and smiling in front of me, and try to remember it being taken. It doesn't have the signature blue marble background of Evangeline school photos. In fact, it doesn't appear to be a school photo, but a candid taken out somewhere—some sort of green expanse barely visible behind my head. My head is the main focus of the photo, which only shows me from the shoulders up. I am turned toward the camera with a big smile on my face, my hair in my normal braid, but it's a bit looser than I usually let it get, with hairs flying around the ends and around my temples. I try to identify the small amount of green background I can make out. I search my mind for any time I visited somewhere lush and green. It would have been some time recently; the photo looks new. It looks like me now, not the way I looked in school. That isn't completely right either, because something about my face is different than how it looks when I see myself in the mirror.

I set the picture aside and turn to the letter. I stop when I get to LeBlanc's handwriting. The words are in front of my eyes, but I cannot read them. All the blood in my body seems to rush to my head and beat hard against my eyeballs. I recognize his handwriting from notes he left around the house during my cold summers there:

Someone fix the back door.
No fish for dinner.
Marigold to stay inside.

I close my eyes and press the flats of my palms hard against my eyelids. When I open them, everything is dark until my circle of vision slowly expands back to a blurred normal, then clears.

Dear _______________,

I've included a photograph. Is that all you'll need? I want to visit and be part of the process from the beginning, but I can't get there for at least a month and I want to make sure this thing is being handled as quickly as possible. My M was about 25 in this photograph. I know this thing doesn't work as an eternity elixir or anything, and I don't mean for it to. I understand she'll look young first and old later, but this is a good benchmark.

Will all of her parts work? I don't ask to be vulgar, I just want to know how close to something "normal" or "real" she's going to have. And what about her personality? Do I do a profile on M and you input that somewhere? Do they have to be taught personality?

I apologize if some of my questions seem stupid, but I am a curious person and want to make sure I understand all my undertakings big or small. This one is rather big, of course.

We can discuss it all further when I arrive. I'll send a note later on to give you a date and time. I just want you to have something to work with and to let you know my primary concerns.

Best,

L

I read the letter over and over again. I think I understand what it means, but I don't know if it means what I think it means, what it could mean for me. I pick up the photograph again and turn it over. Written on the back, in LeBlanc's handwriting is: *M LeBlanc, Beach Trip 20xx.*

CHAPTER TWENTY-SIX

tom

The muck is back.

Marigold sits on my bed. She is wearing a long, white nightgown like a woman in an old novel who carries a candle and lives in a creaky house. It has a high neck and long sleeves that tie at the ends with delicate bows.

"I couldn't sleep," is what she said when I answered the door.

Her braid is loose, only the bottom half of her hair participating.

I am holding the photograph.

"I've seen her before," I say.

"She looks like me."

"No. I mean, yes, she does, but that's not it. I've seen her."

I rub my finger across the woman's face and try to force myself to remember. All I have are those frustrating, swimming memories that swish by so fast all I'm left with is a color, an impression, a feeling, a smell.

"Where do you think she is?" Marigold asks.

Dead, I think. Certainly she is dead. I don't want to say this. I shake my head.

"Who do you think she is?" she asks.

"There are a few choices," I say. "Wife, daughter, sister, cousin."

"They don't look much alike."

"No."

"I've never thought I looked anything like him, no one ever assumed I was his daughter."

"No."

"He's married, then? Divorced?"

I shrug. Still the memory swims past. "I wish I could remember where I've seen her."

Behind the houses on my side of the street, a slow-moving sliver of bayou shoots off from the main bayou below. We stand there in the dark, the strange night sounds shimmering around us, the vague wetness apparent in the scent of the air. I set a small oil lamp on the ground. She has the folder tucked under one arm, a box of matches in her hand. The grass is damp from a storm two days ago, but we decide to sit. We are cross-legged, facing each other, with a gap between. Into the gap she places the folder, then lights a match and drops it on top, casually, like playing a card in a game she already lost.

The burning is painfully slow, not the quick and satisfying burst of flames I expected. The match starts a small circle of flame in the center of the folder, and then the flames begin to walk out from there. We sit and watch. Marigold holds the photograph tight in her hand. She is lit vaguely by my lamp, speckled by the fire. I try to read her facial expression. She stares at the burning folder, the flames inverted triangles dancing in her eyeballs. When the folder is burned, I point to the hand that holds the photograph. She shakes her head. I pick up a cup I brought for such a purpose, dip it into the water, then throw it over the remaining fire. We kick at the ashes until they are well mixed with the grass and mud.

"What are you going to do?" I ask her.

She doesn't answer.

We stand up and walk back toward my house. In the swinging light from my lamp I see that the bottom half of her nightgown is streaked with mud and grass. Something about this imperfection draws me to her, and I place my hand softly on her back as we walk. She doesn't shake me off or accept it, just continues moving in the same way.

When we get to the bottom of my steps, I ask her: "Can you sleep now?"

She shakes her head. "No. I want to walk."

"Do you want me to come with you?"

"No."

It is the way she says things, with no apologies or explanations. She turns and walks down the driveway and out to the road. I watch her, and in that moment she looks so different from me, so much smaller, less solid, less authoritative, a white smudge in the night with a grass-stained dress.

CHAPTER TWENTY-SEVEN

She was in fourth grade when she figured out exactly who she was going to be when she grew up. The school librarian, who didn't seem to have any interest in books, recommended that she read the bridal magazines. Later, she was appalled that an elementary school library subscribed to such a thing, but at the time she liked looking at the dresses, liked that it seemed to give the librarian some sort of satisfaction to see that she was right, that the young girls at the school did want to read this type of magazine.

She liked the pictures of the couples posing together in their nice clothes. They would hold hands against a barn door, walk through a field of corn, stand on the beach. In all of these wilder places, they were wearing suits or tuxedos and pristine dresses, and their faces and hair looked beautiful and they looked like the happiest people on the planet.

She used her lunch money to make copies of her favorite photographs. They were something to treasure, to rub like a rabbit's foot when her parents disappeared, when her sister came home drunk and cried in the living room, when she was home alone, and no one told her where they'd gone. She stared at the wrinkled, black and white photographs of attractive people who loved each other so much that they would wear their fancy clothes to a barn just for a good picture. The picture thumped at something inside of her, made her feel pain and happiness all at once. She felt supremely alone, unable to imagine anyone who would hold hands with her beside a barn, and almost elated at the prospect that this was something that happened when one grew up, that one day the man and the barn would be there, and she would be calm and happy.

In high school there were barn prospects. She became beautiful. She was good at school. Another librarian channeled her romantic interest in bridal magazines into an appreciation for Jane Austen, then the darker George Eliot, the more existential Virginia

Woolf. She mostly read for fun, didn't do any team sports or cheerleading, but this also wasn't held against her, but turned her into some sort of mythical being at the school, mysterious and unknowable.

There were friends, but nothing like she saw in movies or read in books. The level of intimacy required for true friendship was cut off somewhere between her brain and her mouth. She would listen to the other girls speak freely about how they were feeling, about who they liked and didn't like, about what they hated about their parents, about their fears. They thought she was a good listener. They liked to corner her and tell her everything. She would nod, wide-eyed, and offer sympathetic comments. Meanwhile she would scan her brain for things she could share in moments of silence, pieces of herself she could dole out to bring her closer to others, but it all sounded wrong in her head. There was no way to say, "I don't know were my parents are and the lights got shut off," even if Patty had just said something similar. When the other girls said these things, they seemed natural. If she said them they would feel like an announcement, an interruption to the normal flow of conversation.

So she let others give themselves to her and gave them nothing back. They didn't usually notice until knowing things about her became pertinent to another issue. On her birthday she received strange presents: brightly patterned socks, books meant for old ladies to read on the beach, gift cards for frozen yogurt. People would come up to her in the hallway and tell her they just saw this movie or heard this band that they knew she would love, and when she would look into them, it was always something strange, off-putting, sometimes creepy, often poorly made. There was some cohesive version of herself that she was putting out into the world, but she didn't know what it was or where it came from.

When she started having boyfriends, her teachers became concerned. They tried to hold parent-teacher conferences, but her parents wouldn't come. They met with her. They met with the boy. "You could be valedictorian," they told her, "but you don't turn your work in anymore." She shrugged and smiled. "I'll do better," she said. But she didn't. There was nothing special about any of these boys. In her dreams, they morphed into one another and sometimes she accidentally called them by the wrong name. Yet she felt a lightness in her chest each morning, knowing she'd walk into school and someone would be there who would want to hold her hand and give her compliments.

She wasn't valedictorian, but she was an honor graduate and she got into a decent college with a small scholarship and work study job. The ability to pretend like she came from a different place than she did, like her parents loved her, lightened her up, made her more beautiful. She kept her side of her dorm room pristine, even though her roommate, who seemed to hate her immediately, left food containers scattered on her bed and clothes all the way up to the centerline of the room. She made friends quickly: in classes, in the dining hall, walking across campus. People liked to turn to her and make comments, she seemed to come across people when they were having a particularly bad day and wanted to unload on someone. Boys particularly liked to whisper in her ear during class, something sarcastic about the teacher or another student's stupid answer. Usually she would smile politely at these comments and this would be the beginning of a dating ritual. They'd wait for her after class, walk with her to the dining hall, and for a few weeks they'd be inseparable until one of them got tired of the whole thing.

For her work study job, she had to come into the lab at night and take out fly specimens from a freezer, look at them under a microscope and make notes. She didn't understand what her notes meant but was given clear instructions on the words to write when she saw certain things happening. Even though she didn't feel connected to the work, she liked the way it felt to come in the evenings, finishing a to-go coffee from the dining hall, putting on her white coat and working alone in the lab, scribbling and peering into a microscope.

The flies became a variation on the wedding barn photos. When she entered the lab at night her heart went up into her throat. As she walked around carefully following procedures, she felt like she had flashed forward into a future self, a self with a job, an independent self who spent time alone. This version lived in a tidy apartment, bought overpriced fresh produce, and drank wine by herself on the apartment's balcony. She spent her evenings alone watching old movies or reading books and had a fluffy cat curled up on her lap. She had friends and she dated and went out for drinks with co-workers, but at the end of the day she went to her own, clean space, and stayed there alone and felt happy.

The first time she saw LeBlanc was in the lobby of the lab building. He was exiting with her professor and some other department heads. She noticed him because he was wearing a seersucker suit while everyone else was in wrinkled button downs and stained khakis. The other men with him all acknowledged her. She was well-liked in the department. The man in the seersucker suit stared at her until she met his eyes, then he gave her a kind smile, nodded, and the group continued out the door.

The lobby ritual continued for a few days, until one day the group of men from the university got chased down by an administrative assistant. As they gathered around her, listening to the biological emergency, LeBlanc separated himself and approached her as she waited for the elevator.

"What do you do up here at night?" he asked.

"I look at flies," she said.

He chuckled. "Doesn't seem like an appropriate night time activity for a college student."

She shrugged. "I'm not much of a partier."

"Well, that's good," he said. "I was going to see if you wanted to come meet us all for drinks after you finished looking at flies, and it definitely is not a party."

She hesitated.

"They all speak very highly of you. Their most diligent lab tech, they say. I'm sure they'd think it was wonderful to see you outside of work. I'll give them a heads up."

He told her the name of the bar and she said something noncommittal. She pushed the elevator door button and when it opened she got in without saying goodbye.

"See you soon," he called.

She didn't go. At least, she didn't go in. She walked downtown when she was done in the lab and looked in the window of the bar. The men were all there, tipping back reasonable-sized beers at a high top, nodding and smiling gently. LeBlanc began turning toward the window at one point and she walked off quickly, unsure if he saw her.

The night meetings, whatever their purpose, seemed to end after that evening. The lobby was empty when she went up to the lab for the next few weeks. Then one night he was there alone. He sat on one of the hard, vinyl chairs, never sat in long enough to become worn, reading a newspaper. When she entered the lobby, he folded the paper down methodically and stayed seated, like he knew she would come over and talk to him. She did. He wasn't wearing a seersucker suit this time, but a pair of faded jeans and a black fishing shirt.

She walked up to the chair and stood in front of him, not saying anything.

"How are the flies?" he asked.

"I wouldn't know," she said. "I just write down what I see, I have no clue what any of it means."

"You really are a good worker, then," he said.

She crossed her arms and waited.

She thought this man might be handsome. He was probably ten years older than her. His hair was cut short and tidy, his clothes, although unfashionable, were clean and pressed. He had bright, lively eyes, and bushy eyebrows that he rubbed absentmindedly while he talked.

Mixed with a knowledge of his attractiveness was a fear that pressed against her rib cage, radiated down into her femur. She felt like he could reach inside her and pull something out. He was the kind of man who sounded right no matter what he was saying. The kind of man who knew about things, lots of things, and even if he didn't, he could pretend. She knew if she brought him up to the flies he could tell her all kinds of things about the flies and the lab equipment that she didn't know. Maybe none of it would be true, but she wouldn't be able to tell.

It was safe to be alone in a lobby at night with a man like this. This was not a man who would do something bad to you at night in a lobby. This was the type of man who could do many bad things to you over time without your knowledge. In the end, she would thank him for the bad things, thinking them good.

"Summer's coming up," he said.

She nodded.

"I heard the lab closes."

She nodded again.

"I'm always looking for interns. I pay well, too. Room and board included."

She tried to adjust her posture. To seem more relaxed, friendly, and grateful. This was not what she had expected. Not a job offer. Instead she thought it would be an invitation to something unclearly sordid, a party or a weekend away. As the summer approached, a dread crept over her at the prospect of returning home, of the heat, boredom, and loneliness.

To work somewhere, to keep the fantasy life created by the lab alive, that would be almost as good as people who went on vacations in the summer, almost as nice as coming home to a banner and a surprise party instead of two people who forgot you were coming home, possible forgot you'd been gone in the first place. Then there was this other part, this itch scratched by the handsome man who knew so much, who looked at her a certain way.

"I'll need to talk to my boyfriend," she said. She wasn't sure why. She didn't need to talk to him, she would tell him about it, he would nod, and by the time the summer came around he wouldn't be her boyfriend anymore anyway. Saying the words made her feel safe, but she wasn't sure from what.

Then she remembered something else. "Wait, what do you do?"

CHAPTER TWENTY-EIGHT

marigold

Who is M?

I close my eyes so hard that light dances around in the blackness and when I open them I can't see anything and have to stand very still until my vision clears. It feels like there is something there, deep inside my head, that holds the answer, like a very small, delicate cup that I need to tip over. If I tip it over, whatever is inside will spill into my brain and I can relax with knowing.

I call Anna Marie. She doesn't answer.

I call the main number at the lab. It is a Sunday. No one answers.

I run a bath and drop my mud-stained nightgown on the floor. It lies next to the pink bath mat like a deflated version of me. I sit on the bathtub floor as the water fills. It is almost too hot, but not quite, and I let it prick my skin, break me into a sweat, pour and pour until it reaches my neck. It gets so high that it starts to drain out of the safety valve, but I let it run until the water turns cold, a sliver of chill touching my toes. I reach up, turn it off, then lower myself completely under the water. The world is both silenced and amplified, my open eyes seeing the lights around me wave and disperse, my ears hearing the sounds of life muffled and transmuted. Beneath the water, if looked at from above, was I transformed, too? A wavy version of myself, blurred and changing, or a version of her, the smiling M? The photograph lies on the side of the tub. I sit up and look at it again, water dripping from my nose and sliding along the slick paper.

Looking at the photograph reminds me of the time Shelley convinced me to put a battery against my tongue. The sensation was scary, tingling, uncomfortable, but I kept raising the battery back to my tongue again and again. Something inside me turns sharp against me when I look at her face, and I keep looking at her, rubbing myself gently against the sharpness. That is not me. I try to make it me, studying the smile intently, then replicating it on my own face. I stand and look in the mirror, slightly fogged, across from the bathtub. I don't look like myself, but I don't look like her either, my lips frozen in an upward curve, my teeth bared. It's my eyes.

I change into my black pants and one of Shelley's big t-shirts, this one advertising a theme park—the peaks of a rollercoaster faded and peeling over my chest—and pull my hair into a ponytail that sits high on top of my head. It is 9:30 a.m. Shelley is still asleep. I go for a walk.

Sundays on the compound are my favorite days. People hiding in their homes watching TV under the blast of air-conditioning, sleeping past lunch, or sitting on a neighbor's porch lazily chatting and drinking. This early, most people are still asleep. I listen to the sound of my feet against the dewy grass, the gravel kicked up, the birds in the trees.

Once when she walked with me, Shelley commented: "There are a lot of birds out today."

"There are always birds," I had to explain, "Once you know they're there, you can't stop hearing them."

I like the sound of them talking to each other as if I'm not here.

I walk down the main road to the mess hall, slipping around back before any of the few lined up for Sunday breakfast see me. Through the scrub behind the dumpster, I take a branching path that goes to the undeveloped parts of the compound. It is mostly grown over and unmarked, except for the faintest hint of light soil beneath the weeds that shows where people once regularly tread. I walk beneath the overhanging pecan trees, crunching on aborted shells, the weeds scratching against my ankles and gnats buzzing around my head. I remember to hold my hands above my head like Shelley showed me. The gnats swarm to my hands and I keep them raised as I walk, feeling like one of the worshippers at Ms. Odette's church.

The compound used to be a park. The path leads to an old ranger's cabin that sits along a murky outlet from the bayou. I walk up the warped stairs and open the front door. Inside, it looks like the ranger was yanked from her home with no warning. The cot in the corner is covered with rumpled bedding. The remote sits on the arm of the couch. There is a thick layer of dust over all the surfaces, and the moldy smell of past flooding leaks out with each step on the brown carpet. I circle the room a few times, not touching any of the artifacts of the ranger's life, just observing: a glass in the drying rack, a pen dangling from a string on the refrigerator.

I walk out the back door to the picnic table sitting along the water, one of the attached benches broken off and sagging into the waterlogged ground. I sit on the other bench and look out at the water, covered in algae bloom and buzzing with gnats and mosquitoes.

A park ranger might come out here in the morning with her coffee. Might walk around the water a little bit and go back inside, make up her cot, get ready, and start her day. There wouldn't be a plant at the edges of her vision, no beeping of trucks backing up. If she walked to the end of her road, she'd find more roads like it, leading to campsites and boat launches, picnic pavilions and bathrooms with mildewed showers and bugs swarming over the toilets.

Mr. Miller took me to a park like this once during fall break when LeBlanc was traveling and couldn't pick me up.

We left after the last class ended before break, driving in a direction I'd never been. It got dark and the roads grew narrower. We drove past houses standing crouched and lonely against the woods, no windows lit. We crossed the levy against the curve of the river and saw in the gully on the other side a lot with scattered, broken trailers and RVs, a family of dogs greeting us at the side of the road to bark and run next to the wheels.

When we turned into the park, a tired-looking woman slid open the window on the welcome booth, asked for the name, and handed us a map with our spot highlighted. Mr. Miller didn't understand the map and circled around the unlit campground roads until I spotted our site number.

I held a lantern and he had a light strapped to his head and set up the tents while I sat at the picnic table. He boiled some water over a tiny stove that folded out and poured it into aluminum foil bags that had some sort of dried food in them. After ten minutes we ate what was in the bags, some seasoned rice, still a little crunchy and very salty, and he walked me over to the bathrooms to brush my teeth and wash my face. There was only one other site in use, a white RV humming in the night, strung with Christmas lights.

I had my own tent with a sleeping pad and bag. I'd brought one of the pillows off my bed which looked strange and frilly with its eyelet cover next to the slick and shiny sleeping bag and the swishy tent insides. I wasn't sure when I slept or if I slept. I shifted awkwardly on the pad and stared up at the shadows of the branches leaning back and forth overhead in the wind. In the morning we ate eggs out of aluminum pouches that tasted like chalky cheese and Mr. Miller packed our backpacks with nuts and string cheese and granola bars and a big bag full of water and we set off on a hike. The trail took us around the swamp on cool dirt paths and sometimes over on narrow wooden bridges. We stopped after an hour and sat on one of the bridges and ate some snacks. I watched turtles sunning themselves on a log and a nutria on the banks, chewing on the root of something.

That night we cooked hotdogs on a stained grill over the firepit and then sat around the fire and watched it burn out. Mr. Miller told me a story about a tall woman all in black who waited in corners while children slept.

"Why would she do that?" I asked.

"It's supposed to be a scary story," he said.

"Why?"

"I guess it's scary for someone to be around you when you don't know it."

"Why did you tell me?"

"People like to tell scary stories around campfires."

"People don't like being afraid."

"But sometimes they do."

In my tent that night, I tried to believe the tree branches were the arms of the tall woman, leaning over my tent, watching me.

We drove back in the daylight and the roads and houses seemed normal, spread out, but not so desolate and lonely. He pulled off to the side before we crossed the levy and we climbed up the bank in the tall grass and stood on top and looked down at the water, brown and sloshing against the trees that lined the banks.

"Why doesn't everyone camp?" I asked.

"Some people don't like the inconvenience: lying on the ground, getting dirty, only being able to eat certain things."

"But why isn't camping just the way we live? If you didn't have to have so many things you could just camp and not work and walk out in the woods any day."

"For some people that wouldn't be a very full life."

"What's life supposed to be full of?" I wondered.

I call LeBlanc after lunch. I know this is when he will be happy and lazy, sitting in his office, reading. The phone rings for a long time, and I worry that he won't answer. Sometimes he naps at that time, or tells no one to disturb him, or pretends not to hear the phone. Even though it rings and rings and seems like it will never stop, I do not hang up. The ringing goes on so long that when he does answer, an annoyed, gruff hello, it takes me a moment to remember what I am doing.

"Who is M?" I ask, not bothering with greetings.

He hangs up.

I am sitting on my bed, staring out the window. The sun is sickly today, trickling out behind the clouds, the ground and sky an interchangeable gray.

The phone rings.

"I'm sorry," he says.

His voice doesn't sound sorry. It sounds a way I've never heard. Disturbed, I think.

"You just surprised me," he says.

I wait.

"Let's... can you wait a day or two? I'll come visit. We should talk in person."

CHAPTER TWENTY-NINE

tom

I was working for a man that owned the land. He wanted to make sure no one was fishing or hunting on his property, so I watched it. In exchange, I was the one person allowed to fish there. I kept waiting for the man to show up and fish or hunt as well, but he only sometimes drove his truck by, walked around a bit, then drove back home.

I'd gotten out of my mom's house a couple years earlier. Now I spent my days fishing and walking; my nights reading. The trailer was nothing comforting. One side was rotting, falling into the muck in the ground, and I kept it cordoned off from the rest with a heavy tarp taped over the doorway. I had a kitchen, but no running water or electricity. At night I brought in water from the lake and boiled it over a camp stove. I used some of it to brush my teeth and poured the rest in a pitcher that I kept in a cabinet to drink. I bathed in the mornings, jumping in the chilly water, a bar of soap bobbing alongside me. When my clothes got dirty, I jumped in with them on. There was no bathroom, just an outhouse tucked into the woods a five-minute walk away. Mostly, I stood on the back stoop and pissed into the yard. The one functioning bedroom held a blow-up mattress with old comic book hero sheets, my clothes piled on the floor, and stacks of books. At night, I used my lantern to read until I couldn't keep my eyes open. I was never sure what time it was.

When LeBlanc showed up, I was sitting on the back stoop eating Chef Boyardee out of the can.

"This is absolutely shameful," was the first thing he said.

He had walked through the trailer to find me, and was standing in the doorway, looking back and forth between me and the interior.

"You live like this?"

I shrugged and kept eating.

It had been years since we'd seen each other. Since before I moved out of my mom's. The last visit didn't go well. I told him to leave me alone, that I didn't need his charity, that my mom didn't either, that he owed us so much more than what we got, so much more than a worn-down life with no father. I didn't think anything I said actually got through to him, but he did leave me alone after that. Now, as he stood watching me eat cold ravioli, I pictured him spending the intervening time plotting exactly how to manipulate me during our next meeting.

"You're a smart kid," he said.

I debated saying something typical and angsty like: "I'm not a kid." Instead, I just kept eating and staring out into the woods.

"Your father would be so disappointed."

This was an obvious, cliché thing to say.

"Why?" I asked. I still didn't look at him. "I'm happy. He wanted me to be happy."

"You're happy," he repeated. He didn't exactly ask it like a question, but his voice went up a little at the end.

"Yeah," I said. There was a little bit of tomato juice in the bottom of the can. I shook it out into the yard and stood up to face him, spoon clenched in my hand.

"How's your mom?" he asked.

I shrugged. He was standing above me, because I was down the steps from him. I wished I could change this, but I didn't want to seem threatened. I looked up at him and kept eye contact.

"You're shrugging because you don't know. You don't call her, visit her, nothing."

I rolled my eyes and kept my mouth straight. The words balled up something in my stomach, a latent guilt. "I saw her last month," I said.

"You're ten minutes away. You think that's enough?"

I shrugged again. He was right. LeBlanc was often right, which was how he manipulated people so easily. I didn't need him to tell me I needed to visit my mother more. A stranger with the loosest grip on the facts would tell me the same thing. It was his delivery that bothered me, like a tough but fair father figure who was just looking out for my best interest.

"I get busy," I said.

"That can't be true."

It wasn't. I couldn't remember when I was last busy. Maybe at some point in high school when I had two tests on the same day. Somehow, though, when it came to visiting my mother, I was able to become busy very quickly. I thought about her sitting alone in that trailer, the buzzing of the TV, the conspiratorial telephone conversations, the diet yogurts, and I found something that needed to be done. I'd fix a random broken cabinet in the trailer or find a pair of gloves and pull up weeds in the unmowed lawn.

Since my father died, my mother had become a person I didn't know anymore. It was a slow occurrence, so slow that as long as I was in the same home as her, I didn't feel it so sharply: the old her measured up against the new. But once I moved out things changed. The old her was the version I kept in my mind, cradled there in a soft place to pull out with the smell of fresh cookies and laundry detergent. Visiting her, calling her even, muddied up that treasured version, overlaid it with something unpleasant and harsh.

"How long are you going to live like this?" he asked.

"Forever," I said.

I stared at him. I wanted him to believe that I was perfectly happy staying there forever, in the woods with no running water or electricity, my skin becoming a rough hide of scratched mosquito bites and sunburn, my body odor a familiar friend. Because this was what I thought I wanted. Some version of this. The version I dreamed up was a little nicer. The trailer wasn't half rotting and I had a little garden with fresh vegetables around back and a satsuma tree. I had friends in that version too, and we sat out under the stars in my nice lawn chairs, food from the grill laid out on the patio furniture. I didn't imagine clothes stiff from days of dirt and sweat, eating salty canned foods because I couldn't stand one more bite of fish, wanting a hot shower more than anything in the world, but not getting one because I couldn't face my own mother.

"No, no," he said. "You'll come work for me, of course."

But I didn't. I held out and I held out and I held out.

I visited my mom a little more often. Started doing my laundry over there and taking long baths in her tub. All the dirt and grass I drug in with me floated to the top of the water. I sat there and stared at my toes until the water turned cold, then stood up, drained the water, and took a shower. I planted some tomatoes and found a guy who would trade me some venison for the fish. I got a cheap generator that I used sparingly for an occasional night with lights or the relief of a small, portable air-conditioner.

One night I drove into town to visit the sad bar there, attached to a 24-hour diner. It was my birthday. That morning I had breakfast with my mom at the same diner. It was the diner we went to years before so my dad could show me the jukebox. I put on the Wurlitzer song. We both ordered huge breakfasts, because we both liked something sweet and something salty, couldn't have the eggs and bacon without waffles and French toast. She was in a better mood than normal, chatting eagerly about her flower garden and some gossip around the trailer park. She was reading a book I'd recommended and seemed to really like it. She kept thanking me for it and talking about how good it felt to read again.

"I know I haven't been..." she started. She forked up a big piece of pancake and stuck it in her mouth, chewed greedily, then swallowed. "I know I haven't been the best parent."

I hated when she said things like this. The love I felt for her pained me in a way that I couldn't control. It was a mirror of the love she felt for me, but it was harder to give somehow, the other way.

"Mom, I love you. You're great."

"Things weren't..." she stopped, sipped her coffee, started again. "Things weren't always easy for me. Things with your dad. I don't want to speak ill of the dead. I don't want to speak ill of him anyway, I did love him. He's your father and he did a lot of good things for me and there was a time when we were really in love, I think, but he wasn't perfect, you know."

"I know," I said. I said this because nobody is perfect, and that was what I knew. I did not know what she was trying to hint to me, but I didn't want her to tell me. I hoped if I said "I know," she'd think I really did and we'd move on.

She shook her head. "You don't. You can't. You won't."

I decided to just smile and shrug, thinking this would lay things to rest.

"It caught up with him, though," she said. "There's some people... some people you just can't mess with, you know?"

There was no one waiting for me at the bar. I didn't tell anyone it was my birthday, although I'm not sure who I could have told. There was the man I traded for meat, the man that employed me, and my mom. Those were the only people I talked to regularly. There were a few old friends from high school I ran into at the store, painful exchanges where they talked about their kids and spouses and I stayed as vague as possible about my circumstances.

I sat alone at the far corner of the bar. It was a Tuesday night and there were only a few other people there: a man at the other end of the bar, a couple talking animatedly at a low table by the door, and the bartender. I drank cheap domestic beer in cans. I didn't usually drink and started to feel drunk after three. I tried to remember when I'd last been drunk. All of the times I could think of, I was alone in my trailer. A warm feeling grew over me, that nice, friendly feeling of social drunkenness.

"This is a nice place," I said to the bartender, even though it wasn't.

He gave me a look that let me know he thought I was lying, but he seemed bored, so he came over toward me. "What's your business?" he asked.

Because of the alcohol, this was the first time this question didn't make me tense. "Not much of anything," I said.

He nodded, popped the tab on a beer can, and slid it over to me.

"Must be nice," he said.

I wanted to say it back to him, because I thought it must be nice to stand back there and pour drinks and talk to random people. For a moment, I let myself imagine that I befriended this guy, that he got me a job, and that I became a bartender. This was one of my favorite hobbies: pretending I had a different life.

"Today's my birthday," I said.

Only a part of a second passed before he responded, but in that part of a second, I saw a deep pity cross his face. "Happy birthday, man," he said. He smiled at me, then edged down to the other end of the bar to help the other guy.

What I must have looked like to him: a man who does nothing, alone at a bar on his birthday.

That was when I went out in the alley and kicked a wall.

I don't know where the idea came from. I'd never done anything like it before. Even as a child, I wasn't the sort of stereotypical destructive kid. When I got really really mad, I would go in my room and scream into a pillow, or go in the shower and scream, or go out into the woods and scream. I never thought about hitting the pillow or punching the mirror or kicking a tree. But here I was, drunk off four light beers, kicking a brick wall for no clear reason. I wore tennis shoes, and around the seventh or eighth kick I felt my pinkie toe break. I hobbled to my truck and sat behind the wheel, the seat reclined, too drunk to drive. I closed my eyes.

In my dream I was back in my childhood home. My mother was tucking me in and my father leaned in the doorway. I was not a child, though, I was myself, in my man body. My mother pushed my hair back from my forehead and kissed me on both cheeks. My father stayed where he was. He was obscured, in the dark, just a figure. "Dad?" I called to him. I felt an overwhelming need to touch him. I couldn't say it this way, but all I wanted, what my mind yearned for, was just for his index finger, so I could hold onto it for a moment. He took a few steps forward, but it wasn't my dad. It was LeBlanc. He smiled at me, and put his finger forward, but I knew he didn't want me to grab it. He was going to poke me in the chest.

I woke up. It was early morning. The bar was closed, as was everything around it. Mine was the only vehicle in the parking lot. I drove to my mom's house, wincing as I swallowed the stale taste of my breath and cheap beer. I let myself in with the key she kept hidden under the doormat by the back door. It was pitch black and the porch light wasn't on. I fumbled around with the key and the door. Inside, there was the familiar sound of an infomercial. I crept past the living room and into my teenage bedroom, still the same as it was when I moved out. I picked up the novelty phone by my bed—a depressed looking green fish lying flat on a rock—and called LeBlanc.

249

CHAPTER THIRTY

marigold

There is a shift in mood before LeBlanc arrives. People sense something dreadful and act accordingly. It's not that he swoops in and runs around being cruel or critical to everyone. In fact, most people get completely ignored or receive bland compliments. It's more about this seeming blandness, this lack of interest. He doesn't lack interest. But to have the boss you only see a few times a year stop by and yawn and say, "good work," before moving on, deflates you in a way that simple insults can't.

When he pulls up to the compound, there is no fanfare. He always drives himself in his old truck pulling his old camper. This annoys people too. This facade of humility. He wants people to think he is just like them, but still respect him for being nothing like them.

This morning, I wait for him by the gate. Mr. Kenny and I chat about the weather. It is hot. There's not much else to say about it. He tells me a long story about his ex-wife. I love these stories. Some of his stories I've heard over and over again, but he has a nice accent and he always adds something new. I like people who will talk and talk so that I can just sit and listen. It is relaxing. I think this is what Shelley gets out of her old movies and TV shows, but I feel too disconnected from those to enjoy them. It's much more entertaining to hear about how Mr. Kenny, who I know in real life, once bought his ex-wife a sculpted Scottie dog to sit in the front window of their house to act as a guard dog while he was working offshore. Why didn't he buy her a real dog? Well, they actually had a real dog, but it was a tiny chihuahua that slept all day and eagerly greeted all strangers. In the end, the Scottie dog worked out as a guard. When their house got broken into, his wife threw the Scottie dog at the burglar's head while the chihuahua nuzzled against his leg. The Scottie dog didn't do too much damage, but it startled the man, who stepped on the chihuahua, triggering a viciousness never before displayed by the real dog, who proceeded to growl and bite the man around the ankles as he ran out the door.

I'd heard a few versions of this story before, but this was the first time the chihuahua was the victor. The previous versions involved the Scottie dog causing the man to be knocked out and put into a coma, the sharp ear of the statue hitting him right in the stomach and causing damage to his internal organs, or—once—the Scottie being bowled toward him, causing him to trip and break an ankle.

LeBlanc pulls up and Mr. Kenny falls silent. We both wave at him. He rolls down his window and Mr. Kenny gives him a kind of salute.

"Kenny," LeBlanc says.

Kenny smiles at him, jittery.

"Good work."

This is the sort of thing that will hurt Mr. Kenny's feelings. Because he does actually do good work, but LeBlanc hasn't seen any of it yet.

I go around to the passenger side and climb into the truck. Kenny opens the gate for us and LeBlanc drives through the compound, waving lazily to a few people along the road. He likes to park his camper deep in the woods on one of the campsites from when this was a park. We don't talk during the drive.

When he parks, he asks me if I want some coffee. He doesn't look at me. I say yes, and we get out of the truck and walk back to the camper. He stays outside hooking various things up, and I climb in, sitting on the ugly, floral couch while the lights and air-conditioning cut on. He comes in and starts getting the coffee ready; boiling water and finding his disgustingly sweet instant coffee packets in the wood-paneled cabinets. He stays at the stove, waiting for the water to boil, then anxiously stirs the packets into two faded coffee mugs. One says "Florida," with a big orange underneath, the other says "I'm grumpy when I'm sleepy," and has a picture of the two dwarves of that name from the movie *Snow White*. He brings the mugs over, hands me the Florida one, and sits on the couch beside me.

Whether I feel socially awkward is something I think about lately. Lately I find myself hesitating before saying things, even things I know are true, because I'm not sure how they will be received. Now with LeBlanc, my pulse beats violently against my neck and I wish I never called him, that I am not here sitting with him in his camper, but in my trailer doing work.

"Who is she?" I ask, because I am not back at my trailer doing work. I am here.

LeBlanc keeps his hands wrapped tightly around his coffee cup, as if he is cold. He takes a cigarette out of his pocket and lights it, takes a deep inhale, then blows the smoke out of the side of his mouth, away from me.

"She was my wife," he says.

This was my guess, the one I didn't want to say. "You're divorced or she's dead?" I ask.

"She's dead," he says. He smokes and takes some sips from his cup. I drink as well. The coffee tastes sticky in my mouth, like a coffee-flavored syrup. My teeth feel like they are rotting just from the exposure. In my back pocket is the photograph, and I wish I could take it out and look at it.

"Doesn't matter who she was, Mar. She was who she was, and you are who you are. The way you look has nothing to do with anything else."

He throws his sentences at me casually, as if we are talking about a work assignment or a television show. I feel a frustration I can't name, a need for something else from him.

"What do you mean anything else?" I ask.

"Anything inside," he says.

Mr. Miller has not prepared me for this. How to have a conversation about my creation. How to convey to the other person in the conversation that it should matter to him, that some gravity is needed.

"Did you want our insides to match?" I ask.

"Yes."

The yes sits there for a long time. He finishes his cigarette and puts it out in an ash tray on the arm of the couch.

"Couldn't I be trained to be a certain way?" I ask. I'm not sure why. I don't want to be trained to be like LeBlanc's dead wife, but I have a need to discuss logistics.

"That's what I thought we were... I guess not."

"My insides aren't right," I say. It sounds self-pitying or intended to provoke a denial, but I am half saying it in wonder, to myself, to figure out if I think it is true.

"Your insides are fine," he says and then he turns to me and adds "You do good work here. I don't know what I would do without you."

I look in his eyes, back and forth between them. They are a pale blue. They look sad, but also clouded over, defensive. He doesn't want me to see everything that's there.

CHAPTER THIRTY-ONE

tom

I don't know what I am doing out here: my shoes sunken in the mud, my arms covered in mosquitoes, peering through the trees like a kid who just read his first spy novel. LeBlanc's camper hums with the vibrations of the generator and I stand here like an idiot, swatting my arms, and staring at the ugly, stained off-white side of the camper. The camper is called "Adventure Haul." I always love the names of campers and RVs, whimsical hyperbolic titles that make it seem like the driver is about to go on the adventure of a lifetime, when in reality he's probably just parking it in his ex-wife's backyard. How much does he feel like he's hauling himself on an adventure when he's squeezed into the standing-room-only bathroom, the vague mildew from the shower mixing with the smell of his pee?

I found out LeBlanc was coming today from the rumor mill first, but then from LeBlanc himself, who called me up yesterday and told me we should meet and catch up.

"Why are you coming?" I asked.

I knew why he was coming.

I hadn't seen Marigold since the night we burned the folder behind my house, but the timing seemed more than coincidental.

"Why am I coming? Why am I coming? Jesus, boy. It's my fucking company, isn't it?"

After he said that, I was sure why he was coming.

All morning I was agitated. Everyone was agitated. That's just how people are when their boss comes by. For me, an anxiety crawled over my skin and pushed its way into my mouth, tickling my throat. I had to keep stopping and asking myself what I was worried about. And it wasn't that I was worried, not really, I was just anxious. Anxious to know what LeBlanc would tell her. Anxious to know the truth. I guess I am just nosy.

So I followed the camper from a safe distance and parked down on another road that led to a different abandoned set of camp sites, and walked through the woods and here I am staring at a camper as if I will be able to hear the conversation through the walls. After a while, they exit. They stand at an odd distance from each other, a little too far away for a comfortable volume of conversation, but not so far away as to seem rude. They talk for a few minutes, then Marigold turns and walks down the path away from the campsites. LeBlanc lights a cigarette and paces around the truck. I trip back through the woods to my truck, drive down the camp road and idle at the end, where it intersects with the main road, still feeling stupid but committing to my actions. When Marigold comes in sight, walking deliberately, quickly, squinting in the sun, I honk my horn lightly at her. She doesn't startle at the sound or seem surprised to see me. She walks over to the truck and gets in.

We don't greet each other. I drive, not sure where I'm going. At some point, she says, "turn here," and I follow her directions until we end up at an abandoned cabin along the edge of the bayou.

CHAPTER THIRTY-TWO
randy the prophet

When I was young, I ran outside during high tides. Water sloshed over the seawall and filled the streets. The adults griped as they went about their business, rolling up their pants and taking off their shoes, wading across the street to get to the Dollar Store or the bus stop.

"The land's slipping away," my mom would sigh, pulling the curtains so she didn't have to look at the yard, a brown pond, no plants there in years, all killed from the saline.

To me it felt like something else—like the rest of the world was coming to meet me—like there was no more reason to worry about the land falling off into the water because here they were existing together. I was a human and a fish. Up the stairs to my home and I was dry and walking around and dragging my feet even though my mom told me not to. Out in the street I splashed. I didn't roll up my pants or take off my shoes. I went into the Dollar Store dripping and bought a bag of Takis.

Some nights I dreamt the world was covered in water. It was like a snow globe, sitting still on a dresser. The universe was a dome and under it—a stretch of land—Earth. My mom and I were the ice skaters below, but we weren't skating, and we weren't wearing fuzzy ear muffs and scarves. We were in our house, raised so high it almost reached the top of the dome, floating above our beds.

CHAPTER THIRTY-THREE

marigold

He smells a certain way. Out behind the ranger's cabin, I notice it. I've noticed it before without knowing what it was. I breathe it in: cheap soap and sweat and him mixing with the dirt and grass and water.

I am sitting on top of a rotting picnic table. The table is sinking into the mud on one side and I sit on top, with my feet downhill. The sinking side sinks toward the swamp, like the table is pointing to it. I face away from him, toward the swamp, and he stands beside me, on the outside of the picnic table bench, with his hands in his pockets.

Sometimes I forget that I don't have to feel nervous, that nervousness is something I was taught, and the forgetting lets the feeling take over so that it is too late to turn it off. I feel nervous about what he will ask me.

"Why were you out there?" I ask. There are two reasons to ask the question. One is that I want to know the answer, the other is that we are sharing a space in silence, and it seems to be my turn to talk.

"I've never been out this way before," he says. This could be an answer to my question, or a way of ignoring it. People think the fact that they haven't been somewhere is a good reason to visit, as though their historical absence makes it more interesting.

There's a reason he hasn't been here. No one comes here. "It freaks people out," Shelley told me. Humans feel a horror in the presence of abandoned things. I can't tell if this is something learned from books or movies or if there is something about these things—a cabin long uninhabited, a rusted-out car in an empty lot, a jacket in a field—that reminds them of the things they've abandoned, or of the inevitability of abandonment.

Once Shelley and I paddled out to a part of the swamp we'd never seen before. Just as it started to get dark we came upon a boat, half-sunk in the water, the cabin sticking up, a captain's chair dimly visible through the fogged and mildewed window. Shelley kept saying: "Get away from it! Get away from it!" as she dug her oar in frantically on the side where the boat sat, paddling so hard we went in a circle until we faced the boat head-on. She tried to mask her fear as joke-fear, smiling a little and pleading "Get away from it!" in a mock-scared voice, but I could see in her eyes that it was real fear and I asked her to hold her paddle still and let me point us in the right direction.

"LeBlanc likes to be in the remote spots. That's where we usually have our meetings," I say.

It's a comforting sort of hot outside. The sweat settles against my skin. I lift my braid with one hand and wipe the sweat lingering beneath it on my neck with the other.

"Shelley told me," he says. He picks up a tall stick and pokes at the grass.

I pull my knees to my chest and rest my cheek on top, watching him. He pretends not to notice, keeps his eyes straight ahead and toes the ground. The real answer to my question, then, is that he is here to see me, which I knew, but it isn't something I can admit. People aren't supposed to assume things are about them. "Everything's not about you," they say to each other in movies. Usually this is said to someone that everything is about, because they are the star of the movie. Everyone is a star of a movie in their own head, but they have to pretend to be a minor character. "Who, me?" they are meant to ask.

A mosquito sits happily in the crook of his elbow until he feels it, swats it, wipes the blood on his pants.

"What did he say?" he asks.

I shake my head. He isn't looking at me, so I'm not sure if he sees me from the corner of his eye or thinks I'm ignoring him. There is an annoyed anger inside me that makes me not want to speak, to curl myself up and hide from him, to throw a rock at him so that he will stop standing so still, saying things I don't like.

It is cloudy, so the pain of the sun does not come directly, it is meted out through the obstruction of the clouds.

Tom wants to know what LeBlanc and I talked about because he has some anger toward him, or some unresolved issues. He wants me to say the exact right words to LeBlanc, so he can close his eyes and savor them and know that LeBlanc is hurt, that my words magically caused him enlightenment to every bad part of himself. That is justice. That is what people want when they hear about an unjust thing. "What did you say?" they ask, but when they hear the answer their faces fall. It can never be perfect. Someone can't be held down and forced to know his faults. Even if it was possible to find words for every bad thing about a person, he still wouldn't be able to understand it all, to believe it, to weave it into his idea of himself.

Sitting in the humming camper, while he told me about myself, I felt nothing. It was less than nothing, almost, like I wasn't even there to feel it, like I was watching another person sitting in the booth, squeezing a photograph in her hand so hard it left creases. I didn't show him the photograph.

"She was his wife," I say. Because I have to tell him. I wish I had burned the folder behind my own house, by myself, so he didn't know about it, so we wouldn't be having this conversation. Something about it feels wrong, like I'm not supposed to talk about these things.

"She's dead," I add.

He nods. "I think I've met her," he says. "You know how I... you looked familiar when I first met you. When I was a kid. I think I met her or saw her a few times."

He presses a palm against his forehead. "It's all mixed up in here."

"Do you remember what she was like?" I ask, despite myself. I am confused about whether I want to keep the conversation going or end it.

"No. Well, not really. When I think about her I feel sort of sad. I don't know if she's sad or if it's just mixed up with some other memory."

I accept that and don't ask anything else.

"I'm glad you learned the truth," he says.

He thinks the truth is some big shining fish he can catch in his net and clean and eat or stuff and hang on the wall. But the truth is like an algae bloom, beautiful with unclear edges and darkness underneath. Even if you could scoop it all up with a net, strain it out and see it all at once, you couldn't know what once lay beneath it or understand every act that brought it into being.

I get up and join him by the water. He drops his stick into the swamp. It is solid and green here, barely discernible from land, and the stick slowly sinks in until the water returns to normal, covers it up.

I pull my braid over one shoulder and thread my fingers through the hair at the end, watching his face. He doesn't look at me. It seems like he is going to say something else—the space around us is quiet, waiting—but he doesn't. He puts his hands in his pockets, pulls them out and puts them on the back of his neck, then on top of his head, and then one is reaching toward me. His face looks concerned, confused. I think I must have a bug on my head or a piece of grass on my shirt and I try to catch his eye, but he won't let me. Then he is holding my braid. He closes his thumb and forefinger around it and slides his hand down until it meets mine at the end. I forget to wonder what to do. I squeeze his hand.

I think about the stick in the swamp. Not belonging, but surrounded, brought slowly down to its new home.

I ask: "Do you think it matters?"

He pulls his hand back. He tries to close his face off—to straighten out his mouth and blink his eyes.

"Why I'm here," I explain.

Now he looks at me, directly in the eyes, and he is not trying to close himself off, he is trying to pour himself into me. My face feels hot.

He holds my gaze, then drops his eyes: "Matters how?"

I think about this. I'm not exactly sure what I was trying to ask. "Matters for me, I guess. For who I am."

"I guess it could matter. Looking back. It could... I don't know. I don't know much about your relationship with him, but it might shed light on things."

"Yeah."

"Is he... expecting you to..."

I shake my head, and then because he isn't looking at me, I say: "No. I think it was his original plan. Maybe not exactly. He had some sort of plan where I would fill some sort of space she left, but it didn't work out that way."

"That's good," he says.

"You think so?"

"Don't you?"

I look at the water, at the place where it is flat. At the absence of the stick.

"I don't know. I'm not fulfilling my purpose. It's strange to learn."

"Well then it wasn't your purpose."

"What do you mean?"

"If you don't fit that... whatever it was... then it wasn't your purpose. It was a made-up purpose. You can have a different one."

I stand there, arms crossed, watching the gnats swarm around in the late morning sun. The sky is a clouded slate.

"I don't think it works that way," I say. "When you're created like I was, you have a purpose built-in, the purpose of your creator. If you don't match that purpose, what's the point of existence?"

"That's like saying my existence has no purpose because I didn't end up being a doctor. That's what my mom wanted me to be."

"Maybe."

"Definitely."

"It's not quite the same."

He sighs. He looks around like he forgot something. I wonder if he is looking for the stick. He doesn't look at me again. He says: "OK. I have to go," and walks back toward the cabin, around the side, toward his truck. He holds the passenger door open for me, but I shake my head.

"I'll walk," I say.

He nods, closes the door, gets in, and drives off.

The sky is no color now, or maybe it is all colors.

CHAPTER THIRTY-FOUR

tom

"Did I ever meet LeBlanc's wife?" I ask my mom. It's late at night and she is breathing heavily into the phone. I picture her on the couch, with the phone wedged between ear and shoulder. The yelling and booing of a trashy talk show waves in and out of the background noise, mixing with the air from her window unit. We haven't spoken too frequently recently, and when we do the conversations are short, boring. I was excited to have a topic of conversation. My question is met with a long silence. If it weren't for the faint sound of someone on the television screaming, most of the words bleeped out, I would think she had hung up.

"Why are you asking me that?" she says, finally.

"Something came up," I say.

"With LeBlanc?"

She sounds worried.

"What do you mean?"

"You're the one calling me up at night, asking questions. You tell me what you mean."

I pause, unsure how to answer this.

"Are you in trouble with LeBlanc?" she asks.

"No, Mom. This doesn't have anything to do with him. I mean it does, obviously, but it's not anything I've ever talked to him about."

"Good."

"I was just curious... I feel like I might have met her. I mean it would make sense, right? We saw him all the time. Where was she?"

"Dead," she says.

"The whole time?"

CHAPTER THIRTY-FIVE
randy the prophet

"Can I come in?" she asks.

I was asleep. I don't know what time it is. Morning, but not the part where you get out of bed. There is no sun. She is a dark blip against the darker world.

I mumble an assent and she follows me in. We sit on the couch. I wait, rubbing my eyes, stretching, yawning, trying to be awake.

"Can you see me?" she asks.

"Well, yeah," I say. Maybe I am still asleep.

"I don't mean right now. I mean, can you see anything about me?"

In the light from the lamp by the couch she looks different. Her face seems more expressive, older than I remember. There are little lines around her eyes I didn't notice before.

"I see you sometimes," I say. "But if you want me to tell you something... you know how it is. I don't know anything. I'm not predicting anything."

"Have you ever seen LeBlanc?" she asks, blinking.

I stand up and stretch out my back.

"Once," I admit.

"What did you see?"

"I'd rather not say."

"Tell me something," she says. Her voice is at a register I've never heard, with a tinge of desperation, pleading.

"Why are you asking? Is something bothering you?"

She doesn't answer.

"Look, it doesn't matter what I... I'm not helping people, really. Maybe a few times something I say pushes someone in a direction, but who's to say they wouldn't get there already? Nothing I tell you is going to help you figure anything out. You'll end up where you end up."

When she leaves, I watch her from the porch, straight-backed and crunching gravel. It is a marvel that even she can have anxiety about the future, that life can be a mystery to someone with a designed existence. The way she asked, the way she looked at me, made me sure I shouldn't tell her anything.

I know people come to me because they want control, want some signpost that they are headed toward something. It is impossible, even for me, to see beyond the minutes that make up life—to brush my teeth, sit at the counter, count change, call Gloria, swat mosquitoes—to some sort of idea of a life. Who thinks about the life they're living? Who is asked "where do you see yourself in ten years?" and has an answer besides a job, a house, a place, an answer about the person he will be or the stacked experiences that will make him that way? For some reason, knowing something about the future—even if it is that they will be standing on a beach or petting a dog or looking at a painting—gives them some sort of reminder that they are a continuous being, that today they need to buy groceries and at some point in the undetermined future they will be holding a baby.

Marigold should understand this. But the way she looked at me was like a kid with the flu, like she needed someone to tell her she'd be better.

CHAPTER THIRTY-SIX

marigold

I'm not dreaming, and I'm not sure if I'm sleeping. Instead, a narrative presses itself against my brain. I am in a green valley surrounded by tall mountains. A little creek runs beside me. The valley is dotted with wildflowers, and in the distance, before the gray growth of the mountains, crops of trees dot the green around me. I see myself. At first, I think this is the way my mind chooses to process the story, to see myself from outside my own body, but then I realize that I am here too, in my own body, looking at myself, and then I see that it is not myself, but the woman from the photograph. The woman does not look surprised to see me. Even though we are identical, I can see on the outside the ways in which the woman is not me. There is a certain softness around her mouth, a different type of understanding in her eyes.

"Maybe if they tried harder, or I did, I could be you," I say.

"You couldn't," the woman says. "Nothing would have worked."

"Would I have wanted it to work?" I ask. It is a question not to the other version of me that is standing there, but to the version that lives burrowed somewhere beneath my diaphragm.

I don't wish that LeBlanc loved me or that I was a replacement for his wife, but if I had turned out right maybe that is what I would have wanted, and if that is what I wanted maybe things would be easier, maybe I would smile a lot and laugh at little things, maybe I would wake up and hum songs.

"I didn't wake up humming songs," the woman says.

"You weren't programed," I say. "You had a choice."

"If you are programmed, and you are supposed to be me, then why aren't you like me?"

"That doesn't mean I'm not programmed, it only means I wasn't programmed correctly."

A pink light appears around the edges of the story and the woman disappears. I sit up in bed. The sun is rising, trickling into my room, painting the new day. I press two fingers hard against my sternum, pinch my upper arms, kick my feet. I make sure I am me.

CHAPTER THIRTY-SEVEN

tom

When my dad died I was admiring the work of the vanished folk artist. More like, I was trying cigarettes with my friend inside a fake, brick lighthouse.

"This place is weird as hell," my friend said, bent over coughing, holding the cigarette out to me. I stuck it to my lips and pretended to inhale. I hated the taste of it, the smell it left on my hands and clothes. I was ready for this stage of peer pressure to end.

It was my idea to go to the vanished folk artist's garden. I remembered my mother taking me there once when I was younger, remembered the blue-eyed men, the angels, the stone paths, the boats heading down the bayou that ran alongside. Something about the place made me feel like I was living a life, not just a kid biding my time. My mother showed me how to take it all in. We went up to everything. Every piece. We looked each thing up and down and talked about what we saw. We walked around in circles and leaned in close. We guessed how things were made. My favorite part was the blank slab. Something was supposed to go there, but the folk artist vanished and left it undone. My mother and I debated, made guesses. At one point, when she walked off to look at something else, I stood on the pad very still, one leg raised in the air like a karate kick. Waiting for her to notice. When she turned back around she jumped and screamed and we both laughed until we cried.

I stared at the light coming in through the chinks in the lighthouse, watched the smoke curl around my friend's fingers.

"I like it here," I said. I didn't know how to say the other things, how I saw a flicker of the self within myself, how something about the quiet road and the still bayou and the beating sun and the faces—everywhere faces on the sculptures, watching us—pushed something hopeful up into my throat.

At that moment, though, all that was happening in my throat was a tickling from the smoke he blew in my face. When he finished the cigarette, he stubbed it out and threw it on the ground. I waited until he wasn't looking and picked it up with a tissue I had brought and stuffed it in my pocket.

We walked in the slow, dead heat down the road, across a clattering metal bridge. It was the middle of the afternoon. People were at work or napping. We hit sticks against the side of the bridge and listened to the vibration.

When I got home, my mother was waiting in the front yard, arms crossed. I thought she knew about the cigarette, and for some reason I took it out of my pocket, unwrapped the tissue, and held it out to her. She ignored my hand and looked somewhere over my head, at the power lines or the neighbor's roof.

"There's been an accident," she said.

It was water. I thought my father might have liked that, although I never said so to anyone else, not wanting to sound morbid. I wasn't calloused to it, either. Some nights I couldn't sleep, thinking of my young stubbornness, lying in the boat while my father did the thing he loved, tried to share the thing with his son. Then the image changed to my father, alone in the shafts under the plant, a good father, a good husband, a good guy, everyone said so, knocked off his feet by a sudden rush of water, probably confused, or maybe not, maybe knowing "I will die." The water didn't get that high, but the initial rush knocked him against a wall. He hit his head, passed out, and slid beneath. What I wanted was there to be a fish in the water, for my dad to see its disinterested eyes and feel some sort of happiness.

"Were there any fish?" I asked the lawyer.

The man stared at me for a few seconds, then said, "I don't think so. Is that something you'd like us to look into?"

For months I forgot about the vanished folk artist. I spent the summer cooking ramen and beans for my mother and making sure she took her anti-depressants.

Then, one day, he came into my mind again. I remembered the first time I walked into the lighthouse, the faces staring at me, the time I posed on the blank cement for my mother, and I felt a breathlessness, a pressure in my chest, a joy that I didn't know what to do with. In that moment I thought about bringing my father there. I thought if he came back for one day, for a few hours even, that I would take him there, walk him around, watch him while he looked.

Instead, I convinced my mother to go with me. She was pale from staying inside, tired from not sleeping, big bags under her eyes and her hair unbrushed. This was before we lost the house, before LeBlanc bought us the trailer. The house was piled with an old version of our life, my father's things lying casually around as if he'd just left. My mother drove us there, half asleep. We didn't speak. I lay my head against the window and watched the squat, slapped together businesses with their painted-on names and overgrown parking lots pass by. When we arrived, we walked around separately. I watched her from the corner of my eye but didn't push an interaction. She walked slowly, blankly, not looking at much. After a while, I went to the empty part of the garden, to the blank cement, and I stood there, waiting for her to see me. I stood very still with my hands at my sides, a big dumb grin on my face. She was in the lighthouse. I heard her step out, but my eyes weren't turned toward her, and I wanted to stay still, to keep up the joke. I waited.

CHAPTER THIRTY-EIGHT

leBlanc

When I pulled into the driveway and saw his car, I assumed we had a meeting that I forgot. It happened. I'd tell people to stop by at some point, then get caught up at the office and forget. She'd be home to greet them, make them dinner, smooth things over. With him, I wasn't worried about it. We were like family at that point. Me and him and his strange wife and the boy.

When I came inside, the house was different. Usually my arrival prompted various flurries, a few maids wanting to look busy, someone asking me what I wanted to eat, fussing over my lateness, turning on the lights in my study. No one so much as greeted me. The house was dark. I couldn't smell any lingering dinner in the air. There were lights on upstairs, which trickled down enough that I could see my way to the staircase.

I called out, and I thought I heard the shuffle of feet somewhere, but still no one appeared. On the landing, I saw light coming from under her door. When I opened it, he jumped, but she stayed completely calm and still. She was laying in the lounge chair, her knees bent, feet tucked into her body. He sat on the floor with the same easy confidence he did everything.

"What?" I asked.

I didn't know what to ask.

The question hung there. It was so quiet I wondered if a storm was coming. There were no birds chirping. Even the air conditioning wasn't humming.

He blinked a few times, then stood up and said: "Our meeting... I guess time got away from me. You didn't show and..." he trailed off, waved his hand around as if that said it all.

There was nothing I could actually hold onto that made what I saw wrong. She had visitors in her room plenty of times. They were just sitting there. They weren't even touching. It was just something in the atmosphere, how casual they looked, how natural, like they'd sat that way many times before. And when could they have sat that way? Because he and I were like family, sure. His family was my family, I felt, even if his wife might not agree, but my wife was not a part of that. She avoided those get-togethers, the long days in the yard, the movie nights, the home cooked meals. She always had an excuse. I assumed it was her distaste for his wife, a woman who wore t-shirts to formal dinners.

With this tableau in front of me—her still reclining in her chair, looking between the two of us without much interest, him for once seeming less cool than he thought he was—those absences and avoidances took on a different meaning.

CHAPTER THIRTY-NINE

the storm

GLORIA

The scrubby parking lot is gray and still. I look out the window of my apartment and stare at the sprouts of grass in the cement cracks. There are only a few cars. Mine is a faded red box, looking nicer in the cloudiness than in direct sunlight. Front right tail light busted, hanging out, waiting for a visit from my dad. Most people who live here are at work. Some fled.

I moved here to be safe from the weather, knowing I didn't move far enough. I will be safe, I think. I will be mostly safe. At least, I won't be as bad off as I would be if I was still home. Still, though, this anxiety, this stillness, the silence. The realization that no birds are singing. Because even if I won't be in the eye of a hurricane, even if I won't be beside a broken levy, getting rescued by boat, still I may get a tree branch through the window, a blackout, heat pouring in like the air conditioner once did. Still, I won't be able to sleep, drinking coffee and sitting in my bathtub during the tornado warnings.

The tornadoes were always what scared me the most, even though we didn't get them that often. It was the unhelpfulness of the description: it will sound like a train. When wind is flying past your house, everything sounds like a train.

"Is that what a train sounds like?" I'd ask my dad, curled up under his arm, a semicircle, a curled snail, as small as I could get.

"I don't think so," he'd say.

Very reassuring.

Still, I wait for that sound, the whistle, the rumble, whatever it is exactly. Not hearing it is almost worse than hearing it, the hyperawareness of my ears, never quite catching what they're listening for.

I have a shift at the Mart in a few hours. It won't close unless it's in the eye of a storm, and even then, we will probably all have to stay and do inventory or something. Once I couldn't make it in because my road flooded and I was told that was my first and only warning. Next time I would be fired. When I asked the manager what he would have done in my situation, he said: "Swim."

I pull the curtains back in place and make myself a cup of tea. When I moved out here, I had a certain idea of adulthood, of real personhood. The idea involved drinking tea. I never drank tea as a kid, just sweet tea, made by my mother right before dinner, still warm, melting the ice cubes, a lukewarm syrup to accompany our meals. Still, I was sure I needed to have tea. I needed to have hot tea in a cup and saucer and I would sit on the couch in my immaculate apartment and drink the tea and read newspapers.

That is my life now and it is just as nice as I thought it would be. On days when I have the mornings off, I spend a few hours cleaning: scrubbing the grout, beating the rugs out on the balcony, sweeping the floors, wiping the windows. Then I take a long bath, which is always sort of a letdown because the bathroom is old and no matter how much I scrub, the tub is a grimy off-white, and all the collected dirt and dust on my skin from cleaning floats in the water. After my bath, hair in a towel , I make my tea and drink it on the couch. I don't *read* the newspaper though, or not really. I look at the newspaper for anything about LeBlanc, water, the plant, and I read and highlight those things, cut them out, place them carefully in the tidy plastic pockets in my binder.

My apartment isn't anything amazing. It's what I can afford on a Mart salary with lots of double shifts. What it is, though, is peaceful. I know where everything is, and I've picked every object out to look just so. Sure, plenty of the objects I picked out came from the Mart's discount cart or the Dollar Store, but they are coordinated—my blue kitchen towels with the blue oven mitts, my rose-colored candles and rose-colored tea cups, my grey rugs and doormats. All of it just the way I want it to look. All of it mine.

Now with my tea I can't focus to look at the newspaper. I look out the window again. No change. I pace around the room. I call my dad.

We never admit it, but these are our favorite times. Discussing a crisis together. United by worry.

"Any news?" he asks in lieu of a greeting. He knows it is me. I don't think anyone ever calls the store.

We always want to know if the other person has news. If one of our radio stations or television channels is slightly faster at knowing how bad it will be.

The fact that no one ever knows how bad it will be is something we don't mention. Even if, last year, we were warned for days that It Is Coming and many people drove hours and hours out of fear and I took my few days vacation leave to board up my windows and go to work, but not to work, to buy canned food and batteries for my flashlights and gallons and gallons of water. Always all that water, as if I'm suddenly going to become a well hydrated person when my faucets don't work. As if I'm going to have the energy to boil water and bathe myself. Anyway, after all that, It didn't come. It was a sunny day. No rain, even. Schools closed in anticipation and kids ran around in the streets, riding their bikes, yelling, acting like they were personally responsible for keeping It away.

And then that time, back home, when they said nothing at all. Just rain on the weather report, and when we swung our feet out of bed in the morning they hit water. That was when we ran out of the house, Mom, Dad, and I with whatever things we could grab, hopped in the truck, and headed as far away as we could get. The things I grabbed included one shoe, a stuffed animal, five pairs of underwear, one pair of socks, and book five of "Charlie Brown's 'Cyclopedia."

I tell him I haven't heard any news, and he says he hasn't either. I ask him if he's going to get out of there. The compound is the worst place to be in a storm, on a sliver of land so small it gets lost on a map, just looks like a little bit of dirt dotting the ocean. LeBlanc always waits until the last moment to call off work, to let them leave. So far, they've never been stuck there during a storm, but I feel like it's only a matter of time.

"No word from the man yet," he says. "Still here for the present."

I roll my eyes, but I don't say anything. I'm trying this new thing where I don't treat my dad like he's my child.

"Are you going to come here or to that place?" I ask.

When LeBlanc does close the plant, he has a shelter set up where some of them can stay if they don't have family or somewhere else safe they can go. Dad stayed with me during the last storm, but it didn't go very well. By the time he left, all we could muster was a side-hug, eyes averted. I hope he won't try to stay here again, and feel guilty for hoping that.

"I'll probably go to the other place, sweetie," he says.

I hold my breath.

"Just seems like a good idea. Then I won't be in your hair."

I tell him he won't be in my hair. He knows he will and that I'll be in his. We move on. We hang up.

I hear the sudden sound of rain. Hard rain. The kind of rain that sounds like it would bruise your skin if it hit you. Maybe it's hail. I open the curtain again. It is still strangely sunny out, slowly fading to grey, as the rain pelts down.

RANDY THE PROPHET

The year Cynthia died there was a big storm. She was tired and sore and she said she'd rather get blown out of the house than have to sit in the bathtub. I said if she wasn't going to take shelter, neither was I. We tried to lock Gloria in the bathroom by herself, but she cried and screamed so we let her out. The three of us sat in the living room and talked. Gloria complained about a teacher she hated. Cynthia fell asleep and Gloria and I played War. We pretended not to notice or fear the endless wind, the cracking of tree branches, the pelting water. When something that sounded like a train passed by, we pretended to think it was just a train, even though we didn't live near any tracks.

We slept together in the living room: Cynthia on the couch and Gloria and I on the floor in sleeping bags. Gloria kept turning the flashlight on and shining it on her face and trying to scare me. I had trouble going to sleep, constantly sitting up and patting the floor, checking for water, but eventually my mind gave in and I drifted off. When I woke, the sun was shining on me from the parted curtain. Cynthia was still sleeping, but Gloria and I got up and I made some coffee on the stove and let her have half a cup. We went outside with our drinks and our rain boots to survey the wreckage. The house was safe. A lot of the trees were down. Some power poles along the road

291

were bent or completely knocked over. We walked into the woods, climbing over or ducking under the fallen trees. It was very quiet.

"Where do the animals go?" Gloria asked.

I didn't know.

SHELLEY

We drive in the rain. In a long line of buses full of people that have nowhere to go. Another line of buses takes people who have family and friends outside the compound to a central meeting place. Some on the bus are nervous, chatting anxiously, hugging themselves, watching out the window, wide-eyed. Marigold and I just stare straight ahead, bumping along with the bus. Tom and Randy the Prophet are in the seat in front of us, and sometimes one of them will get up on his knees and turn around to say something to us and it feels like we're in elementary school, the fun of it. It is fun.

Everyone complains about going to the shelter. Complains about the storms. I like it though and I wonder if everyone else's complaints are fake, made because they think they're required. There's something nice about the buzz. Even if a lot of it is from fear, I think if we're being honest, some of it is an excitement that something different is happening. Even if that different thing is possible destruction. No, none of us want our property to be destroyed or want anyone to get hurt, we just like having a few days to get away from home, to have something new to think about. Maybe not everyone feels that way. I say, "can't wait," in a sarcastic tone, just like everyone else. But really, I can't wait.

The night before we leave, I have a hard time sleeping. I wake up early. Earlier than Marigold, even, and drink my coffee and eat my breakfast, and when I get on the bus crammed with people, I try not to smile and enthusiastically greet them. I yawn and stretch just like everyone else. Does anyone notice that unlike other times when I don't have to go to work, I've brushed my hair and put on real clothes? Most everyone else is in some form of pajamas or sweatpants, except Marigold, who is wearing her casual look: black jeans, black t-shirt.

I like sitting with my head resting against the window, listening to everyone chatter around me, occasionally participating in a conversation that I'm not a part of, just because I can overhear it. I like the ability to be silent and stare out the window for an hour if I want, or sleep, or pick at the cracked vinyl of the seat in front of me. There is a confined freedom. As long as I am on the bus, I can do whatever I want, or at least some version of what I want that can fit in the seat of a bouncing vehicle.

The shelter is a more expanded freedom. It used to be something else. A government building, a church, a convention center. A space with big stairs, looping hallways, one big room at the center, and other smaller rooms scattered around. Outside there is an old, rusted, dormant fountain and an overgrown garden. Now it is LeBlanc's. This is what LeBlanc does, buys things no one wants and uses them for his own benefit.

Because it is for his own benefit. It may seem like he is benevolently saving his employees from harm, but really he just doesn't want to hire anyone new, or deal with litigation, or have his insurance premiums go up.

When we arrive at the building, everything is set up for us. Who does this setting up? We don't know. Some other group of people who work for LeBlanc in some other capacity. They don't stay here. At least no one's ever seen them if they do. The biggest room, at the center of the building, is filled with neatly made up cots in rows. Each cot has one pillow, a fitted sheet, and a thin flannel blanket. Marigold and I walk in and look around, Randy the Prophet and Tom behind us. Looking out at the beds, I see thick layers of time. Beneath this layer, these beds, there are rows of bleachers set up for a high school graduation, beneath that, folding chairs and a screaming preacher, beneath that, voting booths, old ladies volunteering at a long plastic table. I don't know why it matters to me what was here before, but I feel it sometimes, at night, in the buzz of the air conditioner, as all the bodies around me shift and cough and snore. What was here before and why we are.

Marigold and I head to our usual spot, two beds toward the middle of the outer row, right by a door. The door leads to a private bathroom. The bathroom isn't labeled, the door is discreet. If we are discreet in using it as well, we get our own place to shower in peace. To lock the door when we use the bathroom and stare into space, and not worry about who's listening.

I set up my cot and I've got Marigold on one side and Randy the Prophet on the other. Tom takes the cot on Marigold's other side. I note this as interesting. I smile at Randy the Prophet. I like to see him. Not just for his own ways, his quietness, his wisdom, his stupid jokes that make me laugh despite myself, but also because he reminds me of Gloria. I can see her in half of him, like she's a little shadow on his back that could be peeled off at any time. For a moment I miss her and have a ridiculous wish that she was here too, or maybe that I was at her apartment instead of here. I've never been to her apartment, but the picture of it in my mind is precise and preserved like a ship in a bottle. I see her in a bright kitchen making her stupid tea, barefoot, leaning on the counter and writing one of her angry letters.

I love those angry letters.

All I can express to her is the stupidity of the angry letters. Because they are stupid. In the same way it's stupid to cry during a movie or yell at a driver in another car while you're in your car with the windows rolled up. Writing a letter to LeBlanc or about LeBlanc has to be one of the stupidest things a person can spend her time doing.

"He won't read them," I told her.

That was a long time ago. When I first met her.

We were very young.

We felt old, then. Adult. Me because I had a real job and her because she moved out of Randy the Prophet's trailer and into her own apartment. But in the photos our faces are so smooth, our eyes so bright. We didn't know anything.

He did read them, though. And he wrote back to her. And she wrote back to him. And they had these strange, mostly silent meetings.

But LeBlanc wouldn't change his mind for anything. He could see it all happening right in front of him, see people in poverty suffering, hear an old lady sob. It wouldn't matter to him. Right was right. And what was right was whatever he wanted to be.

But he loves a protege and he loves a lesson, so he loves Gloria.

I love those letters. The idea of them. Of caring about something so much that you take out a piece of paper and a pen and you write out what you think, and you fold the paper up and you stick it in an envelope and find a stamp and write your return address. At some point, you even have to go buy more stamps so you can write more letters. I love to think of her little beating heart caring about things when there's no reason to care, when caring gets you nowhere.

I'm lying on my bed. Tom and Randy the Prophet went off somewhere to explore. Marigold is neatly arranging all her items in the little box that's placed at the foot of each bed. All of my stuff is shoved under the cot. Someone comes by and gives us brown paper bags with peanut butter and honey sandwiches, Fritos, and Capri Suns.

Marigold and I take our sandwiches and leave the main room. We go out into the foyer and up a set of stairs, sitting on a wooden bench in front of a big, arched window that overlooks the abandoned garden and rusted fountain.

People walk by us, some stopping to look out the window, pressing their hands against it, leaving smudges. The rain pours so fast it is impossible to see it. It would seem like the whole world was behind a gray veil if it weren't for the bending of the tree branches, the beaten down grass. Beneath us, children scream and run through the hallway that circles the building, friends and families walk together, eating their sandwiches. Some sit on the steps.

A small memory, now. A vacation with my parents. A beach somewhere. A sudden storm and sitting by a big window, watching the rain beat down on the ocean. Wet hair and a towel wrapped around my shoulders. Soggy bathing suit. My head against my mother's shoulder.

I put my head on Marigold's shoulder. I pretend like we are on vacation. Two normal adults seeing a place we haven't seen before.

"Have you ever been on a vacation?" I ask her.

I am pretty sure I know the answer, but it feels nice here by the window, and I want to hear my words against her, hear her answer.

"No," she says. "Just to LeBlanc's in the summer. One time Mr. Miller drove me to the beach."

Mr. Miller.

"Whatever happened to him?" I ask.

I feel the subtle rise and fall of her shoulder with her breath. "He's still at the school. He calls me sometimes."

"What?"

I lift my head up and look at her. Sometimes I think I know everything about her, because she doesn't know how to keep secrets. But she also doesn't know what's worth sharing and what isn't, so sometimes there are these weird pockets I uncover, little secret holes in her life that are filled in with something mysterious.

"Yeah, usually on my birthday."

She doesn't have a birthday, but a date was picked by someone at some point and we celebrate it even though she shows no interest.

"What do you talk about?"

She blinks at me. "It's Mr. Miller. He usually recommends some books to me. Asks me about you, the plant, tells me I'm doing a good job."

"That's nice of him."

She doesn't say anything.

"Do you ever miss him?"

I've never thought to ask this before. Mr. Miller basically took care of her for years. He was her guide. I never thought about how strange it would be to be completely removed from that person.

"Yes," she says.

And that's it.

A strange moment where the sun shines. The rain is still pouring, the land still beaten, but over it all is a confusing brightness, like the nicest of days, like nothing to do with destruction. We sit shoulder to shoulder on the bench and don't talk. My body feels calm and heavy, my heart light. I see ahead to the next few days, sleeping in the big room, taking stretch breaks outside when the rain lulls, playing cards with the kids, eating so many peanut butter sandwiches that I won't want to touch peanut butter until I have to again when the next storm comes.

TOM

I call LeBlanc. There's a bank of phones tucked in a hallway at the shelter. I haven't seen anyone use them since we arrived two days ago. Kids are running up and down the hallway and a couple is having a fight on a bench a few feet away. I plug one ear with a finger and listen to the ringtone.

"I remember her," I say when he answers.

He doesn't say anything. He might not know who is calling, might not know what I'm talking about.

"When I met her. Marigold. I thought: 'I've met her before.' I was so sure. But I wrote it off. Figured she looked like somebody or maybe I just saw her somewhere once. At a rest stop along the highway maybe. She's beautiful. I would have noticed her."

"Tom," he says. He doesn't sound angry with me, like I thought he would. He is using a voice of pained patience, one I've never heard. "I'm busy."

"But I had met her before. Not her. But her. The other one. Not often. Maybe once or twice. Why was that? She was your wife. Why were you always around and she never was? I remember when I was old enough to think about asking if you had a wife, she was dead already."

"Tom," the same tone. He sounds almost tired, sad. "I don't want to talk to you about my dead wife."

"Right. I understand. But the thing is my mom didn't want to talk to me about her either. And that was strange to me. She likes talking about these things normally. Tragedies. That sort of thing. Newspaper clippings."

More silence.

"And I don't like to push her, LeBlanc. You know I don't. You know how she is. Sensitive. Fragile. But this time I couldn't help it. I pushed."

I wait.

"What do you want me to say, Tom?"

"What happened between you two?"

"Who?"

I am hot. I try to remember another time I've been this hot. I wish I wasn't in public, so I could strip off my clothes, run in the bathroom and get under the cold shower. My ear burns against the phone.

"You and him."

"I'm not sure what you mean, Tom. Do you mean were we friends after I found out about them? Did we have a big fight?" He sighs. The way he talks to me is not bringing me the type of satisfaction I am seeking. I want him to be the cruel way he can be. I want him to be angry so I can yell.

"Whatever. Any of it. What happened?"

"Nothing happened," he says. "We pretended like nothing happened. We worked together."

"And then?"

"What did your mother say?" he asks. His voice sounds soft and sensitive. Who is this man? I wonder, not for the first time. How did this man come to be the center of my life?

"She didn't say anything," I say. Which is sort of true. It's not true because she did say things. Words came out of her mouth and into my ear. But she didn't tell me anything. She didn't recite a story for me.

Silence.

"I can draw my own conclusions," I say. Hostile. I sound like a teenager. I remember it now. Other times I've been this hot. Other times with him, telling me what to do, advising me, interfering in my life. Convincing me, whittling me down. And now here I am in a shelter he owns, stuck. Working for him. Where he wants me to be. Always ending up here like there's no other choice. I think about it at night when I can't sleep. Me in a boat, floating down a river, watching it branch, trying to paddle one way, then the other, but always ending up down the same stream, even if I stick my paddle hard in the water, divert all the way to the smallest path, the strangest, most grown over path, they all converge again, they all lead to the same place.

"You can't draw shit, Son," he says. This is more like it. There is the acidity.

"I'm not your son," I say. Again the teenager.

"You're right," he says. "You're not shit to me. You're just a responsibility I inherited. Some guilt I don't deserve."

"What did you do to him?" I ask. I have to ask it like that. Just exactly.

"Nothing," he says.

"It was an accident," he says. "You want it to be something else, so it can mean something else, but it doesn't. It was just an accident. A meaningless accident."

LEBLANC

It was storming then too. I don't remember which storm. The name of some poor woman. All those Tinas born years before now tarnished by association. "Wasn't Tina the one that wiped out that little island?"

All I remember is that it was raining really hard and that I was wearing those ridiculous ten-dollar white rain boots and carrying a pointless umbrella. The umbrella was pointless because the rain was almost horizontal, pelting me from all sides, none of it coming from the top, pattering on the umbrella like the normal order of things. He and I were inspecting the plant. The construction was complete. We were just waiting on some official stamps of approval and all that and then it would be mine, a running, gleaming example of progress. A saltless crystal.

My wife was dead. I remember that. I remember the storm coming and thinking that I needed to talk to her about provisions. We needed to make our plan. We always made a plan. Then I remembered she was dead. It was the first storm since she died, and something about that was so much worse than the first Christmas or birthday or anniversary. The most married I ever felt was when something bad was happening or about to happen and this other person helped me. When we admitted and accepted that this bad thing was happening to both of us and that we would figure it out together.

And he and I, what were we? I was his boss. Were we friends? I didn't go over to his house for those dinners anymore. We were cordial enough to each other at work, but everything had changed. His family didn't come to the funeral. They sent me some cheap flowers and a generic condolence card. It wasn't clear what he thought I knew. Still, there was a stiffness between us and this strange sadness. We both had the same sadness, but we couldn't share it. My sadness rubbed up against his, became smooth, a pearl for me to hoard.

I wanted to look at the shafts underneath. I thought there would be something romantic about it, seeing them empty and new, before they were filled, slowing, salty, smelly. He came down with me. Both of us in those boots and hard hats, dripping wet.

Maybe it was the fact that we were already so wet that caused the confusion.

Because the shafts were dry. We were wet. It was us. The water was with us.

That was what we thought.

It happened like it didn't happen. It happened like it always was.

We were dripping in the dry tunnel and then we were surrounded. I was surrounded. There was no we. I couldn't see him. There were lamps on our heads and I was yelling, righting myself, falling, standing up again. It wasn't that much water. It was just the force of it, the rush of water from the ocean, it had knocked us both down. I don't know if I had passed out, or if I was just confused. There was no way to tell how much time passed.

My lamp passed across him, a few yards away from me. He was face down. I hesitated. I don't know how much time passed. I stood there. Dripping. Again, I forgot and thought I was dripping from the rain. I thought "I'm never using an umbrella again." It could have just been seconds, fractions of seconds.

I don't know.

I did go to him and turn him over.

I did my best impression of mouth to mouth. I don't say that because I wasn't trying, I was, but I didn't know how to do it, actually. There was a training I attended once. Something about singing "Staying Alive."

He was dead, though.

I didn't do it.

I tried to help him.

I might have hesitated.

I might have hesitated for several seconds, while his lungs filled with water, while his brain shut down.

I might have hesitated for one second.

No one saw.

Later, I could tell, she thought she knew. His wife. She looked at me a certain way.

The next time I saw her, and the boy too, it was raining again. Not a named storm this time, just the usual thunder and lightning and all that. Again, in those dumb boots with the guys from legal and we were at her door and I wasn't using an umbrella, the rain just rolled down my body like I was any old tree or lamppost. The way she looked at me then, at the door. Like she really saw me. Like she was there with me in the tunnel. In the bedroom with my wife and her husband. In my dreams when I thought about it. I did. Putting my hands around his neck. Strangling him. But she didn't really know.

I sang "Staying Alive" in my head and I pushed on his chest and I remembered he was a person and I thought about the boy. Her too, even, but mostly the boy, and I wanted to know what I was doing. I wanted to make my brain remember. How long did I hesitate?

M

The storm put her life in a bubble. She was stuck in this dry little sliver of it. Before the storm, it was easy to let the days roll into one another so that they felt like something outside herself, something she witnessed. They were not her life. Her life was something apart, a floating spectator.

She was no longer useful to him. Or not in the way she wanted to be. There was no internship. There was no job, even.

After she graduated, before they got married, there was a period where it was all nice. She wandered around his cold house in her pajamas. Spent afternoons in the garden. He warned her about the garden. That it was a disgrace. He said it needed her feminine touch. She didn't know anything about having a feminine touch, and when she saw the garden it was nicer than anything she could have imagined: luscious with big-leaved plants and citrus. She didn't know the names of any plants or flowers. She walked the garden paths and talked to the gardener. LeBlanc encouraged her to make plans for the garden.

She started to think: "Did he just want someone to help with his garden? Is that why we're getting married?"

There were no plans she wanted to make. She just wanted to sit in the garden and look at it. The gardener helped. She asked him what he thought could be better. He told her about koi ponds. They planned one. He planned it and showed her the plans and she said, "looks good." And then it was built, and she asked LeBlanc for a nice chair and umbrella and she sat out beside it and watched the fish shimmering around, watched their hungry mouths kiss at her for the crumbs she brought.

It was supposed to be a transition period. They would get married. She needed to focus on planning that. Then she would start living her life. She would work with him, she assumed. In her internship she wrote press releases, helped answer inquiries. She liked doing it. Liked the steady work piling up then winnowing back down by the end of the day. Liked how her wrist got sore from typing, how she could split up her day into breaks, the next coffee always just ahead. Then she planned a wedding. Like the garden, this was something she didn't have much of an opinion about, except for the photographs by a barn.

There was a wedding planner. Like everyone in their lives, this wasn't some outsider hired for the task. It was someone LeBlanc knew and trusted, some woman who did other, unknown tasks for him. One of his People.

Then the wedding happened.

Her family didn't come. She didn't invite them.

Her friends didn't come either, but she realized she didn't really have any.

She decided she was one of his People now, and his People were her People and that would be that.

The wedding was in a big hall at the country club. She loved the country club. She went there every day that summer after graduation, before the wedding, and ate hamburgers by the pool. She liked watching the people there, how much they cared about the strangest things: the way their children's hair looked when they got out of the pool, their bread being too toasted, not toasted enough, buying a new car. Someone was always buying a new car. These people knew who she was. Hated her for it. Were possibly jealous. They smiled at her and asked about what she was up to. She was never up to anything. "I'm building a koi pond," she told them. That shut them up.

There weren't any hamburgers at the wedding, which she regretted. She wished she had mentioned them to the wedding planner. Instead there were various small pastry shells stuffed with small foods she couldn't identify. It all tasted like fish.

When they took their pictures out by the barn door—because the country club had a barn, had horses, although she wasn't sure if anyone rode them

—she tried to feel something. That was her moment and although she couldn't admit to herself that she had been directing her life to such a moment, to such a photograph, the way her heart beat and her smile pulled at the ends of her lips, it all hurt from expectation. But she did not feel it. There was LeBlanc. Distinguished, people called him, because he was old. But not so old. Just older. His hair silvered around his temple. His suit fit him nicely and he looked happy. He looked actually happy and not the kind of happy where he was just satisfied that things were going his way. But she didn't feel it. Whatever she was supposed to feel. She felt hot and hungry.

After the wedding and their honeymoon, a week in a raised house on a lake, him fishing and driving a boat around, her reading on the boat and beside him when he fished, they returned to the cold house. She checked on the koi pond. The fish seemed bigger, brighter, more desperate for her crumbs. She accused the gardener of not feeding them and he just shrugged, laughed. "They're spoiled," he said.

Then he went back to work, and she didn't. She felt too stupid to ask about it at first. Not stupid because it was a dumb question, but embarrassed, helpless, because she shouldn't have to ask anyone about her own life. She should have been doing her life.

One night she approached him in his study. She was wearing a bathing suit under a bathrobe. She always wore a bathing suit or a robe. Since she spent most of the day at the country club and the rest of it in the garden or inside the freezing house, she didn't see any point in other clothes.

"I was wondering..." she started. She had her fingertips on the edge of his desk and he watched her patiently. She thought how strange it was to be married to someone and afraid to ask them a question about your life. "Is there going to be a job for me?"

He smiled at her. It wasn't his nice smile. It was his normal "I'm LeBlanc" smile.

"No worries," he said.

She smiled back at him, a big bright smile to try to convince him that she, too, was confident. She didn't know what his answer meant, but she couldn't bring herself to ask. Instead she started fiddling with different things on his desk.

"You don't need to worry about any of that anymore," he said. It didn't sound like he was clarifying his previous statement, just continuing to talk because it was quiet and he liked to form words.

"I'm not worried about it," she said. The words came out strained, her throat clamped. She cleared it and tried again. "I'm not worried, but I would like to work. I liked working for you."

"Oh," he said. He looked genuinely surprised, like the thought hadn't occurred to him. "Well, there's nothing for you right now I'm afraid. But when there is..."

She nodded.

She should have asked: How long will it take?

She should have said: I'll find something else in the meantime.

Instead she slunk out to the garden and looked at her fish.

It was dusk, and the pale pink sky lay like a skin on the water. She put her robe on the ground and stepped into the pond. The fish came to her, their gaping mouths frantic, their shiny fins slimy against her. Her heart leapt all the way into her mouth and she thought she might die there, and she couldn't figure out whether it was funny or terrifying.

The storm came a few weeks later. She couldn't go outside or to the country club. There was no need for her bathing suit, so she just wore the robe, tied tightly so she didn't accidentally flash the maids. She and LeBlanc didn't have separate bedrooms, but she did have a room of her own, his idea of a female study: a plush, white rug, a lounge chair, a small shelf of novels with pretty, embroidered covers. The wide window, divided into many panes, looked out over the driveway. The road a line, only becoming real when a car or a person moved along it. She lounged on her lounge chair and watched the rain, the way it blurred the view, took away the crisp edges of reality.

She paced around the house. Wandering into rooms she'd never seen before. Unnecessary rooms with big, comfortable beds and ornate bedding, matching curtains and rugs, antique dressers. No one had stayed the night at the house since she'd lived there. She tried to think of one person who might stay there in the future.

The storm lasted three days. There was the warning day—the day where everything grew quiet, still, and then the rain began to pound—then the storm day—the day it hit, the pounding wind and rain, the flying branches—then the day after, the rain drizzling, the air oppressive, the outside ugly in an uncomfortable way: pooled water, dead plants, covered walkways.

In these three days the life in her head, the life that happened before LeBlanc, the life that was always about to happen, collapsed and converged with reality. Gone was the floating possibility. Here was the damp reality. She was a bathing suit wearing, hamburger eating, wandering wife.

A branch fell on the koi pond and broke the glass. They found it waterless, the fish still and nestled against each other.

She cried. She walked away. She closed her eyes and shook her head and tried to remove the image. A deep guilt clenched its hand against her lungs for all the times they swam up to her and she didn't have crumbs, for all the times she walked by and laughed at them, their desperation, their greed. Their water slowly seeped out. Maybe it took longer than it should have, maybe the rain kept it up to a certain point, but they would have wriggled and writhed and tried to breathe. Would they know what was happening to them as it happened, or would the realization come when it was too late, at their last breath, last tail flip?

Did they think: "There is no more water."?

MARIGOLD

I sense him. The rain stopped and some of us are outside, hands on the smalls of our backs, stretching, breathing, squinting from the sudden sunlight. Most people stay inside, quickly acclimating to the idea, becoming people who don't go outside, lying on the bed, staring at the ceiling, or gathered around one of the TVs wheeled out on media carts in various corners and meeting rooms.

There's a little sliver of a creek that runs behind the building. I climb through the undergrowth to it and crouch down with my hands in the water, listening to the pleasant flow of it, a tiny creek made less tiny by the sudden rains, joyfully running faster, fuller, than it's used to.

He is behind me. I don't know if it's his smell or his breathing or the patter of his feet, but I know that it's him. I stand up, cross my arms, and don't turn around. I wait.

"I'm leaving," he says.

There were many things he could say at this moment, but this one surprises me.

"It's not safe," I say.

"Not... not right now. When we get back. I'm leaving the compound. The job."

"You're quitting."

Maybe he nods. I'm still not looking at him. He walks up farther and stands beside me. I turn toward him. We stand there and the creek babbles happily by.

"This is a babbling brook," I say.

"Yes," he says.

I like that he says that, and it makes me glad he is there. Shelley would make fun of me for saying that. Randy the Prophet would extract meaning. Tom accepts it. The stiffness from our last conversation relaxes a little.

"Do you want to know why I'm quitting?" he asks.

We are looking in each other's eyes sometimes, but sometimes one of us looks at the ground, or at the other's forehead. I notice that his hair is frizzed in the humidity, little hairs haloing his head.

"If you want to tell me," I say.

I know this is the wrong thing to say. People want you to tell them you are interested. They need to hear it.

"Yes, I want to know," I add.

"I can't work for him anymore," he says.

That's nothing new for me. That's the most commonly uttered phrase by people who quit. I thought there would be more from him.

"He can be hard to work for."

He snorts through his nose and toes the ground. He doesn't look at my eyes anymore. "You talk about him like he's a normal shit boss. Like he is just bad at communication or too demanding."

"He is."

"Sure."

He sticks his hands in his pockets. I bend down again to stick my hand in the water. I think the water will help me. The water is normal. The water is doing what it always does. It is going.

"But you can't talk about him like that. You of all people. And me neither. Think about how much he has done to us. Think about how much he is in our lives. From the beginning. For both of us. He's not just some jerk I can write a resignation letter to."

"You can't write a resignation letter to get someone out of your life for good," I say. Hoping I am following.

"You can't."

"Do you think getting away from the plant will help?" I ask.

He shakes his head. "It can't hurt."

This makes sense to me. I stand up again and wipe my wet hand against my pants. I realize that I want to talk him out of it. That the plant suddenly seems like a distant gray dream without him.

"I think you need to get out of there too," he says.

"Out of there?"

"The plant. You need to get out. Away from him. I mean, what he did. You and his wife. It's not right, Marigold. And the water, the poor people having to buy that water."

He rubs his hands in his hair and it sticks up in all directions.

"I can't do that," I say. I say it as a fact, because it is one. I don't say it with regret, because I don't know that I feel it. "What happens to me was decided a long time ago. What I am was decided a long time ago."

He gets a look on his face like he is in pain: his brow creased, his lips tight. He starts walking back through the underbrush, swinging at the sickly trees with his arms, then comes back and stands in front of me again, huffing.

"It's not like LeBlanc's walking around with a remote control that makes you do one thing or another. You can say whatever you want right now. You could kick mud at me, or lay down in the creek and roll around, or hit me, or run away."

"And so could you. And whichever one of those things we did, both of us, it would be because of something inside ourselves that we have no control over."

"Marigold," he says. That same look. Like he just ate some cold ice cream and it rushed to his head. The way he says my name, it is a croak, hoarse and sad.

"I think that we are having an argument and I don't understand why," I say. "I don't normally have arguments."

There is a break. During this break I think that something is about to happen, but I don't know what. The creek seems so loud. Like if we talk just now we won't be able to hear each other. Our ears will be too full of creek sound.

I watch him.

"Do you think about me?" he asks. His face isn't so pained anymore, just sort of tired, fallen, blank. He is looking at the water, turning his words that way.

"I don't understand the question," I say.

"I don't know how to have a conversation like this."

I don't respond. Suddenly, he looks smaller to me. I think that I want to walk closer to him, but that would be a strange thing to do. I stay where I am, my arms crossed, squeezed tight against my chest, holding me in place.

"What do you think, when you think about me?" he asks. He sounds annoyed. He sticks his hands in his pockets and looks at me for a moment, then back at the water.

I look at him and try to think what I think. "You are Tom. You work for LeBlanc, like me. You've known him a long time, like me. You seem to worry."

"That's it?" he asks.

"You like Yoo-hoos!"

He smiles a little, then rolls his eyes, then kicks at the ground.

"It's hard to know when you are right here, and I am seeing you," I say. "Because I'm also thinking about you now. I am thinking 'muddy boots' but I wouldn't normally think that."

"Am I the same to you as everyone else?"

"I don't understand the question."

"Like Shelley. You probably don't think the same way about Shelley that you think about Kenny. Like Randy the Prophet."

I have a strange desire suddenly to be sitting behind a door and I think that if Tom was on the other side of the door, and both our backs were against it, that I could feel better. My stomach hurts.

"I prefer some people to others, yes. I prefer you to Kenny."

He laughs. It sounds like a laugh you make when you are relieved that you can laugh, even momentarily.

"I prefer you," he says. "To everyone."

I blink. I push my hands hard into my abdomen. If I were behind the door, my back would relax against it and I could close my eyes. My face might grow red.

"I understand," I say.

"Great." His laugh this time is a little less than the one before. He turns away from me, completely toward the water, so I can only see the side of his face.

"What you're saying, I don't know if it's something I can feel."

"If you could, you would. It's not something you have to think about."

"It's not something that was discussed with me, and I don't know if it's because they thought it would develop naturally or because I'm not capable of it."

I wish I could lay down on the floor and whisper this through the crack at the bottom of the door.

"I understand," he says.

He walks back through the brush. I watch him, shifting my weight in the mud.

Back inside, the rain pouring again, I ask around. Someone has a pair. They are for children, dull with a red plastic handle. In the private bathroom I stand in front of the mirror and squeeze my thumb and two fingers into the small opening. I lift my braid out to the side and begin to saw. It is a slow process, more of a shaving away than a cut. My hair falls in drifts to the ground, some floats up and tickles my nose. When I finish, I keep pumping paper towels from the dispenser, wiping the floor and the sink, until I don't see any more hair. I throw the braid in the trash.

I look at myself in the mirror. I still look like me.

CHAPTER FORTY

marigold

The storm is over. We are back at the compound. Water shopvac-ed out of the low-lying buildings, the landscape a murky brown.

I call LeBlanc and a few days later he shows up in his camper. I see him there, down in the road outside our house, but I don't go out to greet him. I wait on the couch for the knock on the door.

When I open it, he stares at me. He doesn't gape his mouth open or exclaim anything.

Shelley evened it all up with normal scissors and it looks nice now, clean and fresh.

We sit on the couch drinking lukewarm tap water. He keeps looking at my hair, touching his own.

I don't know how to start anything, how to finish anything. I just speak.

"Let them change me," I say.

He shakes his head, takes a long sip of his water. "There's no room for improvement," he says. "You're the most improved version of yourself."

"Maybe. It depends on what my purpose is. Is my purpose to work here? Is that why I was created?"

There is something aggressive in the way he doesn't meet my eyes, looks everywhere else. At the moment he is staring at the kitchen.

"I'm not serving my purpose," I say. "Whatever it was you thought I would do. I have no purpose to serve, so let me be the way I want."

"If you think you have no purpose," he says, now looking at the carpet by my feet, "why don't you just get them to end you?"

I feel something rigid crawl up my body from my heel, through my calves, to the base of my skull. There is a pressure behind my eyes.

"I'm afraid," I say.

It isn't hard for me to say this.

He stands up. I stand up too, out of instinct. He looks at me now, leans in close to my face.

"Of what?" he asks.

I wonder if he is a person who will stand in front of me and shove me. Is he a person who will lean into my face and yell and spit? He is usually a person who keeps his meanness on the quiet side, says something cruel while picking his nail beds. Laughs carelessly at someone's concern. Squared off in front of me, he is someone else. He is trying to force something out of me. Maybe he thinks I will say, "of you."

"Of not existing," I say.

I realize now that he is not standing in front of me in an aggressive way, or if he was, he softens. His eyes look a way I have not seen, like someone tired and sad but also angry and hungry and desperate.

"They really did a good job with you," he says. "Not just Tony and Anna Marie, Mr. Miller too. Even Shelley did...on accident."

"Shelley didn't work on me," I say. I say it like I am sure, but I am not. I am afraid to find out.

"Not technically but she did accidentally, you learned from her."

"What?"

"Probably how to care about someone."

He touches a hand to my cheek. I stay still.

"But how you got the fear," he says. "It could have been a little bit of everyone. People can do that for you, make you think life's something to be scared to lose, as if you have a choice."

"I understand that everyone dies eventually," I say. I back away from him.The back of my calf bangs against the coffee table.

"Even you."

"It's programmed," I say. It's more of a confirmation than a question. It was never spelled out to me, but I thought it was so.

My body feels loosened by this knowledge, like I'm suspended in a pool, weightless.

"You're relieved," he says.

I nod.

"Shelley will die. Randy the Prophet. All of them. And you will too."

The pressure behind my eyes grows. I still feel like I am floating, but that my foot is tethered to something heavy and secret beneath the surface.

"And if you love someone, not the way you love Shelley, but more than that, in a way that hurts you inside but also makes you want to get up in the morning, that person will die too and you will watch it happen or you will get a call in the middle of the night after you had a boring day where you forgot to tell them you loved them and you will be told they are dead. There was an accident."

I am pulled beneath the surface and the pressure is so strong I am afraid something is wrong with my eyes. There is water dripping down my chin, collecting against my collarbone.

"Just let them change me," I say, shocked at the instability of my voice, how it sounds like it belongs to a person much younger, much less certain of things. "I know I should want death, but it's not what I want.

I'm afraid. If I... if they make me back the way I was first, then I don't have to worry. I don't have to care."

"I'll call them," he says. He takes a handkerchief out of his pocket and hands it to me. "They really did a good job with you. Sometimes I forget."

CHAPTER FORTY-ONE

tom

here is she?" I ask when the door opens.

It is night. It is morning, technically. I beat on the door until she came. Because I couldn't sleep, because I saw the strange car drive down the road, because I was packing by the window. It was her in the window, the slow crawl of the car and the crackling street light conspiring to let me see. It was her and she was looking through my window and it seems impossible, too far, too many parts, but it happened that way.

Shelley, always disgruntled, looks angry in a way I've never seen. Her eyes are black, her lips tight. Her hair sticks up at odd angles, here tied in knots, here perfectly straight. She wears the same shirt from the first day we met, one shoulder peeking out from the too-big neck.

"What are you doing?" she asks. She asks it in a calm way that makes her seem even angrier, like she wants to add in expletives, but they would only drain her energy, use up some of the intensity she is saving to hate me.

"I saw her in a car. Where is she going in a car?"

"She'll be back," she says.

She tries to close the door, but I stick my arm in, push it open, doing that thing men get to do. Strong arm.

"I'm leaving, though," I say. My voice sounds pathetic. I want to rewind and do it over. Shelley will pounce on weakness.

"Bon voyage," she says.

Her own cruelty seems to soften her a little. She smiles at her own joke.

"Look. I'm sorry. I don't know... this is a new one for me. She's gone and she'll be back."

"When?"

She shrugs.

"Where did she go?"

She shrugs again.

I want to hit her. Or at least shake her stupid shrugging shoulders. Maybe she can see it in my face.

"I'm telling the truth. I don't know."

"So she left without telling you?"

She sighs.

"No. She told me she was leaving, just not where she was going. I have a guess where she is, but I can't be sure."

"What's your guess?"

"What are you going to do?"

I'm not going to do anything. I just want to say goodbye. That isn't so strange. There are times in my life when I've left without saying goodbye, like when I left my mother's house the first time, and I regret them. There's a relief at first, missing out on that awkward part, the strangeness of leaving but not being gone yet, but then there's the creeping regret, the realization that you missed out on something, some special little pause in life where you could have said something nice, made a joke, given a hug.

Shelley thinks Marigold has gone to this place. This lab. They made her. That night before they came —because that's what happened, some people came and got her, people Shelley didn't know, that she peeked at through her cracked bedroom door— Marigold told her she was going somewhere. She said some other things. Things Shelley thought were strange. Shelley, terminally unimpressed, was worried.

"She was talking to me like someone with a secret terminal illness," Shelley said.

"I love you, you know," Marigold told Shelley.

"You're a really good friend."

"You helped make me who I am."

"Remember that dance? The boy that kissed me on the swings? And Mary Margaret was being mean and then you showed up?"

"Remember?"

Marigold had never asked Shelley if she remembered anything, except to do her homework or brush her teeth.

The lab is a few hours away in an area I've never been. I drive through towns whose names I've never heard. The landscape is the same as anywhere though, same emaciated trees, same garbage along the road, same cracked roads.

I am almost disappointed when I arrive at how insignificant the building looks. It looks like a repurposed apartment complex: an ugly, skinny tower, off-white, stained with algae, with strange square windows protruding like aquariums hanging off the side. It is no longer night morning, but just morning, and the beauty of the morning sun amplifies the desolate ugliness of the building. There are no purposeful markings visible from the parking lot.

I am one of ten or so cars in the lot. When I get to the glass doors at the entrance, I see a vinyl decal with the name of the lab, beneath it a note is taped saying "Ring bell for entry." I look around the door until I find the button to ring. I push it and hear no sound, don't feel the normal satisfactory give. I keep pushing and pushing, hoping to hear a faint ringing from inside.

Finally a voice, crackling, loud. I look up and see a speaker above the door.

"Please stop ringing the bell, sir," the voice says.

I raise my hands up in a show of surrender.

"How can we help you, sir?" the voice asks.

"Is Marigold here?" I ask.

I wish I could say something more forceful, more certain, like, "Let me see Marigold," but I can't be sure she is here. I look around the parking lot hoping for a familiar car, but I saw it in the dark, and I was looking at her through the window. I don't even know what color it was.

The voice doesn't answer me for what feels like a very long time.

Then: "Name?"

I jump at the sudden eruption of sound, the crackling worse.

"My name?" I ask.

"Yes, sir," the voice says. There is an impressive lack of inflection. "May I have your name, please, sir?"

"Tom," I say.

More silence.

I start to count in my head just to make sure it is really taking as long as it feels. Thirteen minutes and thirty-six seconds go by before the voice comes back.

"OK, sir," the voice says.

"She will see you. The door will unlock. Wait until you hear the buzz before you open the door. If you pull too soon we'll have to start over."

I pull too soon.

"Let's try again, sir."

I hear the buzz and click, and I pull at the right moment.

"Please sit, sir," the voice says.

I am in a lobby, silent and empty save for a row of metal chairs against the wall. It is cold in that way of offices and hospitals. I shiver and sit on the edge of the chair, looking down a long hallway, listening for evidence that someone is coming. A black vending machine in the corner hums, its spiral arms holding in bags of mostly air. I contemplate buying a Nutty Buddy.

There are footsteps down the hall and then she is standing there. She looks so different I am not sure it's really her at first. Someone has evened up her hair so that it hits in a straight line at her chin. It looks slightly wet, the part uneven. She wears her black t-shirt with a pair of baggy gray sweatpants.

"Tom," she says, when she gets to the entrance of the lobby.

I am still sitting in my chair, still vaguely thinking about the Nutty Buddy, my stomach in a low growl.

Her voice sounds very calm. She is usually very calm, but this is different. She's not just speaking an uninflected, unaffected voice, but something in her voice seems to reach out to me, trying to infect me with its calmness.

It almost works. I forget for a second my confusion, the drive here, the fact that I'm leaving, her face passing me in the dark.

I stand up.

"What are you doing here?" I ask. "What is this place?" I try to find something condemning to point to, to underscore the fact that this place is strange, but there is only the vending machine, Chili Fritos waiting for someone to mash A4.

"Follow me," she says and turns.

We go down the hallway, passing door after identical door, each marked with numbers and letters. She pushes through a door at the end of the hallway and we are in a stairwell. We climb the stairs, not talking, huffing. She is wearing slippers that slap against the linoleum with each step. The building feels very still. I strain to hear voices or footsteps in the hallways as we pass the doors to each floor, but all I can hear is our breathing, our feet.

"Who lives here?"

She doesn't answer.

We exit the stairs on the fifth floor and go down one hallway, then another, until she finally turns into a doorway: 5P.

"5P?" I ask as we enter. "This is where you came?"

The room is like every ugly apartment I've ever seen. The carpet is beige, the walls are beige with a more yellow tint. It is an open floor plan, meaning the builder didn't want to bother with walls. The kitchen, with yellowing cabinets and a grease-stained stove is separated from the living area by a change from linoleum to carpet.

The living area holds a cot made up with white sheets and a single white pillow. A pink blanket is folded at the bottom. Marigold's bag sits beside the cot, unopened. There is nothing else in the room.

She sits on the cot. I stand in the kitchen, my toe against the metal strip that holds down the carpet.

"This is where I came from," she says.

"5P?" I ask. There's something about it. The ugliness of the number and the letter. The plainness of it.

She clasps her hands between her knees. She looks small and sloppy in the big sweatpants. "This building."

"What is this building?"

She takes a deep breath. "It's a lab."

"Is it LeBlanc's?"

"No."

She doesn't follow up on the no. She tucks her hair behind her ear.

"I came here to get adjusted."

"What does that mean?" I ask, picturing a chiropractor, a cracking back.

"I don't know exactly. I've never had it done, but I will be changed back to the way I was before."

"Before what?"

"Before. I don't know. Before I became like this."

She moves to sit with her head against the wall, at the head of the cot. I sit down by her feet.

"What does that mean, exactly? How will you be different?"

Her foot is bare, she edges it forward and presses it against my thigh, I feel a heat through the fabric. I reach my hand down and put it gently on top of her foot and squeeze.

"I will be different," she says. She swallows. Her voice sounds different, less solid, like a low-quality recording played back.

"You really asked to come here?"

She nods.

"Why?"

"Your hand is on my foot," she says.

I jerk my hand up and put it on my knee, reddening.

"I didn't say that so you would move it. I put my foot there against you. Why would I do that?"

"Do you want me to answer that?" I ask.

I feel embarrassed, but I try to keep my voice low and calm, like this is a barely interesting conversation.

"No. I'm just giving an example," she says. She tucks her knees up under her chin, hugs her legs.

"My behavior has no purpose. They wanted me to be human, really human, but I'm not. There's something about me that can never be free that way. But sometimes I am close, like when I put my foot up against you."

She pauses and looks at me. For a second, I wonder if she is going to stick her foot back out, but she doesn't. I hold her eye contact for as long as I can, then look down at my lap and smooth out nonexistent wrinkles in my jeans.

"And earlier," she continues, "I cried. I'd never done that before."

She scoots toward me on the bed, sits cross-legged beside me, our bodies perpendicular. I feel her hand, soft, cold, on my arm.

"I do those things, the things a human would do, but my mind is still different, it's still thinking 'what should I do?' And for what purpose was I made almost human? So I could be LeBlanc's companion? He hasn't ever wanted me as his companion, though. Since I began, he realized I wasn't what he wanted. So then my purpose became to be another worker for him. Did they need to create me for that? There is a person somewhere out there at a different job who would have mine if I'd never existed and that's my impact on the world. So why cry, why touch you with my foot, why feel pain and worry when I don't even feel it the right way? It's more like sometimes these human parts of me are able to push their way through the other parts, to force their way out momentarily. I want to go back to just existing, performing functions. There's no need for anything else."

Now we are both cross-legged, facing each other on the bed, and somehow her hands are in mine, but my hands aren't holding hers, they are just sort of sitting there, like we are about to perform a seance or say a blessing before dinner.

"You act like humans have perfected humanity." I say. "Like we know how to act all the time and never want to turn off certain parts of ourselves."

"But," she says. "It doesn't really matter, because you can't do anything about that and I can."

I gulp. She turns her hands so that her palms are against mine, and I rub my thumbs against her pinkies.

"I don't want you to do that," I say. I say it slowly, because I don't want to. The words feel stupid. I feel stupid. I look at the floor.

"To do what?"

"To change."

It is very quiet. I realize I am holding my breath. I think she might be too. Suddenly, she lets out a long breath.

"But you're leaving," she says.

"You can too," I say. With me, I think, not feeling like I need to add that part.

"No," she says. "I can't."

"You're not allowed?"

"I just can't."

She moves her hands to play with the end of her braid, realizes it isn't there, and runs them over her scalp instead.

"Maybe what I mean is I don't want to. I can't keep having half a life."

"Why would it be half?"

My hands still sit, balanced on my knees, palms up.

"Because I don't know if I can fully feel it."

I thought I came here with no expectations, but her words wriggle around in my brain, pressing the most sensitive parts. I can feel tears leaking from my eyes, and I push at them with my fingertips.

"OK," I say.

"Tom..." she starts.

I put a hand up. I don't know what she is going to say. I never do. But there is no point. I feel so funny sitting here crying, like someone with big hopes and dreams, not someone who was one place and ended up in another.

"Will you know me?" I ask. "If we see each other again?"

"Yes, but it won't be like this. I will know who you are. Maybe I will have my memories, but they won't mean anything to me, they will just be facts."

I rub the back of my hands over my eyes, then hold them out again. She places hers back down, gingerly, gives me one, limp squeeze.

"How do you feel right now?" I ask. "Still in between?"

"I think I feel human," she says.

The air in the room suddenly feels still and hot, like it is pressing against us. I wish for a moment that I could disappear. The smell of her—powdery, cool—takes up all the space for smells.

"I'm going to miss you," I say.

She doesn't say anything.

Then in the silence, in the heat, in her smell, I say: "I'm doing this for my own memory."

I clench her hands tight in mine and lean toward her. My lips touch her cheek first, then her lips. I pull back and look in her eyes. I reach a hand up and pull loose a strand by her face. My heart feels like it has taken over my body, beating a rhythm to the moment.

"I hope this turns out how you want," I say.

CHAPTER FORTY-TWO
marigold

There was a moment before I was complete when I was born. My eyes didn't open yet and I couldn't move my body, but I could hear, and my brain could process. I wasn't a newborn baby coming into the cold world crying, longing for the warm home it knew. I was something worse than that. Because I wasn't going to be cradled somewhere and shushed and fed and slowly taught what it meant to be alive. I was alive then and no one even spoke to me, and I could compare myself to a newborn baby because I understood what that was, just as I understood that I was in a laboratory and what that was and that outside there were trees and an ocean and people that I would look like. I was nothing but a mind with ears, and then, suddenly, I was more. I had eyes and a mouth and there were faces in front of me saying "Hello, Marigold. Welcome!" and I blinked at them.

"I didn't ask to be born," I tell Anna Marie.

"No one did," Anna Marie points out.

Tony doesn't say anything. He's seemed sad all day. He fiddles with some equipment in the corner.

"Are you mad at me, Tony?" I ask.

He shakes his head but won't look at me.

Anna Marie works on me in a corner of the lab with a mirror and adjustable chair. She is weaving hair into mine, giving me back my braid. As the braid begins to form, I think *that is me*, but I'm not sure if this thought holds any truth. Our faces are so close that I can smell the coffee on Anna Marie's breath, but we don't look at each other.

Anna Marie spins me away from the mirror and finishes the braid. I watch Tony, slumped over a book.

Anna Marie takes a step back and looks at me, nodding.

"It looks good," she says.

She spins the chair around, so I can see myself.

In the mirror I see someone who is me and not me. It is the same face I see any time I pass a reflective surface, but there is something different about this person. This person is walled off, distant. This person doesn't care what happens to her.

"Are you ready?" Tony calls. He was watching me in the mirror, but when I turn toward him, he looks away.

I nod, but since he isn't looking at me, I say, "Yes," just in case.

He pats the chair beside him. I walk over and sit down.

He hooks little pads against my head. They feel sticky and cold. I try to meet his eyes, but he keeps darting them around, going back and forth to his machine, turning dials.

"I think you were the best thing I made," he says. He says it out to the room, to the machine, to Anna Marie.

Thing.

I feel sorry for him. I look at the side of his face, the wrinkles growing around his eyes. When I first met him, he was in his early twenties, smooth-faced and excited. Now he just looks tired. I start to reach my hand out to place on his arm, but the desire fades.

Tony is beside me.

He is Tony.

I knew him when I was born.

He has grown considerably older.

Across the room is Anna Marie, cleaning up her work station.

Anna Marie is also older, the same amount older as Tony, but she takes better care of herself, so she looks younger.

Tony is crying.

"Are you finished?" I ask him.

He nods and pulls the pads off my head. That hurts a little bit, stretching my skin for a moment like a bandage.

I remember something, but it seems far away, or maybe it is from a story someone told me. The edges of the memory fade out into blackness, so that in the center is only a little sliver of it. When I existed but I was not born, I remember words inside my brain. I thought: "So this is life," and with that I wanted my eyes to work, my limbs to move, my throat to make sounds, so that I could know more about it.

CHAPTER FORTY-THREE

tom

There is nowhere to go, or, more accurately, there is everywhere to go. I drive until my neck aches, until my back is stiff, and I am frozen against the steering wheel, peering over, squinting in the sunlight. I stop at a gas station and stretch while the little crutch pushes the handle that pumps gas into my truck. I lean against the bed of the truck to stretch out my hamstrings and look down at my life: a couple of trash bags, a box, a fishing rod, some tackle.

I will drive for what seems like an eternity, but I won't get very far. When I stop, because I need gas again, because I'm hungry, because I don't want to drive anymore, I'll be somewhere that looks like everywhere else I've been. Same empty parking lots, same drooping power lines, same generic strip malls. I will imagine this is just one stop of many on my way to the real place, the place where things are beautiful, with no trash tangled up in the weeds along the road, no fast food restaurants, no inflated gorillas in front of car lots. I will find a weekly rate motel off the highway that advertises free cable and jacuzzis. My room will have neither, just a shower stall, a TV with an antenna, and a heart-shaped bed with a mirror overhead. Driving in circles one afternoon, hot, windows down, my soaked shirt sticking to the seat, I'll find a road that leads to a park, a worn-down baseball field with kids playing tag, hiding in the dugout. A path that runs behind the baseball field will lead to a creek with steep banks and pebbled floor.

In the mornings, I'll go there to fish. I'll catch mostly catfish, whiskered faces blinking at me, good breaded and fried on my motel room hot plate. Before it gets hot, I'll do yard work at the park, mowing and cleaning up the lines on the field, sweeping out the dugout. In the afternoons, I'll work the concession stand, ladling neon cheese and mushy jalapeños onto stale chips.

The nights will be long. I will try to make them short by going to bed early, but will end up staring at the ceiling, listening to the ins and outs of my

neighbors, the yelling, the radios, the gun shots on
TV.

Sometimes I will drive to a chain restaurant with
a bar, double-priced drinks and reproduction sports
memorabilia on the wall. I'll go there often enough
that the bartender will sort of recognize me, but he'll
never remember my name or what I like to order.

Eventually, I am not the self I see in that
unknown knowing in the back of my mind. Looking in
the mirror startles me: my hair graying around the
edges, my gut protruding just a little over my pants,
my face blank. My face is the strangest part. It could
be anyone's face. I raise an eyebrow, give a big
disingenuous smile, just to prove that it's really my
reflection.

He knocks on my door. I look at him through the peep
hole for a long time. I wait for him to say, "I know
you're in there," or "Open up!" but he just stands
there, his hands behind his back. He looks so old and
small, like what I would think of if someone said:
"LeBlanc's grandfather." When I finally do open the
door and when he comes in and sits on my bed and
accepts my cup of instant coffee, I notice he is a little
shaky. I see the thin, pooled skin on his hands, the big
spots congregating around their veiny center.

"I bet you never thought you'd see me again," he
says.

I drink my coffee. It is scalding hot. My tongue goes from burning to numb, but I keep my composure. I don't answer him. I knew I would see him again, though. I didn't know I knew, until I saw him there on the other side of the door and all I thought was: "Here he is."

He has nothing to say to me, really. He babbles about business, asks about my mother, then tells me about her because he still visits her regularly. Trying to patch up a permanently leaky boat, to keep out the guilt. I don't offer him anything but answer his questions politely. The news plays on the TV behind his head, and I have a hard time not looking at it instead of him: a child is missing, a dog is dancing, a politician is speaking.

When he is ready to leave, I walk him back to the door. He stands there and looks at me for a few seconds. There's something in his eyes that I haven't seen before. Something soft.

"I hope you found peace here," he says. He nods at the room behind me and if it weren't for that softness I would assume he was being sarcastic, hoping for peace among the scratchy motel duvet and and buzzing mini fridge.

I shrug.

I don't know if I have.

We shake hands and I watch him walk to his car. It's when I realize which car he's walking toward that I see her. She is standing next to the car, watching me.

It's not her, but it has to be. She is not the same. She is like me in the mirror: softer, faded. Her hair is long again, braided and neatly sitting over her shoulder. She wears a long white dress that grazes her ankles. I feel something jerk inside me, telling me to walk, to get to the car, to say something, but I ignore it and lift my hand and wave. She waves back, slowly, with little conviction, then gets in the car.

The thing about the muck is that it becomes part of my daily life so that I'm so deep in it, I can't see it anymore. I can't see the muck for the muck.

I tell Randy the Prophet this once when he comes to see me and we have too many drinks at the overpriced bar. He just stares at me.

"The muck," I say. "Remember? The muck?"

He doesn't.

It is on my shoes when I walk up from the creek after I fish, more when I walk through the soggy grass to weed eat. I wipe it off to work the concessions but track it into my car on the way through the parking lot. The motel maid comes twice a week, but I know there is no way for her to scrape it all up. It clings to the carpet, the bed, the towels, even the TV somehow. At night, I lower myself into it, let it close up around me. I close my eyes and let it bar me from the world. I close my eyes and I am in the boat with my father, sloshing. I am putting a coin in a jukebox, humming. I am sitting in a room, in a row of identical rooms, crying. In the morning I climb back out.

CHAPTER FORTY-FOUR
randy the prophet

A few weeks after Marigold disappeared, I hear rumors she is back. People stop by the store and talk quietly by the candy bars. I wait, thinking she'll show up, but she doesn't. Neither does Shelley. The whispers by the ice cream case say Shelley isn't coming in to work, hasn't been to the mess hall, that the lights are always out at her house.

When I knock on Shelley's door, I hear nothing. I decide to count to sixty. Around forty-two I hear a thump. When the door opens, I forget to breathe. I've seen Shelley in all states of sloppiness, but this is something else. Her skin is pale with a yellow tinge. She has big bags under her eyes, and her hair is matted to her head. She wears a t-shirt that is covered in stains: sweat stains, food stains, grease stains. I try to catch her eye, but she won't look at me, instead she stares somewhere toward the middle of my chest.

"Yes?" she asks.

"You OK, kid?" I know she isn't, but I think it might help to ask.

She steps back from the door and goes into the living room, lays down on the couch. I follow her in. The house is a reflection of her appearance. Food containers are strewn on every surface, along with dirty clothes and paper towels. There is a distinct smell of body odor mixed with old garbage and stale sink water. I stand in the middle of it all and watch her on the couch. She stares at the ceiling.

"When was the last time you left this place?"

She doesn't answer.

"Could you... do you think you might like to take a shower?"

This isn't something I would normally suggest to someone, but it's Shelley. If it makes her mad, she'll let me know. She won't let a hurt settle on her and fester. She starts to say something, then stops. Tears start leaking from the sides of her eyes. She pushes them away with the tops of her fingers.

"It's too messy in there," she says finally. Her voice is quiet, distant, a floating thing apart from her.

"She always kept it tidy. I don't know... I didn't know that I liked it that way."

"Oh honey," I say.

It's something I've wanted to say to her many times, when she yells at me over some stupid annoyance, when she laughs about something sad, when I see her chinking up her walls against the light. But now I feel like I can say it. And something else I can do now, for the first time: I walk over and kiss her forehead.

"I'll take care of it."

She rolls over so that her face is facing the back of the couch and I go to the bathroom and scrub the grime off the shower, the toothpaste from the sink, pick up the moldy towels and the dirty underwear and take out the trash. I help her up and walk her to the bathroom and while the water runs, I try my best to set the rest of the house right: piling the clothes in the hamper, filling up garbage bags, wiping down surfaces. I find their vacuum cleaner in the hall closet and run it quickly over the carpet. When I try to edge it into Marigold's room, the cord is stretched too far and comes unplugged. There is sudden silence. The water has stopped running too. I push the door open and see a made-up bed, a table with a telephone, and a bookshelf. I close the door.

Back in the kitchen, I take out the vacuum bag, hoping for something. All I get is a plume of hair and dirt. A few blond strands land on the kitchen floor. I pick them up and twist them between my fingers until they fall in the garbage can.

Shelley pads out of her bedroom with wet hair in a clean black t-shirt, three sizes too big, hanging off her shoulder, and four-leaf-clover-printed pajama pants.

In my truck we don't talk. She reaches over and puts her hand on mine as I shift the gears.

The old ranger cabin looks lonely, a thing forgotten, thrown among the weeds. I notice the wood planking outside is freshly lacquered and the stoop rebuilt with raw two-by-fours.

"Have you been here?" I ask Shelley. "Since she moved?"

She shakes her head.

We are parked, and she is squeezing my hand. Seeing her this way is doing something to me. I feel weak, nervous, like I need to lie down somewhere quiet and dark and never come out.

"We don't have to go in," I tell her. "Although she probably knows we are here, so it might be weird if we just leave."

Shelley lets out a snort and then starts to laugh. She lets go of my hand and presses hers against her face. She is crying and laughing, snot streaming from her nose, her face puffy and red.

I wait.

"Sorry," she says. "It's not funny. You know she won't care one way or the other. She won't think it's weird. Only we will."

It takes exactly ten seconds from when we knock on the door until she opens it. I realize I am holding my breath that whole time and let out a long exhale when I see her. She looks exactly the same, and completely different. Her hair is long again, back in the braid, neat little crisscrosses. She is barefoot in a long white gown that buttons down the front.

"Randy the Prophet," she says. "Shelley."

She turns around and walks into the cabin. It looks almost identical to her bedroom at the house, except for the addition of a kitchenette and a wood stove. I wonder why she didn't just move her things over.

"You set all this up?" I ask. My hands are deep in my pockets. Shelley stands half-obscured behind me. Marigold sits on her bed.

"LeBlanc did," Marigold says.

"It looks nice," I say.

Shelley snorts again and starts to giggle.

"Sorry," she says. Her voice is cracking, ragged, not amused. "Sorry..."

"It's nice of you to visit," Marigold says.

I nod. Shelley moves forward to stand beside me, her arms crossed.

"You could have invited us," Shelley says, "but I guess you don't care about such social niceties."

"I don't," Marigold says.

No one speaks for a while. The wood in the cabin pops. Some bugs hum.

"What do you do out here?" I ask.

"I read," she says. "There's a table out back and I can sit and look at the water. I go on walks."

"Isn't reading part of the old plan?" Shelley asks.

"Yes, but now they are just for entertainment. I enjoy them."

"What if you accidentally learn from them?" Shelly wants to know. Her voice sounds tight.

"I will learn, but I won't adapt."

"Whatever that means," Shelley says.

The father in me feels the urge to correct Shelley, to encourage her to be nice to her friend, but I remember they are not friends anymore and this hardness may help her remember that too.

When we leave, Marigold follows us out and stands on the front stoop. She keeps her hands loose at her sides and waves one small wave when we turn to look at her before getting in the truck. With that wave, it's like she is waving away the present moment, waving in the future, and I see her in this same house, learning but not adapting. Her braid stays tidy, her clothes stay white, her sentences short. She adds a rocking chair to the room. Mr. Miller or LeBlanc or some other person who thinks they are in charge of her sends her more books to read and she reads them all. She walks every square inch of the compound and becomes something of a myth to the kids and workers. The woman in white. And then, as it is programmed, she stops one day. Probably long after I'm gone, maybe before Shelley, maybe not, and I can't tell which is worse: to have the phantom reminder of what once was and the unrealistic hope that it can be that way again, or to have nothing, just a memory, a scent, a story, a clinging piece of hair.

ABOUT THE AUTHOR

Sarah Colombo is a writer living in Georgia.

ABOUT THE PUBLISHING TEAM

Nate Ragolia is a lifelong lover of science fiction and its power to imagine worlds more hopeful and inclusive than the real one. His first book, *There You Feel Free*, was published by 1888's Black Hill Press in 2015. Spaceboy Books reissued it in 2021. He's also the author of *The Retroactivist* (2017). His most recent book, *One Person Can't Make a Difference* (2022), was featured on Tor.com's Can't Miss Indie Press Speculative Fiction list, and was translated into Italian for Ringworld Sci-Fi in 2023. He founded and edited *BONED*, a literary magazine, and also created two webcomics. Nate is also a husband and a dog dad.

Shaunn Grulkowski has been compared to Warren Ellis and Phillip K. Dick and was once described as what a baby conceived by Kurt Vonnegut and Margaret Atwood would turn out to be. He's at least the fifth best Slavic-Latino-American sci-fi writer in the Baltimore metro area. He's the author *Retcontinuum*, and the editor of *A Stalled Ox* and *The Goldfish* for 1888/Black Hill Press.